LET THE WEIRDNESS IN: a Tribute to Kate Bush

Edited by Evan St. Jones

HEADS DANCE PRESS

SHREVEPORT, LOUISIANA

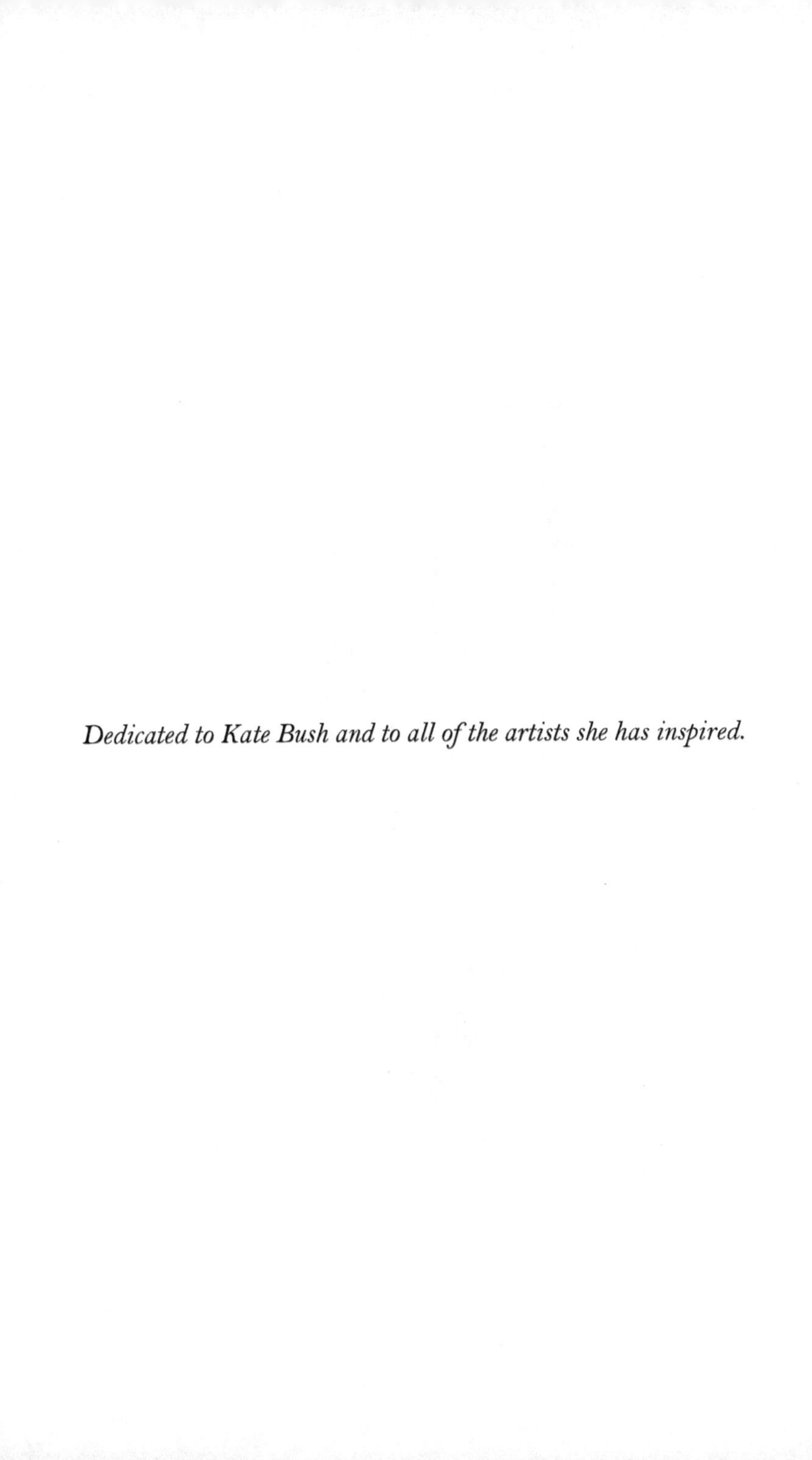

Dedicated to Kate Bush and to all of the artists she has inspired.

LOVE

ANGER

Introduction

Evan St. Jones

I first stumbled upon Kate Bush's music quite accidentally; I was searching for Enya's song "Orinoco Flow" on a peer-to-peer file sharing network (it was 2007) and the most downloaded MP3 was one listed as "feat. Kate Bush." Though she didn't feature on "Orinoco Flow," her name intrigued me enough to open a new search. "Wuthering Heights" was the first result, so I downloaded it—the song was not the original from *The Kick Inside*, but a rerecorded version from her greatest compilation album, *The Whole Story*—and I was fuckin' smitten.

From there, I started ordering her albums on CD when I could afford them as a broke teenager, and I was enamored with her artistry.

Her music was some of the weirdest goddamn stuff I'd heard up until that point; the summer before was when I devoured Björk's discography and was hungry for more of what I would later fondly refer to as *weird lady* music (as in, weird music made by weird ladies), so I fell thoroughly head over heels in love with what I heard, especially *The Dreaming* and *Hounds of Love,* both of which experimented wildly with sonic landscape and genres, often to great effect in building an encompassing atmosphere and allowing the listener to get lost in the stories she weaved for us not only in the lyrics, but in the music itself.

Fast forward to spring of 2021. I was at the height of cabin fever from staying in the house for a year at that point (do I need to mention COVID?). I had been reading a lot of fiction. Lots and lots. More than I ever had in such a short span of time. After seeing tons of themed anthologies in the small press community I became acquainted with through social media during quarantine, I decided to try my hand at a tribute anthology to the art of Kate Bush.

Like her music, I knew I wanted it to be weird first and foremost. So each of these stories is weird—some are funny, some are creepy, others are heartwarming, and many more are very dark. I wanted the book to feel like going through Kate's discography; you can never be quite sure which strange world you're going to encounter next. While editing, I did try to let the stories speak to one another and figure out an order of their own, but I have separated the book into two parts based vaguely on tone: Love & Anger.

I hope fans of Kate Bush will enjoy these stories based on her work. There are references to her music and lyrics galore, and many of the stories perfectly capture the feel of her songs. This was a labor of love from both myself and the contributing writers, and it's an honor to be able to share it with all of you now.

Without further ado, throw the windows and doors open. Prepare to *Let the Weirdness In.*

LOVE

Light Bent Strangely There

Tiffany Morris

Memories glinted coinbright inside the silver lake. Maya spotted her regret, a shimmering bronze fish, darting among the stones. She stood beside the water, watching as the shadows of misshapen birds dove in exaggerated arcs, disappearing and reappearing out of rolling fog.

She walked along the shore's inner edge, its sharp rocks biting into her bare feet. Trees shed daylight among their fallen leaves.

In the distance, the small orange silhouettes blazed. Tapetum lucidum: firefly flashes blinked and bored their gaze into her.

The foxes waited in the dark.

Desire is a bird singing in its sleep. Maya felt Robert's presence behind her as she walked. His presence was gossamer and burning, a molten wisp of glass before it takes its final shape.

"I'm sorry," she said to the night air. "It was the only thing I could think to do."

Silence. She kept walking back to the cabin, lantern in hand, dodging the low-slung branches on the thin path. His presence disappeared at some point before she reached the cobblestone that led to her temporary home that, increasingly, took the shape of something much more permanent.

As she stepped inside and flicked on the light, the large bronze machine resting on the table hummed to life. The smell it emitted from its pink clouds was the ozone before a thunderstorm. Maya had forgotten to open the window. Fear knit itself inside her cold fingers as she pulled it up, praying she would not see her reflection in the warped and stained old glass.

She tried not to think of the city, or of Robert, or of any of the regrets she could weave into a many-colored tapestry, filled with lions and thorn-pricked hearts and the swords of her longing.

The nights by the lake were long, but memory was longer.

Maya sat on the worn couch. She thumbed through a book but couldn't concentrate. Each word snarled and blurred.

Was she crying? She touched her face and was surprised to find it wet.

She closed her eyes and woke in the morning.

Her friend Laura was a great woodland goddess, if ambiguous about the tradition she came from.

"Don't worry about it," Laura had said with a dismissive wave of her hand. Maya watched her clip her black horns, gold-tipped, to a headband, carefully adjusting them to a proper angle.

"It needs something else," the goddess said.

Maya grabbed her pink metallic makeup bag and begin rooting. She had five shades of lipstick, a tube of mascara, some liquid eyeliner in True Black.

Laura grabbed a burgundy lipstick and drew a line above one eyebrow and below another.

"Much better."

It was the same shade of burgundy Maya wore with her Lady Macbeth costume. Dark lipstick villainy, much darker than her fake blood-stained hands.

At the party, she watched *Nosferatu* with an 80s pop soundtrack, pretending to be rapt as her friends disappeared into the crowd. This was not the sort of party where you befriended strangers. She avoided the patio: the only other smokers were the people she already knew. She busied herself at the fringes of conversations and the snack table.

"Those cupcakes have real bugs on them, you know," a Grim Reaper said to someone else.

Maya grabbed one from the cupcake stand. It was wrapped in greasy, thin Halloween-themed paper, covered with cartoon spiders, and topped with traffic-cone orange frosting. From the top, small white worms poked out, as if struggling to air in a rainstorm. She plucked one out gingerly, examining its soft ridges. It was light and crispy and salty on her tongue, a sliver of dried seaweed.

The *Army Survival Manual* and the *Boy Scout Handbook* both outline eating worms in the wild to survive. To eat them safely you must soak them in clean water so that they purge themselves of potentially harmful germs and soil. They can then be eaten raw or smashed into a jelly to be spread on bread.

Maya didn't hate the taste. She could eat them to survive, if she'd had to.

Robert, though she didn't yet know he was Robert, walked up to the table. The chainmail in his knight costume shifted and glowed ghostblue in the dim strobing lights.

"Those are real worms, you know," she said to him.

"Oh, I know," he said. "I brought these." That was when he'd smiled at her for the first time.

"You can eat worms to survive," Maya returned his smile. "You know. If you have to."

"We're eating them now," he said, pulling off the wrapper. "And we don't even have to survive…"

Maya could never really separate Fate from desire. They were tangled silken yarn, slippery in her hands, too strongly knotted together to be destroyed. Instead, they made her want to destroy the universe that created her.

The machine clanked to a stop. The ozone smell dissipated.

"It won't work," she said to the air. She paused and couldn't feel Robert there.

"I'm trying," she pleaded with the emptiness.

Maya didn't know if anything was truly empty. How could it be if everything was energy? The universe was as dense as the center of a collapsing star. Energy was real: you could feel it between two people, the space that fills with whitehot electrical current, a looming thunderclap of tension or passion or possibility. She'd had that with him in so many iterations. She knew she could make something with the residue of it that lived in her, that it could make him come back, to take form again, to be flesh.

Maya shut her eyes tight. The possibility of failure made her ears ring, dying sounds drowning out the world around her. She wished she could forget everything she'd ever learned. Brain a *tabula rasa.* Her sense of self gone through a factory reset. If she couldn't bring him back, she wanted to become a perfect machine, wiped clean of the detritus of being alive.

Robert's angry voice lived as an ache on her neck. She hadn't expected that he'd swerve the wrong way during the fight, that he'd become a distracted, distraught sound crackling through the machine that took him. She hadn't meant it, hadn't meant any of it, hadn't wanted things to go that way.

Desire and Fate. The forces that entwined her, snaketight, coiling and biting their poison into her circulatory system.

It would take something more than machine to bring his voice back to her, to make his ghost real.

There was a lake. Things that froze under it. Truths hidden and uncovered.

Light bent strangely there.

She would find it. She would bring the machine.

Something had to happen.

The research had all led her to the lake at the edge of the country. Perhaps fate, coincidence, or desire: it didn't matter. The whole project had gone surprisingly quickly, and she just had to wait for the right signs to burn into her sight. The fact that his presence came back, more than a voice, the dense energy growing denser meant she had to be close to getting him to return to her.

Maya checked the apples in the front yard. Their crushed rot, bruisesoft, meant the worms would be coming soon.

The air was getting colder. Frost glinted on the edges of the world.

The morning came that the lake froze. The first day of the small thin crust on the top, a clear glass, a mirror shining clouds back at themselves.

It was time. She brushed her hair into a long thick braid, weaving together her three wounds: the fight, his death, her failure. She weaved them with her hope, her longing, her anger.

Maya shut out the images of death: the writhing of soil. Robert had been cremated. It didn't make sense that these nightmares screeched into her thoughts, a bright nuclear light, eliminating her will to live.

Bringing him back would change it. She was sure of it.

She pulled the frozen worms from the pile of rot. The sicksweet decay gagged her, stuck in the back of her throat. She resisted her lurching stomach as she stuck the worms in her coat pocket and slipped on her backpack. Her breath was a silver cloud that stuck between the needles of the evergreens.

The sky was a bright grey, a slate of nothing. The perfect conditions. As she slipped on her gloves, she hoped that it might snow. The soil was frozen, her muddy tracks on the path hard and grey with the cold. She stepped where she had stepped before, a perfect imprint, retracing the past to follow the present.

Robert's shape followed her. She tried not to look at him, but she could see the faint outline, a shadow erased to white. It was barely visible on the bright day. But she knew it was there.

Ernest Shackleton, on his final expedition, imagined an incorporeal being with him and his crew. Perhaps the being was also snowbright on that day: perhaps Shackleton had not been imagining at all. The conditions for birthing energy to presence lived in this cold, this longing for both beginning and end.

Maya walked to the edge of the water. The lake had frozen, but not solid. She tapped a boot to the surface, cracking open a small hole. She put down her backpack on the shore and pulled her fishing pole from its strap.

Threading the worm onto the hook: a sense of relief she didn't need to kill it. She cast the line into the hole she'd cracked open. Foxes shrieked in the distance.

The bronze fish of her regret tugged on the line. She reeled it in, excitement thrumming through her shaking hands. It wriggled, desperate for its freedom. She slashed its neck with a small sharp knife. Its red blood splashed across the thin ice.

She recited the words. Ancient syllables poured from her mouth.

Maya threw the fish onto the ice. As soon as it hit the surface, a fox emerged. It ran to her. She picked it up and knew it was Robert. The fox stared at her, an unusual intelligence in its eyes. Its heart was beating fast against her.

"Okay," Maya finally said. A sharp peace stabbed her chest. She put him down.

The fox ran into the woods, its orange silhouette burning the color of frozen leaves on the forest floor.

Wished

Die Booth

It's not the first voice that's called to him from the woods, but it's the first he's certain he isn't imagining. It's a child's voice. It sounds like, "Help me."

It shocks him to a stop, in the middle of the crossroads just beyond the edge of the village. The air is heavy. There's hardly a breeze, but the trees sway, beckoning him in, the spaces between their branches cradling too deep a darkness for such a sunny day. "Someone help me, please!" The voice calls. It sounds scared. Urgent.

Nick has been frightened by this place since he was little. Of what hides there, in the dark, in the trees, in the places in-between. Of what might follow him out should he ever venture in. Now, he's no longer a child and he's afraid of other things—more grown-up troubles perhaps, but just as ancient and unnameable. "It's coming!" The little voice shouts, and he can't ignore it. Crossing the road, he hesitates on the threshold. The trees close ranks, whispering. Deep within Hellakin Wood, the child starts to sob. Nick sets one foot onto the forest floor.

The canopy of trees turns down the sound as surely as it shades. Stepping into their shadow is entering another world, still and foreign. The air simmers. No sounds of animals, birds, wind—just the level hum of insects and the child's sob that draws him in.

There's a path, sort of. Nick creeps along it, crunching twigs beneath his shoes. He wants to call out, to shout that it'll be all right, don't cry, but something stops him. Some half-remembered fear inside. The voice sounds familiar, picks at the plaster on the cracks of his memory, the damp beneath seeping like tears; no amount of paint can disguise it forever. Our fears shape us. They make us. He presses onward.

Birches full of eyes blink at him, their pearly bark undulating with shadow. The woods are watching. Rising in pitch, the cries grow nearer. There's a smell here: a strange, sweet solvent scent, strong and somehow unsettling. Nick stumbles through tangled nettle and bramble, branches biting at his ankles, to find in a trodden hollow of fern, not a child but a fox.

It stares at him with wild-whited eyes, struggle stilled suddenly but for its ribs heaving in silenced panic. Around its neck is looped a stem, too noose-like to look natural. Where was the voice? Who was weeping? He should go. He should turn around and leave, back the way he came, retracing his steps to the world he knows, but those dark eyes have his, magnetized. Gazing back, he can't look away. Sees in brutal detail the frill of fur and the writhe of fleas amongst it, each arc of bleached whisker trembling as soft lips wrinkle back from curving teeth.

He reaches for it anyway.

The fox grimaces. Tosses its head back, eyes rolling, but otherwise keeps still. Under Nick's palms its ribs vibrate like a struck drum-skin beneath the rough-soft ruffle of pelt. There's no way the knotted vine is an accident: the construction is too clearly a trap. He tests it, but it won't snap. Pulls, but only tightens it. The fox shivers. Who could construct a trap like that? They are both frightened. Something in the humid air is watching. Waiting. Scanning round, he finds a bit of stone, not sharp exactly but roughly pointed, enough to slide beneath the stem and saw. Green bleeds onto his fingertips. The noose, pulping and loosing, finally parts.

Quicker than blinking, the fox darts.

He's alone. The child's voice is no longer, and other voices shadow in his memory instead. *Nick's always been a loner. He'll get a girlfriend someday.* Standing, he brushes the dirt off.

A hound's howl cuts the droning quiet.

Nick's heart ices.

Another sharp bark sounds, followed by another and another. Distant but nearing faster than he thought possible, a pack, clamoring, crashing through the bracken after their prey. He glances the way the fox ran and hesitates. He can feel that tiny heartbeat in his throat. The hounds howl, gaining, and Nick is afraid. Turns his back on what he wanted to save and flees the other way.

The woods whip by, trying to trip him as he jumps branches and banks, the trees reaching for him in his flight. He can still hear the barking. It seems to be coming from all around: a trick of echo no doubt, bouncing off trunks and rocks. What would fox hounds do if they caught a man anyway? They're just dogs. They have a master. He slows, winded, his pulse climbing down. The hounds are still barking, drawing closer, though he ran the opposite way to the fox. Perhaps the fox's scent is on him. Nick realizes with sudden, horrible clarity that it's him they're tracking now. They have his scent; it is the same as the fox's. A howl sounds from directly above him. Fear and need kindle in his heart, burn away to something new. His heart races, and he wants to live—more than he's ever wanted to.

He runs.

Their din is in the sky, their call all around, in front and behind, but they're invisible as yearning. Fleeing between the trees, he ploughs through thickets of fern and towering thistle, creeping soft grass illuminated with buttercups and pink campion, with foxgloves swaying higher than his head, and the breath of the pack on the back of his neck. He smells water before he hears it, hears it before he sees, sliding on stones flocked with moss, down to the bare, brown bank. Joining the chorus of howls and barks is the warning low of a hunting horn.

Nick screams, "Go away! Leave me alone!" Slipping in the mud, his shoe sticks: he tugs off one, then the other, throwing them desperately in the direction of the hounds' baying, wading into the stream in an effort to throw off the scent. The water ticks with frantic insects, skimming and dipping away from him. Pebbles roll beneath his soles, the quick flow colder than the syrupy air. Downstream, the water boils to steam as the pack passes over it. He splashes up the opposite bank, flinging himself into the undergrowth, crawling, desperate.

Perhaps he can hide.

Shuffling backwards, he tucks himself away beneath an overhang of earth held together by the strong, coiled roots of an eared willow. The dogs bark and Nick holds his breath. He hears, in the swish of grass, footsteps. They stop overhead and he hears a voice like the deep creak of timber. "Give up your soul to darling sin."

He's too scared to look at what's hunting him. Pollen sheds like glitter in the filtering shafts of sunlight. The ground is soft with fallen blossom, powdery yellow and thick with the musty scent of May. He leans his head back and closes his eyes, willing it all away. The only sound now is the green quiet, the pop and zing of flies. Hot sap crackling in new stems. His own hammering blood. He's starting to feel light headed from holding his breath. The huntsman knows he's there. He can't hide. He's not sure he wants to anymore.

Another howl and his blood seizes. The fairy hounds, smoking and baying and somehow more alive than he has ever been in his short, dim life. In his head his remembered father says, *he doesn't know which side his bread is buttered* and he realizes the voice of the fox was his own child-voice, crying to be heard, to listen to the dreams he sacrificed to daylight and the narrow path. He ran in the dark after his wishes, until his wishes turned to chase him. He turned his back on what he wanted to save, but his wish-hounds caught up with him anyway. What you want most will devour you. Nick opens his eyes and the shadows look suddenly bright. That odd solvent smell that's been following him has turned to honey. Our fears shape us: he has taken the shape of a man. Of a lover. He *wants* to look.

Turning slowly, Nick peers over the tangle of tree roots. Sees the pack, the dogs of the air, milling around their master. He thought they'd be black but they're white, with pricked red ears and panting mouths and eyes like burning coals. They're big, but the huntsman towers over them. Antlers curve from his head. His skin is green and his eyes are huge and black. He is clad in the forest. Over his shoulder he carries a hawthorn tree for a hunting stick. They said he was unnatural, but they were wrong—he *is* nature, and he is beautiful. "What I catch, I keep." The huntsman's voice stirs the leaves. He holds out a hand.

This is a threshold. This is a choice.

Nick hears the call of the pack. He steps off the path.

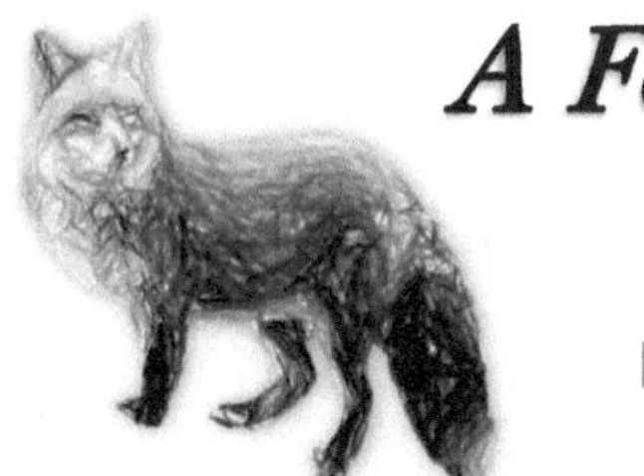

A Fox Caught by Dogs

Leo X. Robertson

"You're all here to stage my play!" At a theatre space in town that I rent at a loss.

Before me are ten whole strangers from different backgrounds. They sit in a circle on a worn wooden stage, framed by heavy black curtains.

"What's it about?" Keisha asks.

I get the feeling she has to be the artistic chick in town, with her black lipstick, tight t-shirt, red Doc Martens and long flared cords. There's a tattoo on her forearm of a uterus with one of its fallopian tubes curled up like a hand extending a middle finger.

It's about me.

Duh, Kate, but I can't ever tell them.

I twist the locket around my neck in thought. Eventually, I reply: "It's about, uh, unavoidable melancholy."

"Sounds great," Dustin says. Chubby bald guy, hi-vis vest, dirty jeans and boots.

The rest laugh.

They're just nervous.

Well you'd never guess who the most nervous one is.

Thereafter comes the barrage of questions:

Trevor: You didn't mention your name.

Me: Jeff.

Trevor: Jork?

Me: What? No, I said "Jeff." Though I guess it sounds like "Jork."

Trevor: No it doesn't.

Dustin: You're like a theatre director or something?

Me: Electrical engineer by profession—

Dustin: You should take my card.

Me: —but I'm not here in that capacity.

Dustin: Whatever, you don't even look like one.

Hair half-shaved, blond-pink. White fake fur jacket, blue tie-dye t-shirt with Laura Palmer wrapped in plastic on it.

Kate, remember you got a VHS copy of *Fire Walk with Me* from a friend at school who'd gone to New York on holiday? You passed it to me in the hallway. Other kids thought it was porn. It was the summer we spent talking backwards together.

Cheryl: Wanna show us the play? Know more about us?

Me: I just thought to assign roles today. We need a flyman and several dancers, but I'll find something for everyone.

Cheryl: So there's dancing.

Lori: And music?

Angie: Less a play more a musical?

Michele: A ballet, maybe!

Bobbi: A multidisciplinary work!

Me: Please debate that in your own time.

Ginger: But we should agree so we can put it on websites and pamphlets.

Me: Great idea! You're in charge of that.

I like to shut down actions I don't care for by putting the suggester in charge of them. People more readily propose work than do it.

>**Shelly**: Can't you help us?
>
>**Me**: I'm not good at categorizing my own work.

I don't care to either.

>**Me**: I'll link you to a Google Doc of the play. Get a majority vote on its labels. I'll accept them.
>
>**Cheryl**: Can't we all read it together for the first time? It's more fun that way.
>
>**Me**: Can you organize that for us?
>
>**Keisha**: You need lighting plans, musicians, costumes, make-up artists, money—
>
>**Trevor**: I can help with funding!
>
>**Me**: Thanks, but we don't need it. I've got it covered.

His revulsion reveals that he interprets this as a flex. To me it's a source of guilt. I'm using an artistic space for my own play, irrespective of its popularity. Sometimes I wonder if we hamper the arts with our own narcissism.

>**Me**: As for the materials Keisha mentioned, I'll supply them all.
>
>**Keisha**: But you can't!
>
>**Me**: Why not?
>
>**Keisha**: You have to specialize if you want anything you do to be great.
>
>**Me**: And if you want the most experience?
>
>**Dustin**: You have drawings? Plans?

Me: Those would be for illustrating the director's vision to other departments. Lighting, sound, costume and so on. If I am those other departments, the plan can stay in my head.

Angie: What will we get out of this?

Me: I'm not sure.

Lori: And what made you think you could do this?

I sigh and think for a moment.

Me: That's the strangest question so far.

Keisha: How so?

All lean in, awaiting my response to this. They are all on Lori and Keisha's side, it seems.

Me: Do you all live as if awaiting permission to try new stuff?

Stunned silence, grumbling, mirth, gossip, half-mumbled responses like, "Well, I would hardly say that."

I wanna go.

I imagine Kate in the corner, laughing, shaking her head. Painted face, flowers in her dark brown hair, long red dress. Neither of us successfully made ourselves understood, so we gave up and just enjoyed life. But once others realized we had lost interest in their opinions, they thought our fun was at their expense.

Stand in a room with someone and they'll make your existence about themselves.

My nouveau troupe disburses soon after, out into the scorching July afternoon. The long side of my hair sticks to my face. The shaved side cools rapidly. Uneven head temperature.

Trevor, the networking guy with the goatee, holds his leather jacket over one arm. "Coming down the pub?"

Dustin stands behind him.

Bemused, I ask, "Are you friends already?"

Dustin mops his brow with a rag. "We're getting a pint together at least."

"Amazing."

"So you'll come?" Trevor asks.

"No thank you."

"Why not? You're one of us now."

I look again. Not a big enough sample size to tell for sure, but "us" probably means "menfolk."

They just want to get to know you better!

Remember our rule, Kate?

Bail from socializing as soon as acceptable. But now that I'm not here, I want more for you.

A well-meaning sentiment, Kate.

"Another time," I say to Trevor, adding a shoulder pat. I accidentally let it linger and it turns a bit flirtatious, so I speedily walk away.

I find a bench on which to eat my pre-packed egg and cress sandwich.

So ended this attempt to find my people. All I found was more reality.

I replay it in my head. I'm surprised no one said "Never met anyone like you!" That apparent accusation usually surfaces during a first impression. Why don't they expect it to be true of every new person they meet?

"You look very glam, son!" An elderly lady stops to stroke my jacket. "Softer than I imagined."

"Thanks!" I respond, quickly getting back up to leave.

I love wearing colorful clothes, but it makes strangers think you're approachable.

Most of my crew return for future rehearsals! I hear a few "nothing better to do" murmurs.

But their motivations are their business and mine are mine.

Me: Raise your hand if you read the play?

One hand, another at half-mast.

Me: Anyway the bulk of the piece is an interpretative dance. Those who signed up to act—

Without knowing the play?

Me: —I'll need measurements for ballet costumes.
Dustin: Making fun of us?
Me: Offering you the chance to express grace and femininity through the veil of theatre. Anyone on the construction site giving you that?
Dustin: Okay, I'm in—
Me: Fantastic.
Dustin: —because it sounds fucking hilarious.

Kate, I can't do this.

I fit them for costumes and rehearsals get going. No further cast members ever read the script. They stand on stage not knowing what to do with their hands. Adorable but useless, like little kids.

Keisha takes me aside one time. "You know, the director usually, uh, directs a little more."

I sigh. "I get that at work too. Other leaders talk far more than I do, but they're rarely saying more. I can't bring myself to placate people with empty speech."

She hooks an arm around my head. "Just ask for help when you need it. We're a big family now!" she adds, loud enough for all to hear.

Pleased looks spread across their faces until I respond "Good for you all."

I get it in the neck enough from what remains of my real-life family. I'm not in the market for more!

Trevor: I have an idea!

Me: Let's hear it!

Trevor: My mate's camera records in 4K. 4K!

Me: Is that like a lot?

Trevor: We put the performance on Vimeo. I know this film producer guy? He watches and then—

Me: That I must advise against.

Trevor: (folding arms) Why?

It just gives me bad vibes—but as I speak, my reason emerges.

> **Me**: You have to be here to experience the play. Most others in the city won't even know about it. Their impression of the world will remain unaffected by this one beautiful thing happening in this one place. And then—it's gone forever.
>
> **Keisha**: And that's what you want?
>
> **Me**: Doesn't matter what I want, it's—how theatre works.
>
> **Dustin**: Can I invite my girlfriend to the premiere?
>
> **Me**: Sure?
>
> **Dustin**: Well, are you inviting yours?

He's in his tutu and ballet costume when he asks. Probably wondering if it's some fetish of mine.

I just wanted to put on a play, but they're all so curious about me! Invites to birthdays, work dinners, brunches. No match for my arsenal of polite declines of course.

> **Keisha**: This is the theatre, darling. Nearly everyone's gay.
>
> **Trevor**: Can you believe I've never met a gay person before?
>
> **Keisha**: That you know of.
>
> **Trevor**: I've always wanted to ask one: Do you ever think about how advanced society is?
>
> **Me**: Where is this going?
>
> **Trevor**: It allows people like you in it who don't reproduce.

Wow.

Look, he's not a bad guy. Just hadn't thought that one through at all. Since I'm five steps ahead of him in terms of what he has accidentally implied, he's shocked by my response.

Me: I just want to put on a fucking play, I didn't come here to debate for the right to exist.

Stunned silence.

Me: I'm disturbed by how you live your lives too, by the way. Like your words and actions don't count for shit, like you have time to spend on activities you don't care about because you have nothing better to do, like it's okay to let others do the work while you contribute nothing but relentless criticism. But did I ever force you to explain yourselves?

I lie in bed that evening, crying to myself. "Picture it, me, a grown man!" I sometimes add in my head, as if it isn't totally acceptable. Wonder where and when I internalized that.

Kate swims in the ceiling above me, like it's an upside-down lake.

You looked like you could use my company.

Mhm. I've been thinking about joining you.

But if you don't learn from my mistake then it really was a waste.

It always will be. Hang around me all you want. Better than nothing. But don't mistake that for my forgiveness.

Someone knocks at the door. I dab my eyes with a corner of bedsheet and get up.

"Keisha."

She's changed into a grey turtleneck and black cords. "Surprise!"

"I don't like those." I'm in a boxers and t-shirt. "How did you find me?"

"You added me on Facebook, remember?"

I walk away, leaving the door open.

She comes in, closes it behind her and starts opening curtains. "Not prepared for guests?"

Plumes of dust billow in light shafts. The ironing board with dirty clothes stacked on top has graduated from symbol of future intent to permanent conceptual art piece. Spirit bottles on tables and counters reveal why all those emptied pizza boxes didn't fatten me up. Alcohol curbs appetite.

Keisha clears a stack of plates from the table and puts them in the dishwasher. "I can't help it, I do this everywhere I go."

I smile softly at her and sit in an armchair.

"I didn't like how things got left at last rehearsal. I worry about you."

"Why?"

She runs a lint roller over the couch. "We've spent some time together over the weeks and I've come to enjoy your company. Or your presence, at least. Whatever you would call it."

"Wow." I lift my legs so she can sweep the floor beneath them. "Sounds like you're really trying to put things in my language."

"Guess I'm quite intuitive that way."

"Keisha, can you sit for a minute?"

"Thought you'd never ask."

I take a deep breath. "There's something I'd like to tell you."

I had this sister, Kate. We made art together our entire lives. Drawings, cartoons, short stories, novels, films—stop motion things with Lego figures. Unreleased videogames about the mundanity of adolescence. Our own version of Monopoly—Ournopoly—made from cardboard and filled with locations from our own neighborhood. Do not pass Go, go directly to your bedroom.

Some might say we "did the Henry Darger thing." You ask me, the notion of outsider art has been co-opted by middle-class Hunter S Wannabes who once did cocaine in Goa. Like, who didn't?

After school Kate went to uni to study law and drifted us apart, deliberately, like I was an unfortunate phase she had outgrown. The calls got fewer and further between. I'd send her links to stuff that reminded me of her. Michel Gondry music videos. Japanese performances of Sarah Kane's plays. A clip from *The Holy Mountain*. She'd occasionally respond "Weird" or some terse remark.

I was studying electrical engineering at the time. Wasn't trying to "grow up," I just liked it, I don't know. One afternoon the students invited me out for Wasted Wednesdays. I called Kate and basically said "What the fuck?"

I remember how her response felt more than its details. "Weirdo," "working world," "adulthood." Fill in the blanks, you might've heard it yourself.

I thought we'd remedy things that Christmas. Before we could, she killed herself.

Keisha, Kate was my person. Soulmate. Sure, fuck it, it's my soul, I know what it was. We vibed through life together. We hadn't meant it to be the two of us against the world, the world made it so.

Now it's just against me, and I don't know what to do.

Keisha is perched on an armrest, hand on my knee as I choke back sobs.

"So that's what the play is about," she says. "And why you couldn't tell us."

"It was years ago now, you know? But—goddamn it I'm still not ready to talk about it."

Her hands are in her lap now. "You know, Jeff, every time we get figures like you and your sister—and it is rare—it's so beautiful. Yet the Jeff and Kate team never shared its talents with us. It's not a loss the world feels. You can't know what you never got. But it's a loss nonetheless." She grips my arm for emphasis. "Now you're doing it, man. You're gonna put it out there and make people look." She kneels and envelops me in a hug. "I'm so proud of you."

I melt into her.

When she pulls away, my locket gets caught in her hair.

"Sorry," she says. She pulls at the fastening and the memory card falls out.

I pick it up. "It's—a video. Of how she did it."

Keisha gasps. "My god."

"Her final gift to me." I flip it between my fingers. "I clicked play on it once."

She flinches.

"A stony beach. Cool colors, everything cast in blue. Deliberately underexposed. The way life felt sometimes to me, and inescapably to her, I guess. The video goes on, but I stopped it."

Keisha grips her chin in her hand in thought. "I'll talk to the others. I won't tell them much, just enough to get their confidence back."

"I'd appreciate that."

She heads to the door, adding, "Thanks again, Jeff," on her way out.

The first in a long time that a social interaction has ended sooner than I would've liked.

Keisha: Here he is!
Cheryl: Hi, Jeff!
Dustin: Good to see you!

A little patronizing, but I'd take it.

Keisha: We're ready to rehearse again.

Trevor approaches with his arms out. He thinks better of it and bumps me on the shoulder with a fist.

Trevor: Sorry, Jork. I was talking shit earlier. I didn't know about your dead sister.

Keisha groans. She'd probably coached them on what not to say.

I resist the urge to ask Trevor whether it would've been okay to treat me a certain way if my sister was still alive.

Me: Apology accepted, Dork. Let's get back to it.

Opening night comes around. We stand backstage, twitching the curtains to see the early arrivals.

Trevor's in place by the fly system, checking the cables and ropes. Keisha gets the main cast to stand in a circle, put their hands together and chant "Energy, energy, energy!" with increasing, uh, energy. The sound of it sends me into a full body cringe. I almost pull a muscle.

Dustin slaps his hand on my shoulder from behind. I gasp in fright. He points to a group of construction workers sitting at the closest table. "All the lads are here."

Why?! "I appreciate you inviting them. Curious what they'll make of it."

"They insisted on coming!" He shrugs. "But don't worry, I warned them it won't be any good."

I shake my head, trying not to react, and make my way to the lighting bay.

The performance begins.

Fake flowers spring through holes in the plywood of my raised stage. My pre-recorded synth music plays. Spotlights, programmed wirelessly through a tablet, wash the stage in yellow.

Keisha and Dustin, in ballet outfits, run in together. As the Ournopoly board floats by, Dustin mugs to his peanut gallery mates, who laugh.

The light cools, casting everything in blue. The stage is almost too dark by the time we reach the scene of Keisha in her suit and tie, hunched over like a chimpanzee, dragging a suitcase and wailing.

Later Dustin returns, his beard flecked with purple glitter. He spreads his arms to release his dragonfly wings, fluttering his hands like dying doves. A rain of blue sequins scatters across the stage.

We reach the denouement. Dancers prance back and forth, clutching silk scarves in tow, in various shades of blue, making an impressionistic sea.

Keisha takes to the high board in her blood-red dress. My vision goes blurry at the edges as I watch her, the piece culminating in my mind. A mixture of what I intended and what the cast brought to it. An extension of my internal world made real for all to see. The expression of what I wanted to say, which I could do no other way. Not a conversation, an essay, a song, no. This and only this.

Keisha dives. Trevor, with pinpoint accuracy, pivots her to the vertical and lowers her gracefully into the silky murk.

Fade to black.

Scattered applause. Oh, but it hardly matters.

Keisha carts me around the tables afterwards. Michele and Bobbi, two hipster students who attended the first meeting, sit at one of them. They're pleased with how it turned out and want to join in next time.

Next time?

"You must!" Keisha grabs them by the shoulders. "I'm finishing up my play now."

"Your play?" I ask.

She nods at me. "You inspired me."

Huh. I should've asked her more about herself.

"Michele, Bobbi?" she says. "I've got an important task for you both. What's the name of our troupe?"

Dustin's table of construction workers ask me what their mate was doing in a tutu.

"Expressing feminine beauty, supposedly," I reply.

"I didn't get that," one says.

"Dustin!" another exclaims. "Why didn't you express your feminine fuckin' beauty like the director wanted? Arsehole."

Trevor's girlfriend, a glamorous wag, waves at us. We head over to her.

"Jeff," she says, "I bet you take your creativity for granted, but"—she points a thumb at Trevor beside her—"people like this big lug here need it. He could never come close to creating something like this. He was thrilled to be a part of it. All he talked about from day dot."

"Ah," Keisha says. "That explains all the networking and crowdfunding suggestions."

She nods. "Just trying to help how he can. Jeff, we're going out for drinks after, you have to join us!"

At this, Trevor places a gentle hand on her forearm. "Not his style, honey. Have him over for dinner sometime. And give him plenty of notice!"

How kind of him to have learned about me. Yet I worry our future friendship will be forever tainted by what he said to me in ignorance that one time. God, I hate myself—for something he said, sure—but I don't know if I can get over it.

Keisha leads me to our table. Champagne sits in an ice bucket beside it.

"You're wired differently, honey," she says. "It brought everyone here tonight. Aren't you proud?"

"Oh yeah."

"But you seem disappointed."

"Not at all. I was just thinking. When I ask myself what I wanted from this, it's something like, 'I want my sister back.' Can't have that, so maybe a boyfriend, friend or piece of art. In that order."

"Huh," she says. "It wasn't much about the art for any of us."

I nod effusively. "You're right."

"Jeff?"

"Yes?"

She looks at my locket. "Do you want to watch Kate's video together?"

Wow. It's like she just reached inside me and opened a little concrete door that held back a deluge of emotion. In response I start wailing uncontrollably. Like an exorcism. And isn't it?

Heads turn my way.

"Forget it." She puts her hand on mine.

Others, seeing I am comforted, go back to their various chats. Between them I imagine Kate in a puffy white dress. It glows as if viewed through a silk stocking filter.

I look Kate in the eyes and pour myself a glass of champagne. Condensation gathers on its side. It will be cold, crisp and delicious. Before Keisha can object, I take the memory card out my locket and dunk it in the glass.

"Uh, Jeff?"

I look back to Keisha. She looks scared, like I will regret my haste.

I shoot her a smile of reassurance. "I would never have made you watch it. But I sincerely believe you would have, if it's what I needed." I raise my glass. "I am overcome with emotion to call you my friend. A toast to you."

She raises her glass too. We clink them and sip.

Kate nods to me slowly.

Yes, a tribute to you too, Kate. Our friendship exists in worlds of our own invention. But reality can rob one of fantasy. You deserve a death more poetic than any finite gesture might afford you. So no one will ever see it. Your infinite imaginary deaths will forever populate my imagination and enrich the art I make for the world.

I look across the room of chattering folk. "There's a party going on."

"In your honor," Keisha replies.

"Come on, then." I reach my hand out to her. "We must meet all our people."

You Without Me

Katie Young

I don't know what I've done this time. This morning when I woke up, he'd gone. All his clothes have disappeared from the wardrobe, and his toothbrush is not in the cup by the basin. I didn't hear him leave, but he's taken the car. Great.

We didn't fight, and I've been wracking my brains trying to think of something I could have said or done to make him leave, but I'm drawing a blank. He'd been quiet for a while. Pretty much totally ignoring me. Come to think of it, he hadn't spoken to or acknowledged me at all for days. Weeks maybe. I lose track.

I'm used to the cold shoulder. He withdraws and becomes distant when he's stressed about work or generally feeling anxious, but this feels different. In hindsight, I should have tried harder to coax it out of him and find out what was wrong, but his default is to clam up and give me the silent treatment. He hates confrontation—even when it's well-intentioned. And now he's gone.

The other night, I woke in the shallow hours of morning to find he wasn't next to me in our bed. The sheet was wrinkled but cool. I needed to pee, so I got up and padded to the bathroom, and as I passed the spare room I poked my head around the door and saw that he'd crashed out in there. I'd probably been snoring. Too many glasses of wine with dinner. It really got to me, for some reason, this inexorable widening of the fault line forming between us. I sat on the toilet for long minutes after I finished emptying my bladder and let the tears come. I looked in on him again on the way back to bed, and this time he was awake, sitting up, his eyes big as dinner plates. He stared at me—no, not at me; through me—as if he were still in the grip of a nightmare. I started toward him, to comfort him, but he pulled the covers up over his head and turned to the wall.

I wonder where he's staying. Maybe with his sister. She's only an hour's drive away and they've always been close. I worry. I keep meaning to call him, or at least send a text asking if he's safe, but I can't seem to find my phone. I hope it turns up soon.

Things haven't been easy for a while now. I haven't worked since I was signed off long term with these migraines a few months ago. I was finding it harder and harder to focus on my job, and finally my boss picked up on it. I was making silly mistakes—forgetting to send important e-mails or dial into client calls. I was lethargic all the time, and found it hard to keep up with what was being discussed in meetings. It wasn't like me at all. I started losing things too, misplacing my handbag and locking myself out of the house. I'd joke about it being early menopause or senility, but it's scary, becoming someone you don't recognize. Bloody terrifying, actually. I feel much better now, and the pain is mostly gone. I get a touch now and then—like a hangover. I see lights dance in my periphery then I feel the aftermath, a dull ache in my temples. But it's not constant anymore. It doesn't make me throw up. Maybe it was stress after all. I've always had broad shoulders, but I guess we all have limits. I don't think I'm ready to go back to the office yet. I still have trouble remembering things.

Then there was the cat. Tom and I always said we wouldn't get another after our beloved Bengal had to be put down. It absolutely broke our hearts. But then Lucy at work found a stray, only she couldn't keep it because it kept fighting with her dog. She showed me a picture of this wretched, skinny little thing, and before I could help it, I found myself saying, "I'll take him." Tom was annoyed for a few minutes when I got home and told him that night, but then I showed him a picture of this bedraggled creature with huge orange eyes and knobbly bones too visible through his matted fur, and he relented immediately.

We called him Beans, on account of the shape of the soft fleshy pads on his feet which looked so pink and adorable nestled in messy tufts of black fluff when he stretched out on the sofa between us. Tom would gently stroke them as Beans spread his little cat toes and purred, and my heart would feel like it was swelling in the cage of my ribs, like all this love would come bursting out of my chest like that scene in *Alien*.

But a few weeks back, Beans seemed to change overnight. He was always so affectionate, and then suddenly he started acting strangely— spitting and hissing and lashing out. He'd be fine one second, sitting on Tom's lap, and enjoying a scratch behind the ears, and the next minute I'd go to pet him and he'd shrink away from me, ears flat to his head, and scoot away. If Tom tried to restrain him, Beans would go crazy, even drawing blood with his teeth and claws on a few occasions. He started to explore outside for longer and longer each day, only coming in for food. He even started staying out at night, eschewing the warm luxury of our bed for the suburban wilds, getting into scraps with other cats and skulking about the neighborhood in all weathers.

One morning, he didn't come back for his breakfast. Or his lunch. Or dinner. Tom waited until the weekend and then put posters up in all the surrounding blocks for a mile or two, but we haven't seen hide nor hair of Beans since. Maybe that's part of why Tom left. Maybe he blames me for bringing the cat home and letting Tom grow to love the scruffy little sod without thinking about the fact he might have been mistreated in the past. It's always a risk with strays. There's no guarantee they will settle down. I should have thought about that before I said we'd adopt the poor thing.

The house is so quiet now. I keep feeling the phantom brush of Beans' tail against my ankles or imagining I can hear Tom clearing his throat in another room. I should probably go shopping for groceries, but I've lost my appetite. One morning, when I go to the cupboards for cereal to stave off the gnawing hunger in my belly, I find them crawling with tiny, dark brown insects. Weevils. They must have hatched from eggs in old flour on the top shelf. They are in everything—in the box of cornflakes, in a bag of rice, crawling purposefully around the bottom of the biscuit barrel. My skin crawls, watching them teeming in our food. It feels like a huge violation, and I am close to weeping again as I dump ruined packet after nibbled box into the trash. I disinfect everything and hoover up all the dead insects I find scattered about the worktops. But by the next day, there are dozens more of the little bastards scaling the pantry doors. All the cobwebs I swept away the previous day have been re-spun and there are maggots in the bin, writhing in my discarded food with the beetles.

The joy has left this house. For all the time and care I spent picking paint colors and wallpapers, furniture and textiles, tiles and art, there is nothing here that brings me comfort now that I'm alone. This used to be our sanctuary; a place I adored coming back to at the end of a long day. I'd lie with my head on Tom's chest, listening to his heartbeat and to rain lashing against the sash windows, as Beans dozed at the foot of the bed. I'd read by candlelight in the bath, drink wine by the open fire in our cozy front room. We'd spend leisurely hours in the kitchen at the weekends, baking bread and muffins, slow cooking ragu and stews. In the summer we'd have friends over to sit in the tiny garden, sipping cocktails as the sun slid behind the roofs of the houses opposite. I always planted wildflowers for the bees. I was proud to host and share my space with my nearest and dearest, but now everything seems to be decaying and moldering and gathering dust and grime, and I can't seem to keep on top of it.

I need to leave the house and get some essentials. Bread, milk, coffee. Something green and nourishing. Perhaps if I try to eat healthily and drink water and sleep properly, things won't feel so insurmountable. I just need to take better care of myself. I'll track Tom down and make him speak to me. I know he still loves me. He must, because you can't fall out of love with someone overnight. He probably just needs some distance. Things have been hard for him too, worrying about me and losing Beans. His job is pretty demanding, although he never talks about it. I can't blame him for feeling strained. I know I've not been easy to live with recently. I forget things, you see.

I take several deep breaths and open the front door. The light is blinding. I hadn't quite appreciated how dark the house is with the curtains all drawn. The fresh air is shocking. It's a sharp contrast with the damp, musty smell of the hall. Moths have started to eat threadbare patches in the woolen carpet. I really need to get a handle on the cleaning. I step out onto the tiled path and look up and down the street. It's quiet and the sun is starting to burn the early morning clouds away. My knees feel like they might buckle as I make my way to the garden gate. Weeds are sprouting up around it—dandelions and bindweed, nettles and storksbill. I put my trembling hand on the latch, but I can't bring myself to lift it. Some unseen force is rooting me to the spot, filling me with a creeping sense of dread. I stand for several minutes trying to overcome this strange inertia, but eventually I give up and go back inside.

I think maybe I need to call someone. I think I need help. Maybe I need counseling. I need pest control. I need groceries. I need Tom.

It's dark when I hear a voice on the landing. Not a voice exactly. Someone humming slightly out of key. My first thought is Tom is back. It sounds like him. I leap out of bed and run to the top of the stairs. But it's not Tom. It's a strange man walking into my bathroom. He's on the other side of middle age, getting thick around the middle, slightly stooped, hair thinning on the back of his head. I slam my hands over my mouth to stop a scream escaping. There's an intruder in the house! I run back to the bedroom to grab my phone but I can't find it. It's not charging on the bedside table where it should be. Shit, shit, shit. There's a trespasser in the house and I can't even call the police. What am I going to do? I could hide and hope he leaves. Perhaps someone noticed our car is missing and the place has been dark. Maybe they've been casing the joint and decided it's empty. Vulnerable. Infested with moths and maggots and beetles. Maybe I should confront him and hope he bolts. No, no that's insane. He might have a weapon. You hear about burglaries going wrong all the time. People getting killed trying to act the hero. I pad to the window to see if I can alert the neighbors, but all the blinds and curtains are closed. I'll just keep really quiet and still and wait for him to leave.

Somehow, I must've fallen asleep while I was cowering under the bed, listening for the burglar. When I wake, there's light streaming through a slit in the curtains. I stay where I am for a few minutes, straining to hear any signs that he's still in the house. It's silent. I stand up and stretch my aching muscles, and gently tiptoe to the landing. I listen again and then descend very slowly. Every time a step creaks, I stop dead and wait, my heart racing. But when I get downstairs, there's no sign of anyone. All the doors and windows are closed. Everything is in its place, nothing broken. It can't have been a dream. I am certain I was awake. But then again, I have been under a lot of pressure. Could I have imagined the man on the landing?

The house is haunted. I know now. Either that or I'm certifiable. I have seen the man several times since that first night, but every time I follow him, he disappears. I've tried calling out to him, but he doesn't seem to hear me or see me. He just looks through me and trudges from one room to another, then vanishes. He seems benign—familiar even—but I don't want him in my space. First the weevils and the moths, now this. My house feels wrong. Like it doesn't want me there without Tom. I should leave—go and see a friend. Maybe things will seem better if I can just get out of the house for a while. If I could just go to the shops (*when was the last time I ate anything—I forget*) and see people and have a conversation and feel the sun on my face. Maybe I could do a spot of gardening. I go to the kitchen window and look out, but my garden isn't my little garden anymore. It's been paved over. There are a few pots here and there but no borders, no shrubs, no fruit trees. Just grey slabs, a patio set and a few miserable pots. What is happening? I start to wail.

There's a new ghost. I know she's a ghost because she can communicate with the other one. I've seen them together in the garden on the ugly rattan patio chairs that aren't mine. I've heard them together in the living room, laughing and talking long into the night. Ghosts are like weevils. Once they infest your house, they multiply. They take over. They're persistent. I try everything I can think of to get rid of them: prayers, incantations, sprinkling salt about the place. But they always come back.

It's a chilly, grey day when the ghosts appear in the bedroom. I'm lying in bed watching the mizzle blur the edges of everything through the gap in the curtains when they materialize either side of me. I freeze. I am no longer exactly afraid of them, but this is new. Different. Intimate. They are close enough that I can see their flesh overlapping mine, passing through it, insubstantial, reaching for each other. Their spectral fingers intertwine, and the ghost woman says,

"How are you doing, Tom darling?"

I turn to look at the man. My heart stutters. I see him now, my Tom. His face is lined, his edges softened, but the eyes are the same. How can it be? How have I never noticed until now?

"Hanging in there, love," Tom's ghost says.

"It can't be easy," his companion says. "Anniversaries are always hard." I lie between them, frozen in place.

"Twenty years," Tom says. "Twenty years since I lost her."

"Do you still feel her here? Her presence?"

Tom turns his face so that we are nose to nose. For just a second, I think he's looking at me. Not through me, but at me. He smiles.

"Sometimes," he says quietly, embarrassed. "I don't know if I ever told you, but I moved out for a while after she died. It was her dearest wish—in the lucid moments—to spend her last days here. She would forget things. The tumor made her…confused. But she loved this house. When she'd gone though, it felt changed. Restless. Hostile even. We had a cat once. A little rescue called Beans." Tom chuckles at the memory. "He was a soppy old thing, and then after she passed…he just changed. He'd run up and down the corridor all wild-eyed and spiky-furred and hiss at nothing. Maybe he just missed her like I did. Then I started hearing things…seeing things. It spooked me. I couldn't sleep in this room. I'd wake and think she was next to me in the bed. I'd forget, for just a split second, and remembering was like losing her all over again. One night, I woke in the spare room and I could've sworn she was standing there at the foot of the bed, watching me.

I let the house go to seed. Moths got into the carpets. The garden was overgrown. I thought about selling up. But it was home, you know? I had to come back in the end. It *is* home. Our home."

"Oh, my love," the woman says. She moves her head towards Tom. I brace for impact, her skull on mine, but she passes through me and kisses him on the forehead. "I can't imagine how painful it was. She was no age at all. But you survived. You lived. I'm sure, if she could see you now, she'd be so happy for you. So proud of the life you've made for yourself."

I lie between them, numb and cold as the grave.

When I next wake, the ghosts are gone. The sun has come out. It's summer…no spring. I'm not sure. I should try and call Tom. He must still be at his sister's. I'm worried about him. I'm not sure what I've done this time. I've misplaced my phone again. I miss him.

I'd lose my head of it wasn't screwed on! The hedge out front needs pruning. I should go to the shops. Get some cat treats for Beans and something for dinner. Something green and nourishing. When did I last eat? It's these headaches. I forget things, you see.

The Man on the Hill

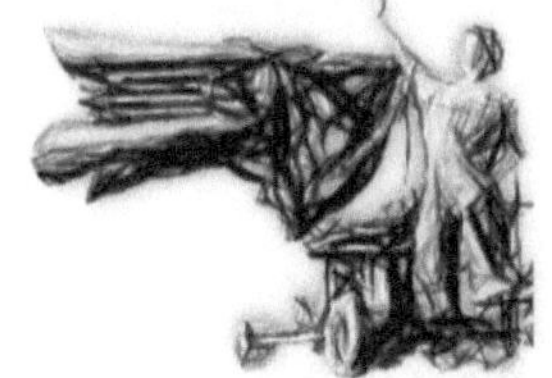

Adrienne Clark

15 June

Dear Peter,

It's raining again today. It rains every day now. I don't know that I would have noticed such a thing if I was free, but now that I am without my freedom, observing the weather is one of the few ways I have left to occupy my time. I can almost hear you scoffing. Me? The very idea of your dear old dad ignoring the weather does seem preposterous. But I truly had stopped paying attention to the weather the way I used to. And I think that might be why I'm in such trouble.

If you're worried, don't be. The wardens stationed to guard me are kind. They are used to watching over men much more violent than me, and my gentle disposition seems to be a respite for them. I wish I could say the same for myself. I don't mean to seem ungrateful. After all, these gentlemen gave me paper and pen to write to you, which is something they didn't have to do. But no one will listen when I speak about my work. Peter, something is terribly wrong, and without my machines, I don't think I will be able to fix it.

I can't say more just yet. After all, a scientist shouldn't speculate further than necessary. But I will tell you all I know in the coming weeks—once I have a firmer grasp on what has happened. If only I could have a better look at the sky. But, alas, my guards are not keen on letting me out into the yard after everything that has happened.

Please pray for me; I do the same for you every night.

Love,

Dad

20 June

Dear Peter,

My cell is on the top floor of the building. If I climb onto my bunk and press my head against the window, it feels as if I'm on top of the world. Like I'm looking over the edge into the vast unknown. Of course, that is only because I can see so little. Just a strip of sky and the tips of the lush summer tree line. If only I could get a better look, I might still be of some use.

Do you remember those summer days when you were little? When we would place one of my smaller machines into your red wagon and drag it out to the fields? We'd point it toward the sky and just see what happened. I loved those days. I didn't know what would occur any more than you did. You probably didn't know that, did you? I had my theories about orgone, and what it was capable of, but no proof. No one had proof! We were all simply experimenting. That much is clear now.

But we were on to something, weren't we? For the rest of my life, I'll remember that day when those black clouds rolled—no, not rolled—*formed* above us. The way the sky stayed bright at the edges but turned black and beautiful just where we stood. You had that little yo-yo in your hand. I remember looking down at you—my small, sweet child—and seeing it gripped in your palm. It was glowing. Seems a small detail, doesn't it? But that glowing, cylindrical toy was what proved to me that we had done it. With the help of my machines, we had brought the storm.

If that was all we had done, I feel sure our circumstances would be different. We'd be living like kings. The lords of the elements. That would be us.

Oh Peter, but that wasn't all, was it? Please write to me. Tell me you're safe.

Dad

23 June

Dear Peter,

I don't have long to wait now. Soon those men who came and took me away will be back. They'll come for me again, and then, only heaven knows. I feel as if I'm living between two worlds. There is the plane of my corporal predicament: I am to be tried for my alleged transgressions, and, if I am found guilty, sentenced by a judge who neither knows nor cares about me or my work. But that work is the substance of the other world I'm forced to straddle. The world of my work is ethereal, changing. It's not something I can easily explain to these humorless men in black.

It is hard to write to you. I want so badly to speak of pleasant things. What fun is it to have a father who is always fretting? So, at much risk, I will tell you something of the marvel that led to my situation: I have found something.

Discovered is a better word. I have discovered something for which I do not think there is yet a name. It's true that I began my work with orgone to attempt to master the elements. But in that endeavor, I have uncovered the unbelievable.

There is something more beyond the clouds than mere atmosphere. It came through the last time I pointed my machines to the sky. It—*she*—came right through the billowing clouds of my own creation. But then the men appeared and took us away. She's here now. She's close by. I can almost hear her breathing.

If I could only see her again.

With hope,

    Dad

30 June

Peter,

Something spectacular has happened. This morning, one of those ghastly pale men came to my cell, and, without a word, he opened the door and led me away. Although they never speak, the man who guided me gave the distinct impression that something was wrong, and when they opened a dark wooden door into their laboratory, I saw that it was so.

When I first saw her come through the mists of my clouds out in the field, she was magnificent. The sun glinted off her skin creating an iridescent rainbow of pinks, blues, and shimmering, impossible purples. She looked just like an angel. Not one of those cheap plastic girls abandoned on the tops of Christmas trees, but a proper angel. The kind that the Bible describes as greeting onlookers with the pacifying *"be-not-afraid"* in an attempt to counter the terror of their fearsome visages. Even as I looked straight at her descending form that day, I could not comprehend her beauty. Did she have two eyes or ten? I couldn't say. Were the wispy coils of pale organza that flowed out from her center clothing or flesh? Even after examining her today, I cannot answer for certain. But I can tell you that she is incredibly old. Ancient by any estimation. Today's encounter has assured me of that.

As soon as I entered her room, I could see what was wrong. These evil men had my angel restrained. She was prone, tied down tightly to a roughhewn examination table. Her skin was blanched in places, leaving her colorless. I'm sure I saw her face, but all I can remember now is a vague impression of sadness. Such deep sadness. I could weep at the thought.

The men wanted me to help her. They wanted to know what was wrong with her. But I was at a loss as to how to reason with them. It was clear the issue stemmed from her captivity, something I dare say they were unlikely to change.

I touched her gently and felt her soul ripple underneath my palm. She needs me, Peter. Before she burst through my clouds, she was more powerful than any creature living on this earth. It is my fault she is here. It's my duty to free her from this place.

Pray for us,
    Dad

14 July

Dear Peter,

You'll think me a fool, but I've begun to get my hopes up. It seems that my captors are invested in keeping my angelic discovery alive. How could I have ever thought otherwise! They let me see her every day now, and while she has not greatly improved, some daily interaction has done her good.

I'm continually fascinated by her, even as her visual form fades from my memory just hours after seeing her. I daresay she is deliberately playing tricks on my mind. Or perhaps she is just too magnificent to stay fixed in mortal recollection. Either way, it's clear there is much for me to learn from my new friend. Yes, I said friend. For that is how I think of her. It may be naive, but I believe she thinks of me as a friend too.

Your jailbird pals,
    Dad and Angel

2 August

Dear Peter,

I hope you'll forgive me for my silence. I have been focused on my work, day and night. Although I am trapped between these walls, I have found a way to continue experimenting with my machines!

It was all her idea. One day, not too long after my last letter, I was sitting by her table. The men had allowed me to remove a single restraint, and my cherub and I were exploring each other. She, by running her feelers over my arm. Me, by placing my ear upon her side and listening to the notes living inside her center. We had been that way for some time when an idea formed quite out of nowhere. I heard the voice in my head, but it wasn't my own. It must have been hers. She spoke in pictures, but I understood her meaning clearly. My machines. Me. The Sky. Black clouds. And behind the clouds, thousands like her. Healthy, sweet, beautiful spirits.

I looked up into her eyes with shock, but she gave no knowing glance. No indication that she had shared such a precious secret with me. She simply conveyed peace down her appendages and into my soul.

Armed with her holy benediction, I went to the men by the door.

"I must have my machines," I told them firmly.

They looked at each other with pronounced lethargy (it is their manner to move at an unearthly pace, I have found). They seemed to confer for some time, although I never saw them speak. After a time, I tried again.

"The . . . creature. You know it came from behind the clouds. Perhaps if I could continue my studies, under your supervision, I could learn more about what is happening to her."

I waited, but they said nothing. They only opened the door and led me back to my cell. Oh, how I quaked that night at the thought that I had ruined my chances! I was certain that they would never let me back to see her. I had pushed too far, and now I would spend the rest of my days between these stone walls. But then morning came, and with it a silent invitation from the men in black into the yard where one of my machines stood waiting.

Now I split my days between my machines and her. I know I am on the right track because whenever I am with her, she twists her limbs around my body and fills me with warm light. It feels like nothing I have ever experienced. And while I am in her arms, I want little more than to stay there forever.

I'm sure I sound like an old fool in love. I suppose, in a way, I am. Even when I was a virile young man, I never tingled with sensations quite like these. What human alive could have known it was possible?

If you have ever tingled at the touch of another, I ask you, Peter, to meditate on that feeling after reading my letter. Meditate on it as hard as you can and know that it is but a fraction of what my angel has given to me.

Your old fool,
    Dad

13 September

Dear Peter,

I feel I am at a crossroads, once again. Every day for a month I have worked in the yard with my machine. My machine, which my captors have allowed me to have. And yet, two days ago, I was plucked away from my work and locked within my cell. I have no idea why, but I can tell from the lack of bread and water that I'm being chastised for something. They will not even let me out to see her, at their peril. They know how important I am to her. She is only content when I am near. Whatever they think I have done is serious in their eyes.

Peter, it has been so long since we have stood face-to-face, and yet as I write these words, I can see your accusing glance staring down into mine. I can just imagine what you would say to me now.

"Father, that can't be right," you'd say in a more paternal tone than I ever took with you. "If you are suddenly being punished, there must be a reason why." Yes, I can see you in my mind's eye. That knowing glint in your look, so full of excitement and hunger for knowledge.

Fine. I will come clean. I know why I'm being punished. They've caught on.

All these long weeks, I've had them convinced I was recalibrating my machines to heal their prize. My angel, my sweet, their victim. But I never had any intention of helping them. As I have alluded to before, she is speaking to me. My guardian, she knows what is best for her and her kind. She has been helping me to fix my machines. We had almost completed our mission when those black-clad bastards caught on. Now I am trapped. Trapped, once again, in this damp, godforsaken place.

But they can't keep me here forever. I can feel their hunger for her knowledge growing. It seeps through the walls, weaves through the bars of my cell. Without my help, they are powerless to understand her. It's only a matter of time before they let me out. And when they do, my angel and I will strike.

Alone, but not lonely,
    Dad

2 October

Dear Peter,

Weeks and weeks. Weeks and weeks. I have been here waiting. But they do not come. What are they waiting for? I must get back to work. I must. I must get back to work. I must get back to work, get back to work, get back to work. It's been weeks and weeks. Week after week after week.

I can feel her now. She is inside me. Her spirit is calling to me. These men. These stupid men. They do not know what they hold. They understand she is special, but nothing more. They'll never understand her. They'll never understand us. What makes us special makes us dangerous. But they'll learn. And they won't forget.

Soon,
    Dad

30 October

Dear Peter,

I am free. Last night I feigned a terrible pain in my side and begged to be examined by a doctor. I let them take me down to their special room. Their room from peering and poking. I had hoped she would still be where I saw her last, but when they led me through the door, I found her table empty. Just a day ago I would have despaired, but I couldn't spare the emotion. I had a plan to enact, and I did.

Just as the doctor arrived, I flung a chair through the window and dove out between the falling shards into the little yard. I ran through the grass, grabbed my machine, and made for the distant tree line. Never in my life have I run so hard! I thought for sure they would catch me, but my guardian angel was guiding my steps. Soon I was deep in the forest and safe. I am safe, my son. And now I can do her work.

We begin tomorrow night.

31 October

Peter,

I am punching holes in the sky. Me and my magnificent machines. We have done it. We have completed her mission. All this time I thought my angel was looking for escape, but I was wrong. As I sit here in a little hut hidden in the forest, I see now. I understand what she wanted all along.

The recalibration of my machine wasn't to make a portal for her escape, it was to make a doorway for her friends. Even now, as I write this, they are coming through. Massive. Taller than the house I raised you in all those years ago. They tower through the holes of my manmade clouds. How they float and sway, like something in the ocean. But no jellyfish was ever so holy. They do not speak to me, not with words, but I can understand them. It's here in my head.

A long time ago, they lived on his earth. They were the rulers. They are our rulers. Only we never knew it. Instead, we transferred their stories onto men. Because we could not understand them, we made them in our image. Oh, what a sorry, insignificant thing our stories are in the face of angels. In the presence of gods.

There are at least a dozen of them now, hanging above the tree line. They pay little attention to their host, the man in power of the machine. And that is as it should be. I am nothing more than a humble servant to their needs.

It's raining again. Little drops fall into my eyes as I watch them come. I hope you can understand. I will never forget you, my son. Every time it rains, you're here with me. You're here in my head.

They are descending now, into the world. Oh Peter, I hope you can see it. It's beautiful. I just know that something good is going to happen.

A Song of Seeds

Leee McHugh

His face is a Swiss cheese moon, glowing faintly as he steps nimbly along the sagging dock. My heart rate increases with each catlike footfall. Ten jazzy beats later I can see that it's only white greasepaint highlighting the subtle craters on his cheeks; there's a smear of the stuff lining the brim of his hat. Three yards outside of my lamplight, he rolls to a stop with a supple sort of grace.

We stare at each other, and even the sea seems to stop its shushing and wait. I don't move a muscle. A moment later I see all of his relax. He leans one shoulder on a salt-rotted post.

"Is it you?" he purrs, his expression carefully nonchalant. One slim ankle crosses over the other, the long legs of his sharkskin suit catching the light.

Is it me? I wonder, but only for a moment. "They told me you knew where to get in."

The alley cat before me picks his front tooth with a painted claw. A thoughtful frown pulls at his face. "I can tell you where to go." His answer seems directed at no one in particular, so I don't reply.

It seems like that passes the test. My shepherd straightens up and strides past me. I pivot around to follow, wrenching my stupid ankle. It's a scramble to catch up to the Italian-cut shadow flitting in and out the circles of lamplight along the dock. It's a struggle not to lose sight of him in the salty mist fogging up my glasses. Everything smells like rotting kelp. But after what feels like an oddly short walk, he stops.

I wipe my glasses. It makes them worse. My guide is leaning on another post, gazing out at the sea. I open my mouth on a query but can't force it out. My jaw clunks closed, and I let my eyes wander.

In front of us is a short, squat little hovel, made of cinder blocks held together with seaweed and spit. There are no windows, and one door. The door is salt-scarred and gnarled like driftwood, but it looks solid. There's no knob or knocker.

"How do I get in?" I wonder aloud, running my hand across the door. The wood is cold, clammy, and wet from sea spray. Little mollusks cling to it, forming elegant arcs like pearl necklaces dropped on bedroom floors.

"Ahem."

I turn my head only an inch before there's a sharp *flick* of coated paper next to my ear. Two cold fingers are holding a tarot card next to my face. It's a little theatrical. My eyes can't help but roll.

I still snatch up the card. The Wheel of Fortune. I know this card. But I've never seen one where the wheel was spinning. It seems to hum in my hand, the symbols on its face a blur. I stare at it, hardly remembering to breathe.

"How—" I start to ask, and don't finish, because as soon as I glance up from the card I realize I'm alone. I look left and right and see no one, and that's all I see before the vibration of the card in my hand suddenly reaches a feverish frequency and the card bursts into flame. I drop it with a yelp. All that's left is ash by the time it reaches the dock, soon picked up by the brackish breeze. The wind blows, and the ash swirls up and dances through the now open door.

I tip one toe closer. Through the doorway, I can faintly see into a dark room with a low ceiling and a packed earth floor. Indistinct shapes move around the small space. I step inside.

The room is brighter on the inside, or else my eyes adjust to it very quickly. Does that explain why it seems a little bigger now, too? The moving shadows from before are the bodies of dozens of people, undulating around the room. I stand at the edge of the crowd, transfixed by the motion. The dancers move like ink dropped into water, blooming out of themselves, seeming to diffuse into the space.

No one looks at me. I realize I hear no music, but the dancers move together in some languid rhythm I can't quite discern. I take a step further in and turn, searching for eye contact, looking for anyone who isn't dancing. I find no one, turn again and notice, with a flash of adrenaline like an icy zipper opening my chest, that I have lost track of the door. The room is square, and all four of the dusty cinder block walls are unbroken by any sort of egress. No windows, no doors—how did I even get in? My heart throbs sickeningly loud in my ears.

The taste of coins fills my mouth. I realize my whole body is vibrating to the beat in the pounding of the dancers' feet against the dirt floor. The sound rises, rattling my chest, shattering the brittle thoughts clattering around my mind. In the emptiness left behind, I begin to feel my body moving. I didn't ask myself to move. I don't think I want to. I can feel my own blood rushing in my throat. I try to stay still and I can't. My limbs rebel, somehow flowing with whatever strange time these dancers keep.

I see myself joining the dance, at once in my body and out of it. My motions appear smooth but I feel like I'm jerking, internally fighting against this urge.

Why am I fighting? Isn't this what I came looking for?

I glance around the room and no eyes will meet mine, though every inch of skin calls to me in a yearning voice. Hot desperation wells up in my eyes, but it doesn't fall; it just makes everything sparkle.

Everything. Sweat dripping off skin, teeth glowing white inside open mouths slack with ecstasy. I shimmy without my permission around the room and see that piles of fruit glistening with juice line the walls, heaped in every corner and scattering toward the center. Broken pomegranates spill their arils, and squashed bananas lay naked in piles, their peels tossed carelessly aside like so many dressing gowns. Roughly split papayas drip with juice, black seeds sparkling on the dirt floor like gemstones.

Fruits squash underfoot and squeeze through grasping hands as the dance goes on. Dancers pluck the skins off mandarins, popping the pieces into gnawing mouths. Juice runs down chins and chests in shiny streams. My skin feels impossibly hot, stretched tight over my bones like it no longer fits.

Unknown hands start to skim my arms, sticky fingers catching on my sensitive skin. I reach for their owner, grabbing for whatever hands might hold mine. I find what I'm looking for and enjoy one moment of fingers intertwined before I realize I'm holding two fistfuls of fat caviar limes. Their knobbly green skin lets off a bright aroma as my hands close on them tightly, juicy vesicles squeezing out through broken rinds.

I drop what's left of the limes and reach for the nearest dancer. My fingernails scrape down a skinny spine. Sultanas scatter on the floor. A sob rattles around my wet throat. I reach out again and grasp at whatever is there: shoulders, a collarbone, a pair of breasts that fill my palms like ripe mangoes. No, these are mangoes, heavy with juice, so ripe the skin ruptures easily as I clutch them. I let them go. They splat onto the floor.

My body is still moving. The beat is still pounding, louder than ever, resonating through my shuddering chest. The dancers around me are tugging at each other's bodies, tearing flesh into fruit. No one speaks, no one leads; all are dancing, all are pulling and being pulled apart.

Torn skin drips with juice from ragged wounds filled with clusters of blackberries. I slap at the hands clutching for me. My feet slip on pulverized plums. Without meaning to, I cry out and the sound of my voice is crunchy, unused.

A lifetime or maybe a moment later I feel a breeze wash over me and all hands withdraw. My head snaps up. A woman is standing before me. Her eyes meet mine and my overripe heart splits open. She's the one I came here to meet. I don't want to meet her. I freeze, unable to dance, unable to flee. Her fishnet dress presses tightly into her pregnant belly, causing deep red grapes to round off and drop to the floor. They bounce over my toes as she steps toward me—shining, pulp-covered hand outstretched.

Her fingernails touch my chest and don't stop. They sink into my skin with no resistance. My flesh parts around her wrist like a cracked coconut. Sunny heat bakes through me as her hand closes tightly around something inside me. She yanks it out. I choke and grope for the hole in my chest, juice running down my belly. The woman thrusts her prize in front of my face: a golden pear, whole and perfect. She holds it against my lips.

"Eat."

I open my mouth and set my teeth in the flesh. Brightness bursts on my tongue as juice flows down my chin. I glut myself on the gush of it, sucking at the flesh, gnawing down to the seeds. I swallow every bite but my belly aches more than ever.

I look up, the tears in my eyes finally falling. The woman stuffs the core of my pear into my mouth. She grasps the edges of my gaping chest and unpeels it. Juice splashes and seeds scatter. Darkness clouds my vision before I hit the floor.

When I know myself again, I'm on the beach. My skin is salt whipped, raw all over. For a moment I just lie there, feeling the sand firm and wet under my body. But I have to see. I put my hands in the sand and lean up high, craning my neck to check how far I am from the building.

The dock is barely there. What's left is a ruin, claimed by the sea who knows how long ago. There is no building that I can see, only some crumbling foundations. I try to stand but my limbs shake. Pebbles scrape my palms and knees as I scramble for a closer look. Leaning on the cracked concrete I pull myself up and peer over.

Seedlings. Inside the foundations hundreds of tiny green tendrils poke out of the dark dirt. Gratitude and trepidation fight for a seat in my chest. My lips clamp down on something between a breath and sob. I decide to stop shaking.

They'll need fresh water. I push myself up and walk away from the sea.

Magari!

Remo Macartney

After I fled the nest, my parents went sex-crazy. I was away studying social work, and grant writing, and blah blah. Meanwhile, my father was sealing his head inside of a plastic grocery bag and going to town with my mother. I didn't mean to find this out. But I blame it on housing prices. I get an MSW and I have to move back home because rentals in San Jose cost a soul and a half.

Anyway, it means I'm back in my old room with my collection of art pop cassettes. I bought them back in the days when my parents had quiet sex. I'm sitting out in the living room every night writing grant queries on behalf of non-profits. I say things like, "Write your little donations off of your company's taxes. Put a leash on how we spend every cent you grant us. Please, please, blah blah." While I'm writing something like this, I look up and see my dad walk out of the bedroom in his grocery-bag mask. His ragged breath rustles in and out of a fresh-poked hole. He's got his boxer shorts on, and he's feeling his way down the hall from memory. I know my mom—who has bouts with Pica— is in the bedroom oiling up some pennies so that they're easy to swallow. As a matter of fact, she named me Penny because she said I was lucky to have survived birth. Her chronic iron deficiency meant that I came out two months premature. I was like a little crying lima bean. She should have been eating her nails, her screws, her nuts, her bolts. Keys are her favorite.

I'm sitting there, and I'm listening to my dad piss with the door open. I'm hearing him stuff his plastic bag into the trash. I mean sex ed does teach you to cover your head, I guess. But what I realize, in that moment, is that I need to get out more.

For my sake, I met Veronica a few weeks into my confinement at the family home. She's the type who thinks everything happens for a reason. She works at a hippie shop that sells herbs and flowers. She's always telling me about names, "Matthew over there. He drinks *Matricaria chamomilla* tea because his bowels move like wet cement. Allie, who's in on Mondays, likes *Allium tubersoum* on her potatoes. I myself adore the *Veronica alpina*. Names are important."

"You and my mother agree on something."

I started dropping in most days to bother her at work. Then we started seeing each other for real. And then we started playing games together.

I enjoy being stuck or trapped, and Veronica's glad to help. Elevators make some people nervous, but they make me horny. If I don't have anywhere to be, I get in an elevator and hope for a power outage. But you don't want to get stuck with some panicky guy. You're blissed out and he's hopping, screaming, and begging. He's pushing the "door open" button a million times as if that will help. Phone booths with sticky doors are cool, too. I shed a tear every time the city tears one of them down. Or when someone calls them an endangered species, artifacts of a bygone era, blah blah.

On our third date, Veronica wrapped me up in a tennis net that she snatched from the local park. She let me writhe around on the carpet in the net while she sat on the sofa and got off.

This past week, I figured out a way to increase the intensity. At the same park that provided the net, there's a small bathroom. Veronica schmoozed one of the maintenance guys for a key. Once all the families leave, we can have fun with that bathroom. Veronica will wrap me in the net then lock me in the bathroom for a half an hour.

Afterwards, we'll walk over to her place and watch reruns of *Gilmore Girls* or something like that. We do the same thing on our vanilla nights, though.

Veronica gets off faster than me, so I told her, "Once you've had fun, grab us some decaf coffees." Stupid me. Stupid, stupid me.

So, it's a Saturday night, and Veronica kisses me, tells me to have fun, and closes the door.

The bathroom has three stalls, two sinks, and a vent over the window that lets in parallel lines of light. July means that it's still light out when we start the game.

Earlier in the evening, Veronica said to me, "I've got the place ready for you. I came by an hour ago and sprayed everything with ammonia. I don't want you getting E. coli while you hump around on the tiles."

"I'm kinky, but not kinky enough to get super sick for an orgasm."

"Do you remember the safe word?"

"Seedcake."

After Ver locks the door, I warm up my voice with a few repetitions of, "Hello, is anyone there?" Then I start with the screaming, the calling, the crying. I've heard dopamine and cortisol can either make you excited or anxious. The two emotional states aren't that different. So now that my brain is full of the stuff, I'm sure my voice passes for frantic. I try to squirm and flop. The tighter the net coils around me the hotter this is. I picture Veronica out there with her hand stuffed down the front of her jeans. I picture her head thrown back, breath hissing through her bottom teeth.

I roll on top of my hand and try to slide it down the front of my humid sweats.

"Please, my queen. Let me out," I say.

I scream and listen to it bounce off the hard tile.

"I'll do anything you want." The arousal should make it sound like I'm panicking. In reality, I'm edging myself towards an orgasm.

I reach my first climax as the sun sets and the last light goes out in the bathroom. I roll myself so that the exposed skin of my forearms is against a cold patch of tile. I take deep breaths for a few minutes and prepare to work up a second climax. I've got my nose pressed against the floor. I can smell the strong scent of ammonia. The maintenance guy, who gave Veronica the key, should be paying her for doing his job.

As my breathing slows, I first notice it. My mind seems to reach out in the blackness. Then it's there: the presence of something else in the bathroom.

I turn my head and try to focus my eyes in the dark. The blackness is so dense, it's as though the darkness is reaching out and wrapping itself around my eyes. I listen for sounds. There's a hum from the pipes. There's blood rushing behind my ears. But even in the silence, the presence seems to expand. If the bathroom were to function like a pair of lungs, it's as though those lungs were inhaling a dense gas. Images move through my mind. I'm picturing feet dropping down and touching the floor. I picture the toes, shriveled fig toes. Adrenaline blushes my cheeks.

I try to slide my stomach along the ground towards the door.

"Seedcake," I say.

No answer.

I turn my head to look towards the stalls, as if that would help anything. I turn back towards the vent.

"Seedcake," I say, again.

No answer. My breath is getting high in my chest.

"Seedcake, seedcake seedcake."

I start shouting; I'm repeating the safe word again and again. I'm shaking around like an idiot, shouting the word "seedcake." What a nightmare. All I was trying to do was get off.

I turn around, again, squinting my eyes, like I'm expecting to be able to see with zero light. What's worse is that the enhanced realism, the fact that Veronica isn't answering, is turning me on again. Other people get off with regular sex, or with plastic bags, but for me, it takes a fucking locked bathroom. My mother used to use the Italian word "*magari*," that she took to mean "if only." Add what emphasis you will. I used to dream about a vanilla sex life. *Magari!* If only. Now I've gotten myself into trouble.

Veronica and I checked the bathroom before we began the scene. No one could have snuck in.

"Is anyone there?" I say. I'm like Velma from *Scooby-Doo* when she's pawing for her glasses.

I can't tell if something's happening, or if I'm losing it. But it begins to feel like there are waves in the blackness. Like energy is passing through the blackness itself and making it ripple. My adrenal glands are exerting themselves.

"I'm sorry," I say. "I got stuck in here," I say.

No answer.

Magari! If I could move and confirm that the bathroom was empty, then I could get back to orgasms.

When I told Veronica about my paraphilia, she nodded. Adrenal glands blew out all the capillaries in my cheeks.

"I get that. I've heard of that."

I told her, "I used to go to bed every night saying, '*Magari*.' I used to read the Edgar Allan Poe poem "Alone," again and again. I used to take people home, let them do what they wanted with my body. I remember a party. Everyone around me looked like they wanted to hump and thrust and that's it. But nothing could turn me on like my kinks. I felt ashamed. I never told anyone I was different. Instead, I hoped that it'd go away. That one day, I'd laugh and ridicule the idea of trapping myself."

Then she'd said, "But why not indulge in it? In spite of the shame. I could hold the key."

A child might have a tea party. They might reach their hands out and shape invisible cookies. They might lift dainty tea cakes to their lips. They might wipe away imaginary crumbs. They pour fake tea and watch fake streams of steam. They take the nothingness before them and shape it like clay with their minds.

I try to focus beyond my eyes and reach into that void. The presence vibrates like the waves in the darkness passing before my vision. A panic-sweat beads up on the backs of my shoulders. My heart beats too hard.

I remember the fig toes. Like a dream, images pass through my mind. I picture each toe growing thick and purple. I picture each toe bursting and spreading a thousand seeds. The seeds drill through the tiles. They leave needle-like holes. Blackened stalks grow from the holes and thicken until fissures form in the ceramic tiles. The foundation of the building begins to warp and crumble. The walls fall. The earth swallows the patch where I lie. Once swallowed, I'm covered in an infinite darkness. Within this darkness, there is no motion. There isn't even a blackness that I could compare to any familiar color or hue. There is nothingness.

"You know," Veronica said.

We'd been drinking tea made from *hibiscus sabdariffa*.

"I like to break down the Latin names for plants. *Atropa Belladonna*. Atropa was a Greek Goddess. *Atropa* also mean a person who can't be set aside. *Bella donna*, you're Italian, you know that means beautiful woman. So, string it together and you have the name of one of the deadliest plants. I bet a man named that one."

"I bet he thought he was being poetic, too."

"Think about that idea," Ver said. "To be incapable of putting a person aside. Apply it to your sexuality. If something is a part of you, Penny, then you shouldn't put it aside. We'll be dead soon enough."

"And yes, I suppose this is the moment where you say, 'plus you're already a *bella donna*.' I mean, you wouldn't be wrong."

She smiled.

I imagine where Veronica must be. I see her, elbows on the counter at the coffee shop, ordering our decafs. She sees a dried rose in a vase next to the register. She says something like, "Strawberries are a member of the rose family."

I inhale a deep breath and let the fear, the adrenaline flow through me. The presence feels like nothingness itself. Like death. Like the loss of the flesh. The loss of a cheek pressed against the hard tile floor. The loss of the squirming. The loss of the heat, the trust, the orgasms. The presence feels like that stillness. The thing that makes these achievements impossible.

So, on the patch of tile, inches from what might be oblivion, I return to everything that brought me here. I lie on the edge with nothingness and feel a rush.

"Veronica, let me out! Help, help! Please. I'm begging you."

I twist and turn until I can get my hand back down my pants.

"This isn't funny. Please let me out."

Something is working. There's heat moving through my body. I sense the future possibility of an orgasm. I search my way towards it.

I scream again, hearing the reverberation.

I thrust myself about. A woman. A *bella donna*. Named not for her luck, but because her mother enjoyed swallowing lubricated coins. Her mother might even take a big clanging shit in a bathroom like this. A bathroom where a woman is flailing about in darkness, turned on.

Then I gasp; I shudder; I come.

Some time passes. Then I hear a key slide into the lock.

Veronica opens the door. She's got our coffees.

"Those last few shouts were hot," she says.

She unties me. I kiss her so hard that I mash our lips between our teeth. I taste coffee on her tongue.

"You started drinking it without me?"

"I couldn't wait. Ready to go? I recorded the episode where Lorelai and Rory reunite after half a season apart. The one that always makes you cry."

I move about, stretching my arms and legs. I walk to the stalls and look inside each one. Nothing.

"What are you doing?"

"I guess the dark creeped me out," I say.

"Did you have fun?" she asks.

"Yes. Though I'm sure I'll have a wicked sub-drop tomorrow."

We walk down the path and out of the park.

Veronica can figure anything out. She knows how to get an elevator in an old apartment building to stop mid-trip. I let her trap me in there sometimes. She'll put me in a large suitcase and take me to the airport to ride around on the carousel. We'll play together with the crawl space under the bed. Or under the house.

Once in a while, I go back to that bathroom. Veronica will blast the floors with ammonia. She's started covering up the nasty ammonia smell. She mists the floors with a homemade, pennyroyal-scented spray.

"I insist that names are important. This plant's for you," she says. "But pennyroyal can be toxic if ingested."

"Again, I'm not kinky enough to lick the floors and get sick."

When we plan a scene, I use one of the other definitions of "*magari*." Instead of "if only," I use it to mean, "I'm ready to do this."

So, it's a Tuesday night, I've finished a grant proposal. My parents are producing uncomfortable noises, so I'm lying on the floor of the bathroom. This time I'm tangled in a web of pantyhose that Veronica tied herself. I've heard about sensory deprivation, hallucinations, blah blah. But I'm here anyway. I'm lying on the floor. I'm horny and strung out on endorphins, and I'm trying to stretch my mind to contemplate nothingness.

Please Press One

Sarah Karasek

When the doctor asks her, Courtney realizes she doesn't even know what her job is anymore. People transfer phone calls to her and she answers, "Hello, Hammer Industries. This is Courtney speaking. Please hold." Then she transfers the calls to some other people who transfer those calls to some other, other people. That's her job description. That's exactly how her boss trained her. She's thought about asking why, but her boss is the most intimidating human she's ever met. Besides, Courtney's fine on the phone when she's working—it's all scripted—it's ordering pizza or calling off sick that makes her anxious.

She swings her feet forward and back off the end of the examination chair, like she used to do as a kid, with the hope that the steady movement will keep her head from twitching, something she wasn't concerned about until the doctor stuck the otoscope inside her ear and she imagined what a pain in the ass it would be for Dr. Radnowski if her head was moving during the exam.

It's staying still, really, that seems to be causing the anxiety. She wants to tell the doctor this, but instead she says, "Well, it usually happens when I'm on Zoom. When I need to talk on Zoom. I think about my head twitching and then my neck tenses up and then—it's really embarrassing."

"So it usually happens when you need to speak in public?" the doctor asks. Courtney nods, partially to stop her head from twitching, and the doctor kindly explains that performance anxiety isn't uncommon; that some high percentage, the exact number Courtney forgets almost immediately, of singers and public speakers experience the same thing and take pills for it. Courtney could take pills for it. Courtney nods and thanks her profusely.

Doctor Radnowski, or Diane, she'd told Courtney she could call her Diane, steps around the examination chair to view the other ear, check her breathing, all that. Everything's in order. She moves back to her computer chair and types a bit while Courtney reads things on the white tiled walls. *Hazardous Waste. Please Refrain from Cell Phone Use. Hand Sanitizer.*

"All right. I'm prescribing you the ten-milligram for now. Do you have any questions?" Diane asks.

"I don't think so. Thank you."

"Is there anything else you want to talk about?"

Courtney shakes her head no. She thinks about the sense of doom that happens deep in her gut sometimes, the sense that something terrible is about to happen. How she feels it more and more often. She used to trust her instincts, but now it's all imminent death and ultimate failure. She'll wait and see if the meds make any difference with that.

"Then we're all done." Diane gets up and holds the door open for Courtney, and Courtney wanders out meekly into the maze of hallways and exam rooms to find the checkout desk.

Courtney's phone vibrates audibly to tell her that her prescription is ready before she even gets home. But as she pulls into the pharmacy parking lot, that sense of disaster grips her again and she finds herself sucking down a cigarette before getting out from the safety of her car. It doesn't get any better inside—the line stretches half the width of the store, and standing in line is nothing if not staying still. Or maybe nothing and staying still are exactly the same thing. She taps her foot, unclips her phone from her pocket just to put it back just to unclip it again, types half a text then deletes it. When it's finally her turn, she takes a deep breath.

"Hi, I think you have a prescription for Courtney Blush." She feels her mouth twitch a little.

"One moment please," the pharmacy tech says before turning to rummage through paper bags. When he returns, he looks stricken. "Um, are you aware of the price of your medication today?" Courtney's face goes blank, and he continues. "Your insurance is willing to cover $50, but that leaves $302."

The grip on Courtney's solar plexus tightens. It's a one-month prescription. "Oh. No, I was not. Um, I'm gonna pass on that then." She smiles at the pharmacy tech. At least she knows what the disaster was now, she thinks. Maybe her instincts aren't as out of whack as she thought.

"It looks like your insurance isn't willing to cover anything until you try Penitral. They'd cover all of that. If you like, we can talk to your doctor."

"Yes, please."

"Okay, we'll give you a call."

Courtney wakes from a dream of being unable to answer her phone no matter how many times she touches the green circle to answer it. Its buzzing grows to a preposterous intensity, the caller ID displaying the names of friends and relatives now distant or deceased. She wakes to the sound of her phone buzzing. "Hello?" she asks groggily.

"Hello," come the even tones of a robot. "Your prescription for PEN is ready. Press one to speak—"

Courtney hangs up and begins the slow process of dragging herself out of bed. It's Thursday, she double-checks her phone to make sure and to comprehend that it's 11 am, which means it's the start of her weekend and she'd hoped to sleep in a bit later. She throws on a t-shirt and some baggy shorts, sans underwear, to trudge into the kitchen. Misha is, presumably, at work, and Ronnie is, presumably, still visiting his parents, but Courtney knows better than to make assumptions, especially after the time Misha left all the curtains and blinds open "to let some sun in" and Courtney didn't realize until she made eye contact through the kitchen window with the old man across the street. She'd stopped shoveling snow for him after that, but sent Ronnie over since it really wasn't the old man's fault.

She groans a few times, loudly, while pouring herself a glass of water, to announce that she has risen from the land of the dead to anyone who might still be in the house. No response. She drinks half the glass before stumbling off to the bathroom where she showers, digs through the laundry for underwear, puts her shorts back on, and finds a new t-shirt. Then she drinks the other half of her water while she waits for a cup of coffee to brew. She reasons it might be her last cup of coffee for a while, since caffeine is supposed to void the effects of her anxiety meds. Once the coffee is done, she sits down with it to watch the news.

She imagines all the rabid Facebookers in her area telling her that watching the news will increase her anxiety, that it's probably the sole cause, but she'd rather know what's happening. Besides, she doesn't need to immediately respond to the news. It's nothing like ordering pizza. She leaves to pick up her new prescription when she finishes her coffee. The television is playing a segment about a baby jaguar who befriended a wolf pup before she turns the TV off, which isn't news, but maybe it helps those Facebookers.

The pharmacist wants to speak with her when she gets there. There's no line, most people being at work and all. "You understand that Penitral has just reached the market?" she asks. Courtney nods and the pharmacist continues. "It's still in its early stages. If you have any side effects, please contact myself or your doctor immediately." Courtney nods and the pharmacist takes a deep breath. "Penitral is the first ever anxiety medication in ear drop form. Have you used ear drops before?"

Courtney nods.

"Well, just because Penitral insists that I tell you, you'll want to apply them in a mirror to ensure that you insert one drop in each ear in the morning and one drop in each ear at night."

"Okay." Courtney nods again.

"Just sign here then," the pharmacist says. She does, and the pharmacist hands over the paper bag and sends her off.

Courtney gives herself the first dose when she gets home. It's about the time she wakes up for work, so it seems appropriate. She's not used to staring at her reflection for so long. There's bags under her eyes. She's used to dark spots, but the bags are new to her. She chalks it up to aging until she remembers the bagless eyes of the pharmacist. And the bagless eyes of Diane.

Ronnie gets home before Misha. He finds Courtney sunk into the couch, legs splayed, eyes glued on the television. He hears groaning, rushed breaths.

"Another zombie movie?" he asks.

Courtney presses the pause button. "Yup." He's wearing infallible jeans and a stylishly faded blue and white striped button up. "You weren't just visiting your parents, were you?" she asks.

"No. Well, yes. I was visiting them to see if I could borrow their house."

"For?"

"A ten-year anniversary appreciation party for Gravy."

"And the verdict?"

"After a couple glasses of wine and the cruise tickets I saved up to bribe them with, a resounding yes."

"Cool."

Ronnie nods and heads to his room and Courtney unpauses the movie. The zombies are chasing a woman through the woods. Her clothes are nearly torn to shreds from branches or some shit, but its late in the movie, so Courtney knows someone is about to sweep in and save her. The question is if he'll survive.

By the time Misha gets home, Courtney's made a casserole and Ronnie's made a pie. Misha tries to keep frowning, but the apartment smells too good. "You two should be off work more often," she says. "Today was a shit show."

Courtney realizes her ears are clogged. "Ronnie's got news," she says and heads back to her room to examine any side effects printed on her prescription bottle. Instead, she finds printed on the bottle, "If experiencing side effects, please call…" followed by a 1-800 number. "Fuck," she says out loud. Worse than ordering pizza. If it keeps up, she'll just let the pharmacist know the next time she picks up a prescription.

Misha raises an eyebrow at her when she comes back into the kitchen. Courtney pushes a chuckle out of her lungs. "Good news, right?" she says.

"That why you shouted, 'Fuck?'" Misha asks.

"Gravy did always wanna fuck her," Ronnie laughs.

"Some respect for the dead," Courtney quips. "But no, my hearing's muffled and my meds say I need to call them about any side effects."

"Your anxiety meds?" Misha asks. "Oh, the irony."

When Courtney's alarm goes off at 1 pm, she awakes from a dream that she's inside herself, only she's not herself, and she's waiting to spring from her head like Athena from Zeus. She springs from her bed instead, from the strangeness of the dream or nightmare, she's not sure which. She remembers to grab her bottle of ear drops on the trip to the bathroom. She puts on some music for her shower. This is the type of day that begins with her not caring if anyone can hear her as long as she doesn't know they can hear her.

Halfway through her shower the music muffles. It's only been two songs since she dropped the meds into her ears. "Well, it's official. Today is fucked, too," she mutters. She feels the death grip start to well in her chest, but then she feels a mumble of calm take over. It'll be okay. Her hearing's back to normal by the end of her shower.

She spends some time browsing art online—virtual museum tours, Etsy shops, Pinterest boards, the collection of Gravy's paintings saved to her desktop—until Pinterest leads her to some new recipes. Some of them, she already has all the ingredients there in the kitchen; when Misha and Ronnie get home, they find a spinach quiche and a strawberry-spinach salad waiting for them.

"How goes it?" Courtney asks once they're all sitting down to eat.

Misha wraps her lips around a forkful of quiche and points to her mouth. After she finishes chewing, she says, "Better now that I've got this. I haven't eaten anything you've made in like nine years, excluding yesterday." She pauses, chewing and thinking. "Yeah, nine years, senior year of high school."

"I thought I was the pie guy," Ronnie says, pretending to pout.

Misha rolls her eyes. "Oh please, quiche isn't pie." Ronnie feigns dismay.

"Glad you like it," Courtney says.

"In other news," Ronnie says, "Official date for the party is Saturday. Court, I'm sorry, I know it depends on your work, but I guess my parents were already planning to visit the beach house. Misha, can you make it? I'm trying to get a good count so I know how much food to order."

"Close enough fucking notice," Misha says. "I'll be there. Just gotta get my nails done first."

"Tomorrow? I'll try," Courtney says.

Courtney dreams that Spot, her first dog, is licking her ears. It's a happy memory until she wakes up to face the facts that Spot is dead and she's an hour late for work. Her phone shows two calls from her boss. It also shows that her alarm clock is still going off. She jumps out of bed, still groggy, and even though she vaguely considers that if she's already late, she shouldn't rush, she trips over the rug in the living room. She doesn't hear herself hit the floor. Slowly, she gets up, remembering to take deep breaths, remembering to make sure the curtains are closed before walking to the kitchen and banging a metal spoon against a baking tin. Nothing.

"Well, shit's fucked," she thinks she says out loud, but she only hears it in her head. "But it'll work out," she hears in her head and wonders if she's said it out loud. She gets decent and goes to the internet for aid, perched on the edge of her rumpled bed. She finds a website for Penitral—a real, official dot gov website. On the website, she finds directions to take her medication orally if she experiences any hearing loss. Also, to call the number printed on the bottle, but she can't really do that until she can hear. She takes her medication orally, which is weird as fuck, but it tastes like dandelions, so whatever. Then she sends an email to her boss explaining that she woke up deaf, but she's taking care of it, and can start taking calls as soon as her hearing comes back. Part of her knows it won't take long, that her boss will understand. Part of her knows that this is the low of the valley and things are going to start looking up any time now.

Courtney puts on a subbed anime she's been meaning to watch and makes some toast with apple butter. There's seven main characters, all of the global powers are against them, and the fate of the world is at risk. Perfect relaxation. It's the last jar of her grandmother's apple butter, but Grandma would've wanted Courtney to eat it, not waste it. Two hours in, she can hear again. At first, it's just a weird sort of slurping sound that makes her imagine holding a super-powered mic up to a slug. A really cute slug. Then it gets fainter and she starts to hear the characters talking. Then it's just the characters. She finishes the episode (there's only twelve minutes left) then calls Penitral.

After a couple rings, a bot speaks from the other end (she's never understood why the phone rings at all if it just goes to a bot), "For a list of possible side effects, please press one. To report nausea, please press two. To report hearing loss, please press three—" Courtney presses three. The bot says, "Please enter your zip code." Courtney enters her zip code. The bot says, "Please enter your birth date using two digits for month, two digits for day, and four digits for year." Courtney does. "Hello, Courtney Blush," the bot says a few seconds later. "Thank you for reporting your hearing loss. Please begin taking your Penitral orally. If you are experiencing other side effects, please press two. For more information, please press one. To end this call, please press five. To hear this menu repeated, please press pound. Thank you for calling Penitral." Courtney hangs up and calls her boss. She's ready to start taking calls.

Her boss understands. Five minutes after their call ends, just enough time for Courtney to set up her headset, her phone buzzes with her first work call. "Hello, Hammer Industries. This is Courtney speaking. Please hold."

Normally, Courtney doesn't get off work until 8:30 at night. This evening, her boss calls her at seven. She knows Courtney's had a rough a day, and she wants to make sure she'll be in tip-top shape for the rest of her work week. Consider the last hour and a half unofficial paid vacation. Courtney doesn't argue; she gets changed for the party at Ronnie's parents'. Before she leaves, she gives her Penitral bottle another read. Not only does it say nothing about alcohol consumption, it looks like she could've been drinking coffee this whole time.

Ronnie's parents live in a small mansion on the other side of town. His ancestors managed the coal mine that essentially created the town, and it's been in the family ever since. When Courtney rings the doorbell, Ronnie grips her in a tight hug. Courtney tries to grip him just as hard, but she doesn't have private gym muscles. Once inside, she takes her time at the hors d'oeuvres table where Ronnie deposits her, and where she'd be spending time with Gravy, were he still around. Eating, avoiding people. Maybe laughing at them.

Ronnie quiets the music to get everyone's attention and proposes a toast. "So, I know we're just a little shy of the ten-year mark, but I want to thank you all for coming out anyway to celebrate Gravy's life. Gravy was real family to me. You're all real family to me. Today was the only day my parents would let me borrow the place, and you came out here to celebrate Gravy. You're welcome to all the liquor you can find in the house." His audience laughs. Everyone drinks.

Courtney realizes she's incredibly thirsty. She takes a plate of melon balls before going off in search of water. She bumps into Misha, who's just ended a week of office work and is approaching sloppy drunk already. Misha still finds Courtney some water before planting a fancy vodka drink in her hand and saying, "You know what Ronnie's parents said? They're okay with the party since Gravy was '*only*' bi. Ronnie's never gonna come out to them." She throws back her drink to dislodge the anger. Music blasts. They dance. They separate and dance with strangers—friends of Ronnie's they've never met. Courtney talks to some of these strangers, effortlessly, like the words aren't even her own. Like her tongue isn't even her tongue. Five glasses of water and a tequila shot with extra salt later and Courtney feels queasy. She finds Ronnie and thanks him before heading back to the house.

Courtney drops Penitral on her tongue at exactly one in the morning. Even though she feels queasy, she knows it's all right. Actually, really, she knows something good is going to happen. She gets a text from Ronnie that Misha is too drunk to drive and she'll be crashing on the couch there at his parents'. Shortly after that, Courtney pukes. For a split second, she thinks about calling Penitral, but everything feels so right. Between spewing hors d'oeuvres into the toilet, she fills up the bath tub and adds some pink salt.

Then she vomits a tiny gray blob into the bathtub. Tiny gray tongues wriggle out from it. It's almost two in the morning, but she feels like the sun's coming out. *We've got this*, it says in Gravy's voice.

"We've got this," she says, before passing out.

Courtney wakes to a gray blob in her bathtub humming a song she almost recognizes in Gravy's voice. *It's gonna be all right*, the blob says in her mind. She checks her phone for the time. It's just after noon. "I won't leave you here," she says. "But I need to start working now." She runs to her bedroom where she grabs her headset and laptop.

When she gets back to the bathroom, the blob is peddling its tongues through the bath water. *If you're already late, don't rush*, he says. Courtney sits on the toilet, sets her laptop up on her lap, and turns on her headset. Within minutes, she's got a call. "Hello, Hammer industries, this is Courtney speaking, please hold," she says.

You're doing so well, it says. *You don't need to worry.*

"But… how do I get you out of the bathtub?" she asks between calls.

Don't worry about me. All I need is salt water. We've got this.

Three calls later, Courtney hears the front door open. She hears two sets of footsteps tip-toe across the apartment towards her.

Misha asks outside the door, "Courtney? I really have to pee."

Courtney speaks without thinking, "Misha, I'm so sorry, but I can't stop puking." She makes a gagging noise.

"I need a shower, too. I can just pee in shower."

"I puked in the shower, too," Courtney says. "Like, it's full of vomit. Just give me a few minutes to clean it up."

Ronnie says, "Oh, honey, I'm so sorry." He opens the door slowly. "Let me help you clean it up." Once it's fully open, Misha screams.

Courtney removes her headset and gently sets her laptop down. "It's okay, it's okay. I'm sorry I lied to you. He's a side effect of my meds, okay? I've got everything under control. If one of you could just run out and get a fish tank… I didn't have time with work."

Misha continues screaming. "A side effect?! You said you called their number about side effects. I'm calling them right now!" She runs to Courtney's room in search of the bottle.

Ronnie takes a deep breath. "Are you sure?" he asks. "I have some questions about the brain-tongue thing, but if you're sure, I'll go get the tank. If you explain later."

Courtney nods, but soon she hears Misha starting to dial on her phone. "I'm sure. Please, hurry." Ronnie runs from the bathroom and soon she hears his car speed away.

It's gonna be all right, Gravy says. *Focus on you.*

Courtney has another call coming in and she answers it. Two calls later, Ronnie enters the bathroom with a ten-gallon aquarium. He apologizes, "Biggest they had in town." She takes it and begins filling it with some of the bathwater. Then there's a sharp knock at the front door.

"Emergency services," says a deep voice. Courtney hears Misha open up and say, "In there."

Ronnie says, "Fuck," and backs the hell out of the bathroom. Courtney draws the shower curtain. When they storm in, Courtney glares at them and their neat black suits. "I'm not experiencing any side effects," she says.

They pull the curtain aside and scoop Gravy out of the bathtub with the aquarium. *I know it's looking bad, but everything's gonna be all right,* he says. *They're gonna keep me up in Alaska, nice facility, right next to the weather-control machine.*

"How do you know?" Courtney screams as the men carry him away. They exchange glances like she's crazy.

I've been talking with the others. One day, you're gonna be so confident and relaxed that you can just break right on in there and see me. But for now, just focus on you.

Behold! The God at the Top of the Hill

Patrick Barb

You send me, your heart, across the universe, propelled by a cursed world's ending. The recording orb fails to capture your final whispered words. They're lost in time, swallowed by my pod's thick layers of shielding. Whatever you say, it's not the talk of gleaming towers, no recited names of the loftily-ambitioned aristocratic intelligentsia, or accounts of noble purposes designed for the betterment of existence, the kind which your partner, my father, offers time and again in the pulsing databanks of the glimmering orb. The same orb powers my pod with calm artificial intelligence, ferrying me past black holes, dying stars, and riotous asteroid belts.

Your lips, a pale blue, unlike my Earth mother's cherry red vibrancy, press against the glass. As though you hope to capture all the good nights, good mornings, "I'm sorry, please forgive me, I'm so proud of what you'll become or what you became" in one action. A shocking moment of emotional release before I'm gone, before I'm made another shooting star.

Despite the pod's planned stasis program meant to keep me in slumber, I remember everything about my journey to Earth. Sitting in the clouds above my new home, this new dying planet, I close my eyes and, for the briefest moment, I remember clapping chubby fingers in delight as space whales spray cosmic dust from blowholes, swimming in the primordial soup of a newborn galaxy.

There, in this memory, I pull the swaddling blanket to my drooling, gummy mouth. I savor the memory of your embrace.

Somewhere on the other side of this new dying world, a stranger—they're all strangers to me—cries for help. They want someone, anyone to listen and act.

I oblige. After all, they accept my strength and power only relative to my servitude and sacrifice.

When I emerged from between your legs, pulled from your body a civilization's lost lifetime ago, did you sense how far I'd travel?

Did you understand how far you'd go for me?

You can't fly. Father can't fly either.

For all the advancements bringing a utopian planetary society to a state of nonchalance and beyond to a state of annihilation, your people remained grounded until the end. Until the planet's molten core expanded at a shocking, unnatural rate, and cracking fault-lines leaked your planet's life-blood through countless mortal wounds.

My father enters wild-eyed, suffering from too many sleepless nights under different stars than shine above my head on Earth. He shows you the plans he's made. A pod capable of deep space travel, it's designed to carry you away until it finds a safe harbor somewhere, anywhere.

I'd tell you not to act surprised I know this truth, but I'm play-acting familial banter with a ghost I don't even know. Your responses are nothing more than imagination trying to fill the gaps of impossible, unfathomable loss.

You pick me up and hold me. The soft bare skin of my dimpled backside touches your pale cheek.

You won't shed tears for my father.

My tiny fingers flutter like a damaged butterfly's wing trapped in a spider's web here on Earth. Doomed beauty, lovely despite the inevitable ending.

Or because of it.

My new-formed fingers touch the ceremonial headpiece father wears to distinguish himself as someone who matters. My spit-covered digits divide the holographic light show, producing smaller parts of the whole out to infinity.

We make him understand:

How I will live and you will die.

Earth mother—nurturing, but tempestuous, sometimes still alive and sometimes long dead—calls me by another name. In dreams and in memories unraveling like dreams when picked apart, she performs alchemy. She transforms your blanket into something new, a symbol of something greater. Trimmed tights provide something blue. I borrow her love, connecting me to the place I'll call home whenever someone asks me. She stands in a field plentiful with the harvest, like an oil painting of a better, simpler world.

And then, she lets me go.

Her fingertips slide from my grasp as the pull of the skies takes over. Earth father's there as well, or he's gone already too. He holds her as a man or as a memory depending on those circumstances.

They give me to the world. A one-way relationship in many ways. I'm a visitor, and I strive to prove myself worthy of this planet's shelter every day.

On this new dying planet, I thrive. Earth's lone satellite influences my powers—strength, flight, speed. Like I'm some four-color action-

and-adventure man here to "bam, pow, zoom" the indifference of evil, sending it soaring into the sun.

Still, my heart breaks the same as anyone else's. I say goodbye, imagining what parallels lie between this farewell and the one we shared so long ago.

You can't understand how small I am, yet still alive. Still, I breathe in your hopes and exhale possibility. A dreamer's smile crosses your lips, watching my arms tucked against my chest. The sight reminds you of the stranger birds gliding through your world's pink skies.

"He's got his grandfather's eyes."

But my father's lost, running calculations in a head filled with worry—for his world, for his family, for you, and for me. You clear your throat. The lingering pain from my birth sits on your chest, your breasts sore and swollen. Dried blood flakes onto the interior of the recovery chamber, falling from the hard-to-reach places on your legs. You persist despite sleep's alluring call.

Father's cheeks flush with shame, acknowledging abrogation of his familial duties. "The seismic activity increases every day. No one provides any explanation, no theories, *nothing*."

"Your son's awake."

He protests but moves closer to your bedside all the same. "I'm talking about the end of the world."

"Here's the beginning of your world, my love." You bring his hand up to touch my face. I pull away. Blue lips purse. Eyes blind, I'm an earthworm led to the surface after the deluge, seeking sustenance in the richness of the soil.

Except, this world—your world—never held any creature by the name. These words come from a dream neither of us dreamed. Yet.

I feed on you.

There, I'm nothing. One more child, soon to crawl, soon to walk, soon to live, soon to die, and nothing more besides.

There, you're a part of my everything.

I kiss the woman who tells my stories.

We fly to the moon. She's not afraid. She's never afraid.

But I feel obligated to tell her she can breathe because of my powers, my connection to her Earth's moon. Like the tides, I grow stronger in proximity to the satellite. Enough power flows through me to share my strength with her.

Not like she needs much help though.

She's the one who makes me a hero. Pursuing the truth, she pushes through the awestruck mobs with their necks angled to the clouds. She calls me down from the sky, catching me by surprise.

She doesn't fear me. I think she loves me—even then. She shows the people how to co-exist with me. No miracle from deep space, but a man born under different stars. If she can stand beside me and demand an accounting of my origins and intentions, then what do they have to fear?

You gave me a name for *your* world. Earth mother gave me another name so I could hide in hers. And this girl gave me my final name, a pulp hero moniker for a world of imagination and her paper's bombastic headlines. One of the last truth-tellers, she spins adventures into a web designed to capture the hopes and dreams of a better tomorrow. I keep the first article she writes about me close to my heart. Folded, yellowing paper, smudged printer's ink declaring: "Behold! The god at the top of the hill comes down to meet humankind halfway."

She fought her editor for hours to keep the line. Years later, when we lie in bed, I ask her why. She kisses me on the forehead like I'm some wayward child. "You deserve poetry."

On the moon, I reveal the name my Earth mother gave. She laughs and laughs. "Of course, I always knew."

Listening to her heartbeat, I confirm the truth between syllables.

Now, when I save the world, I save it for her first.

I wish you could meet her.

Too many faces surround you, belonging to elders with more names you'll never remember. All your life, you've carried more names inside than should be in your head. Anything new exists as a touch on the back, a hand hovering above your belly. Some stand behind you whispering promises in your left ear and preaching cautions in your right.

You search for father, hoping for an embrace, a loving smile, or even a nod of understanding. But he's far away from you, suffering through the Father's Craft, in the top of the birthing temple as tradition dictates.

Someone's whispering voice breaks through, like a pick shattering a thickened ice sheath. "It's good to find those strange purple lips of yours turning a proper blue at last. Now, you're one of us."

You reply with an anguished scream. You collapse onto the crystalline floor. All those faces swirl and swirl. Until, there's one face, one voice.

"Son?" you ask.

My answer comes in time.

Take me ahead to the end of the world. Relieve me from preventing the countless false ones every day. Bring me to the last gasp of this rock, far past the point of humanity's final bow.

Will I remain when the true last day comes? Will meteors slam into the moon, pushing my power source closer to Earth? Will waves crash, towers of poisoned seas rising toward rotten skies? At this true ending, will I change? Will I burst apart with power and resurrect as some new god?

Will there be no one left for saving?

Does this planet require more saving now because I'm here? Or was earlier destruction inevitable without me—a fate played out on some parallel world where my pod never landed?

Here, I come to save the day, the night, and the year after year after year. Others follow. They all dream of a better tomorrow, whatever their version might be. Mortals—strong men, wise women, strong women, wise men—draped in cloaks and capes, masked secret-keepers all of them. They act like they cannot die. They play out their cops and robber melodramas or science adventure mega-exploits on a planetary scale.

Pantomime villains engage in japes and madcap capers, before settling into brutal sadism and death marches to the beat of mass murder's drum. Distracting sagas and innumerable epics give way to bleak, torn-from-the-headlines tragedies. When I embraced the hero's role, I committed to simple, fundamental concepts. Standing for what's right, fighting against the corrupt and powerful, ensuring an equitable future for all children no matter where they came from.

Somewhere along the way, those ideals fell out of favor. Razor-blade shoulder pads and pouches filled with bullets and bad dreams: "This is what they want. This is what the world needs now." Or so they tell me.

I've never believed myself an outsider.

There's the lie I always tell myself.

Forgive me, I'm not the same.

My wife's dead. Died in childbirth of all things. Her last words were, "Funny, I always figured I'd die telling people about how you saved the world again."

I scream into the molten hot faces of a star. I pick a fight with a bad dream and bend the abstract concepts until they plea for mercy. I forget your face and the way you whispered words I still don't know.

Then, they find me returned to my Earthman's disguise—the rumpled clothes and tired eyes, the skin-tone lipstick applied every day to my lips to help me blend in. They call me by the name my Earth mother gave me.

They want me to know one thing—the baby survived.

It's a girl.

"How long have we known each other?" my father asks. You wave your hand across the surface of the silver water, countless years represented by the ripples produced.

"Our reproduction time is here according to the elders. Don't you want our line to continue? The life we'd create contains a potential for greatness beyond what our people ever imagined."

You kiss him, pressing your violet mouth to his blue. He pulls you into the silver water and the liquid comes alive at your touch. He takes your kiss as an admission of defeat, of giving in. You know because he tries to pull away, to make the kiss of his own doing.

But you hold him there. Your teeth bite his tongue and you let him bleed into you.

Moments later, the silver water recedes. You rise from the pool. "We're having a son," you tell him.

My father's wounded tongue sits heavy in his mouth, so words come slow. "How?"

"I feel it. Deep down inside."

My little girl flies too. She goes in fits and starts at first, but soon she soars. Even dreaming, she ascends. Pushing her tiny body through too many ceilings and rooftops, floating like a lost balloon until I fetch her back into my arms.

The years soar past, begging us to keep up. My girl speaks words the way her mother spoke them. "Love you" sounds like an atom bomb. "Forever" forms a black hole, a dying star imploding on the edge of a neighboring galaxy.

Strange how it happens, the way you never understand it's the end until you're past the point of no return. My cape becomes her blanket. She holds it to her cheek. Then, I hold her and we fly to observe the imploding star. We go because I want to see something even I can't hold in my hands or my head.

"Daddy closer. Closer." Her cheeks dimpled, she laughs where there's no air to breathe.

And I oblige because she's now my world.

I don't forget about or miss the black hole. I know it's there. I know we're too close.

We fall into its matter-obliterating embrace. But there's strength left in us yet. We fight, pushing against annihilation. I change in the process. I feel her change.

I feel *you* change. She *is* you after all.

Always has been, always will be.

We reach the other side. Under different stars, in a time before my birth, I fall from the heavens. Bursting with energy, molten-hot with power, I hold you tight. And you never let go of the cape that served as a blanket once and will do so again for the first time.

I leave you on a dying world. I melt into the center of the planet, swelling with destructive energy—a ticking timebomb set to explode and destroy this new-old world. Someday, but not today.

You never fly again. A patrician family with aspirations to power takes you in and claims you as their own, despite the tell-tale physical signs you could've come from somewhere else, somewhere beyond their stars. They talk of their stars as your own. And you're young enough so their words become your truth.

You meet a boy. His ceremonial headpiece is too large for a child's head. It slides off and hangs around his neck. He makes a light show on the ground, an infinite constellation of self. When you stare at the markings, you observe how they illuminate the blushing boy. He dreams of science and using it to save your world someday.

You help him. He thanks you. In these smaller moments, life begins.

They're as profound as the separation of a cell.

I breathe. I burn. I grow. I vibrate at a frequency where not even the advanced technology of your homeworld finds me. My father fails because he cannot see me. I won't let him.

You move above me. You place me into the pod, the one you'll send away with words I never learn.

When the moment comes, I stretch out, destroying the planet you've called home, and returning to gaze at stars I've never known.

I'm sorry for the pain I cause. The last "human" part of me whispers a silent prayer, wishing for a swift end to this planet's death. I hope it comes fast, in the way mine did not.

I find you holding onto my father. Your grandfather. You speak your final words to me, understanding the truth of who you are to me and who I am to you and the doubling-up of our roles. The cycle ends this rotation and prepares to take us around again.

"Hi, Dad," you say, but you're already gone.

And I'm going too. I'm floating toward those unknowable stars.

Up, up, and away.

The Treacherous Terrain of Sunbaked Skin

Nikki R. Leigh

The ground is tan and stained with footprints. The paths of past racers mar the skin of the giant, the outline of toes and heels and balls of feet digging into a memory foam of detritus.

The Dancer opens her eyes, taking in the topography in front of her. She remembers that her child held her hand as she died, waiting for the heart monitor to fall flat like her face, devoid of the valleys and peaks.

Flat, unlike the peak the Dancer will be chasing momentarily.

She jumps from foot to foot, jogging in place, warming up a body long dead. The ground moves beneath her bare feet, spongy, weathered. The back of the giant feels strangely like the terrain of a bog drying in the sun. Clumps of hair sit like peat against leathered skin.

The Dancer looks ahead to the long stretch of hillside, the small mounds where the giant's spine pushes through. The twin peaks of shoulder blades. The thinness of the neck compared to the trunk of the large form.

The Dancer sees the head, bowed, ready to straighten at any moment to make the last stretch as hazardous as anything that has come before. On top of that dome, sticking out in odd arrays, is the hair. The dandelion of it all. The prize.

The Dancer has surveyed her path, so next, she observes her competition. One winner, three racers. One life reclaimed, two left to slide back down the back and through a pinprick hole in the ground. An eternity shrouded in shadows.

The Dancer feels the comfort of his presence. She looks to her left, sees her childhood best friend who she still shared everything with, even in her own old age. The Boy died a year before her, cancer taking his body. His old, wrinkled face turns, smiles at her, winks as it turns into a younger version of itself. The Boy is a child again, waving to her like he did back when they were kids from across the street, a basketball in his hand. Their souls were tethered then. They reunite here on this back of a giant, sun-bleached skin stretched between them.

The Dancer gazes in the other direction, feels the pull of love from a life lived with her Partner. Her Partner who had stayed with their child when the Dancer worked long hours. Her Partner who she had loved liked nothing else from the moment they met eyes. She'd have traded all her creativity, her work for her Partner, every last tenner.

The Partner smiles back at her and the Dancer's heart melts, the viscous liquid spilling between her bones. She knows that if it comes between the two of them at the top of the giant's head, she'd hand the seed to her Partner, let her take it in between her hands that gave so much in the life they shared.

She'd live in the darkness so that her light can shine again.

The Dancer, Partner, and Boy glance at each other, small grins gracing their features, encouraging them to do their best and their worst to reclaim a life. They arrived knowing the rules, as if not only their unearthly forms had been transported to the giant they now perch on, but that their minds were filled with knowledge they should not know. They don't recall who poured the awareness into their heads, but they are grateful to move forward, together. Three lives held with threads conditioned by love.

The sky above the giant opens, a beam of light directing the competitors on their journey. The light rains yellow, staining the ground in a golden hue. The skin of the giant flexes in return, the spotlight urging pockets of terrain to emerge from its back. The Dancer contemplates how beautiful it is, despite the strangeness of it all.

The Dancer's heart leaps, stands on its toes like she had at the ballet so many decades earlier. Her stomach pirouettes, turning in on itself mimicking the crumbling passage of time in this space between a heaven and a hell.

The giant opens its mouth, its head turns around with a wide scream splitting its face. It has no eyes, no way to see who rides its back and who might win the right to reincarnate. It wants to know who will pluck a hair from its head, the root grasped and planted into ground anew, a sapling of life to be relived. It wants to know who won't.

The giant knows nothing, only able to play the role of the obstacle course, feeling the torment of the sky thrust upon its back, so it howls. The Dancer feels it under her feet, rattling the giant's ribcage, rippling through its skin and reverberating through the calloused toes of the contestants. The percussion of the outcry makes their bones groan in response, as if each have grown mouths of their own and moan in unison.

The runners sense the yowl reach their chests, grab hold of unbeating hearts, and they take that as their cue. The Dancer, the Boy, and the Partner begin their ascent, a starting horn if ever they'd heard one in the afterlife. The Boy sprints, his bare feet clapping against the sun-tanned skin. The Partner begins her walk, slow and steady, calculating the dips and peaks and partitioning out energy to exert to maximize success.

The Dancer moves her hips to the beat of the giant's movements. Hears the rhythm of the giant's breath. Her toes needle into the back, finding purchase in the rough pockets. After a few moments, she notices her muscles do not grow weary. She continues to let her body sing, until she begins to feel pain nevertheless. Her muscles know no boundaries, but her feet burn from their contact with the skin of the ground. The Dancer ruminates, wondering why the giant has sweat that is toxic to those that are forced to do nothing but run across it. She doesn't have time to look at the soles of her feet, skin coming away in chunks.

The three dance, sprint, and steadily walk their way to the head. Their feet grow blistered no matter their pace, so they continue in the manner that seems most appropriate to their core. They know they must not only beat one another to the top but also outpace their corroding terrain.

The Dancer reaches the lower back of the giant first. She twirls in place, absorbing her next steps, noting how the skin dips into caverns near the spine. Takes in how the spine protrudes from the back like an infinite canopy of bones. But most of all, she realizes that the sky has trembled and opened above the giant's titanic form.

Rain falls from the clouds, a vitriolic green dripping from the sun-filled sky. She sees a water drop target the ground before her, striking a patch of the giant's hair, sprouted from its back like trees. The tips of the hair fizzle, burn, an acrid scent tantalizing the Dancer's nose.

The Dancer does not relent in her momentum, moving forward and into the caustic rain. It hits her arms, bubbling her skin in its wake, her hands now matching the bottoms of her feet. The only way out was through. *No,* she thinks as she surveils the bones arching into the sky, *the only way out is in.*

She dives beneath the giant's skin, into a pore. She sees red around her, scarlet burning from inside the giant as she tumbles through the opening. Her body gyrates forward, dancing to her internal drum synced with the giant's breathing.

The Dancer leaps across the ground, underneath the curvature of the giant's spine above her. The bones are bleached white from their exposure to the sun, and the Dancer wonders if the giant aches. As she jumps and the impact bounces through her knees and up her own vertebrae, she feels echoes of her own back pain, throbbing and strained as she aged. A fizzy welling blazes in the Dancer's guts, a twinge of happiness that she is on her feet again, her limbs cutting through the air just like when she was at her best in her youth.

She is alone—until she isn't. And while she expected her companions to arrive, she did not anticipate the maggots that lived in the giant's hollows. Each the size of her arm, the maggots are also wriggling in time with the gusts of air the giant breathes. She hopes they are unaware of her intrusion, that they are primordial in their ability to do harm, but she's proved wrong again and they turn to her and face her with eyes—human eyes. She wishes to scream but forces it down to her gut.

She hears the gasps of her competitors, the soft thumps as they disappear into their own foxholes. The Dancer hears them intake air again, turns to face them with a finger across her mouth. The maggots stay in their place. She can see the end where she can climb the neck of the giant.

But they don't let her.

The larvae pounce from everywhere at once, and the Dancer feels their gelatinous bodies thud against her blistered limbs. She thinks of the caustic rain she tried to avoid and frustration wells within her, having traded one ghastly encounter for another. She shudders as she feels tiny mouths suckle her skin. But like the mouths of newborns, they have no teeth. It is unpleasant, but not debilitating, so she presses forward.

Within the giant, the three continue, through the sea of insects who are so, *so* hungry but can't quite find the purchase to consume. The Dancer ponders if they ever devour each other in their panic.

The three, armored from the acid rain by the bones of the giant, but striking out against the hundreds of grey maggots, continue their path upward. The Dancer lets out a sigh of relief as she reaches the final cervical vertebra, finds a pore nearby. She grips the skin, feeling almost like it is crumbling under her fingertips, and pulls herself upward. She emerges once more to feel the sunbaked skin beneath her feet. Her own skin relaxes as the weight and slime of the insects vanishes.

At the base of the skull, the Dancer eyes her prize: the dandelion flower sprouting from the head of the giant, a single golden seed there for the taking.

She climbs. The Partner emerges, her head just below the Dancer's feet as they work their way to the top of the giant's skull. Below them both, the Boy grabs a thicket of hair and reaches above.

They know they should be ruthless, kicking in each other's faces, grabbing ankles and pulling down to better their chances of winning. But they love each other. To destroy one would destroy them all.

Skyward they go, despite knowing they'd have a decision to make at the top. They each want to live again, but to do so at the expense of another…

The Dancer's stomach slides on the lip of the scalp, reaching the peak. She grabs tufts of hair, slithers her body forward. Walks slowly in awe at the dandelion in front of her. To take the seed, almost blinding her with its light, would be so easy. She can almost imagine the way the wind would feel on her blistered skin, torn from the acid rain and erosive skin of the giant, puckered from the suckling of the maggots. She sees plains from her perch at the top, spread out as far as her eyes can follow, patched in green all waiting for her to plant the seed of new life.

She reaches out, ready to take her prize, but feels the presence of the Boy behind her. His youthful eyes bore into her back, yearning to grab the stem before she does to secure his reincarnation. The Dancer tells herself she deserves this, that she was good in her life and that she would be again. Her fingers stretch out.

The fuzzy seed is almost within her grasp, but a stab of pain through her heart tells her that the Partner has arrived as well. She feels the Partner pushing her love towards her, urging her to take her reward.

That their child would be so happy to have a mother back with her. The unbridled support almost brings her to her knees.

She turns, wordlessly, not sure she can even speak. Her lips are sewn together by invisible thread, commanding a silent victory.

She reaches again, this time for the hands of the souls who are most closely aligned with hers. A best friend. A lover. A life.

The trio grasp onto each other and extend their hands towards the dandelion stem together. Fifteen fingers curl around the glowing reed. Three arms encircle three torsos.

They jump, as one. No longer the Dancer and the Boy and the Partner but the People who are intertwined in life and death. They hold the dandelion close, hold each other closer, hope the earth will accept what feels like a cheat.

The unit aims for the field before them, littered with golden dandelions from winners before their time. The yellow flowers dotting the green below releases a wave of joy within the group, excited at the prospect of a second life without having had to sacrifice two of their own.

They float for miles, thousands of life-plants underneath their combined form. The People feel their bodies buzz, like a bumblebee ready to pollinate the earth, as they near the ground below. The field approaches, the flowers blurring together with each second passed. The People had won—

The earth says, "no." The green space they targeted opens its mouth, becoming a void of itself, their heaven now a tunnel to hell.

The People are sucked into the pinprick black hole back miles from the head the giant. Angered, they feel it fitting in their cheat, hoping that a place devoid of morals won't balk at their lie. They wonder if though alone they may perish, their triad together as one can have a chance to regrow goodness into the shadows of the universe.

The People, in their bleakest hours, oh how they still had their hopes. But as they approach the darkness, feel the pain emanating from the gap in the earth, they realize they are fools. Tears shimmer down their faces as they approach the void, no way to change course. The dandelion dips, sending their interlaced bodies into pitch black.

They sink for what feels like days, floating downward, the ground never closer until all of a sudden they crash into the crusted soil of the bottom of the pit. They hear skittering all around them, the whip crack of hatred and anger rolling over them in waves.

The dandelion roots itself immediately upon kissing the ground.

The seed is planted, the People should begin their new life, though it may be a life unwanted.

As the People feel themselves separate back into the Dancer, the Boy, and the Partner again, they kick themselves for having fool's gold hopes. The shimmer of a loophole had been attempted before, and as the once golden dandelion glows a new fierce red—they are exposed to their folly.

With voices that still do not work, the three scream. Their faces are twisted into surrealistic portrayals of what they once were, reliving the pains of their past all at once while they simultaneously discover their anguished future. The Dancer, the Boy, and the Partner observe a field of underground dandelions, wilted, with their victims underneath. They witness how an endless field of others fared when they did not abide by the rules of their purgatory. Their bodies…they aren't just bodies anymore.

The trio feels their own skin and bones meeting the same fate, melting into a pile of themselves, a screaming agony that makes their already tortured skin, welted and raw, twist into new levels of pain. They scream. They melt some more.

The DancerBoyPartner become one once again with the howl of the giant in the distance. Liquefied, they'll exist. As nothing more than a conjoined puddle of who they once were, they'll wish they had remained on the treacherous terrain of sunbaked skin.

Eclipse, Embrace

Joe Koch

The huntsman's axe in miniature cleaves the tough pad on the earth side of the animal's paw. Howling skyward, claw extracted, the animal forgets the small wail of stolen blood. As a magical artifact, the claw's lost consciousness resonates in isolation. Inaudible to the huntsman, the animal, and the blade of the infinitesimal axe, the remains of keratin sheath and mangled vein rotate in discordant harmony as if the sun circled a singing planet or the moon maneuvered a new-found orbit.

First the capillaries extend outward, rooting through stone, finding footholds in the flawed rock of the abandoned quarry. Next the blood groove of the claw thickens, re-fossilizing in concordance with protractile mineral tendons inside the curved structure. Passages narrower than single threads vibrate with a venous amniotic message of growth. Perception and penetration fuse. Flesh and fur encapsulate raw stone.

This wolf will not be weighted down and stitched together by huntsman's tricks. Red cloaked in the guise of a child, this wolf of stone and claw rises with the buoyancy of shed tears. She fills her grave with weeping. From her saltwater slurry, the animal Sophia stays afloat even as the quarry floods. Swollen generosity deposits her ghost in piled sediment on the graffiti-marked cliffs.

Sad enough to split constants, Sophia feels like she has two heads. It's hard for her to be alone in theory; impossible in practice. Deva's due back from town to rescue her again, but Sophia was born in the quarry, born from a claw. Through unforgiving seasons of loss, through arterial congress, through petty theft from kids who vandalize the abandoned quarry for kicks, it's the place Sophia will never leave.

She's pleased when Deva fucks up. It's the same with every job they get. Deva promises to save Sophia from the wild and comes back from town broke again with ridiculous offerings: potato chips, a handheld marine radio with a blown fuse, a lost cat. This time it's fireworks.

The campsite is far enough from the quarry that they don't worry much about cops. Public land allows two weeks per month residence before it's a criminal offense.

Deva sets up their haul around the fire-pit left over from the last class of seniors celebrating graduation. In the deep well of the abandoned quarry, sounds bounce off the severe surface of abused basalt and rise into a company of echoes that puts Sophia on edge. A murmur magnifies into a laugh, a laugh into a newborn's scream, and a scream into a chorus of moon-mouths howling as though a cohort of wolves and lovers sprang into orgiastic life from stone.

Sophia listens for intruders between echoes.

Graffiti disappears as the sun sets. Messages lost in the dark. Unspeaking stones circle the monolithic walls of the manmade cavern. Deva unpacks missiles, tubes, and repeaters, happy doing all the labor. They gather branches for the woodpile and get the fire going. Sophia's darting eyes light up with reflected flames.

They're useless, Sophia thinks with gleeful approval of Deva's misplaced enthusiasm. They're serious about putting on a good show, serious about growing old together, serious about providing for the family they fantasize having with Sophia someday. Deva doesn't realize an apartment isn't much different from a cage in a carnival or a museum diorama that turns life into a display. Deep in the woods is the way to run free, love free, and stay off the taxidermy grid until Sophia decides she wants to end it all and get stuffed.

Young as ever, Sophia with her high pretty voice and dark animal eyes watches Deva by daylight and firelight growing older, rougher, less sinuous but no less sensual. Deva prods the logs into a tripod shape, caretaking shy flames at the base. Forearm striations flex. The lines in their face suck down shadows with the fierce thirst of time. Life in the wild is hard on mortal flesh. Deva's meat grows lean from circumnavigating death.

"Go up on the ridge, love," they tell Sophia. "You'll be able to see better from there. Won't be so loud for you."

"What about Cutter?"

Sophia named the cat after bug spray. Deva worked hard to domesticate him when he following them through town to the edge of the asphalt and into the brush. Cutter's been missing for who knows how many days while Deva was off losing another job. Without saying anything out loud, they've agreed never to discuss how animals act around Sophia.

"Just go."

Sophia wants to say *I'm sorry*, or *won't the fireworks frighten him off for good*, or *we could get pregnant together but not in the way that you think*, but instead she obediently climbs the gravel rise to the lip of the quarry in diminishing luminescence. Slippery bits of rock don't slow Sophia's nimble pace. Nor does her red hooded cape, threadbare on its ravaged hems and overly long for her childish height. It whips around her sure-footed steps without a mishap.

At the crest where Sophia exits the steep quarry, five boulders perch, sentries over the gulf of denuded earth marking a gateway between worlds and lives. The open pit gapes empty with decades of disappeared rock. Beasts abused of stone and claw dash down to start anew. Mortals flee for fear of falling. Hawks lift up and away, carrying the sun over the horizon nightly to sink under the earth in slumber. Sophia's unique in holding a mutable and mutated form on the borderline.

The huntsman and his axe live within Sophia still, though surely he's forgotten her face and the sound of her cries for mercy. Murdering wolves is his habit and his calling, and he must be called. *So much time has passed*, she thinks. The spaces between echoes can't possibly hold his footsteps. She climbs on top of the highest boulder to watch the show.

Small and powerless below, Deva bends, a huddled creature scampering to craft flame from sparks. Sophia perceives movement more than identity, will more than art. Untouched by light pollution, the quarry's darkness inks over the edges of Deva's fledgling fire and paints kohl onto the axe blade forever red emboldened with Sophia's blood.

Here in the place where she was murdered, Sophia feels most at home. The past threat of her disgorging veins is ever-present. A thriving hunger ignites within the strata of inert rock where she intersects with the huntsman's path. Aroused by her touch, the quarry got a taste for sacrifice. Exploited geology throbs with loss and a need to live. Sophia feels the cold desire of stone through her cloak, cross-legged atop a boulder.

Hissing, a firebomb shoots upward and vanishes with a whistle. Seconds later, repeated detonations clamor over the basalt expanse. The quarry shudders loud at percussive sounds reminiscent of its broken past. Lights flash and sizzle near Sophia's eye level. Expectant rock beneath Deva's feet trembles at the next launch. Multicolored lights bloom from the arms of smaller and smaller pinwheels of light exploding in the sky.

Like starfish being born, Sophia thinks. She has the inexperienced and vague misconception that everything in the sea sparkles.

"You wouldn't like it there, no matter how many stars." The huntsman's shadow speaks from behind Sophia in a tone as dense as clay. "You'd sink like a stone. The ocean's made of a million people's tears."

Because he's a shadow, he's invisible in the dark. Sophia's thighs chill through the worn threads of her red cloak. The boulder underneath her freezes in anticipation. The huntsman tests his axe.

Deva hollers up joyous and unaware between blasts. The shotgun sounds of festivity have roused the huntsman's curious aggression with real or imagined war.

He leans over Sophia's shoulder, pulling back the lip of her red cowl. "Let me kill the animal and save you from all this." He whispers. "I'm an expert. No one will be able to tell the difference."

No doesn't sum up every reason his war isn't hers, how the animal is inseparable from the sacred meaning of pursuit, or how the fur and tooth of one girl can swallow as many men as it takes to conquer and close a threshold. Silent though his axe may strike and miniature in its surgical penetration of Sophia's anatomical vice, the secret damage inflicted on her hits home hard. As it was in the past, the endless forever moment of trauma cracks Sophia in half.

Lights, colors, and shooting arcs: a claw within a claw. Sophia hurls her halves apart. Stone meets axe. Wolf meets man. Sun meets coma. The smell of struck matchsticks writ large and drifting across the quarry undermines the explosive magic of soaring, sparkling lights.

Deva sets off the last and biggest blast with a warning yelp. A cannon sound precedes the finale. Like a vivisected starfish, arms depart the central disk in the sky as stones fall like innards into the huntsman's hands from Sophia's ripped-out stitches. The hot smell of sliding gravel weighs down lingering smoke.

Noises lapse into echo. Memory of sound makes a dying sound.

Hewn by the huntsman's shadow, her heart home to the spirit of his axe, Sophia stops struggling against the forearm crushing her throat and enters the final stages of becoming a statue. The pain from behind guts her like a forsaken clock. She cycles through memories of the future. Above the celestial roof of the quarry she sees into a world that is always spinning, a world where Sophia is always murdered, a world where one single capillary thread must be stronger than stone to survive.

Pressed under layers of sediment, Sophia feels the flow of ground water replacing her soft tissue with minerals. The process fossilizes her vulnerable remains and hardens the tiny spaces between her bones. Her image crystallizes in rock. She ceases to age.

Fixed in time, Sophia's terror casts a shadow with seven heads: a three-headed wolf bites a two-headed man wielding a double-bladed axe. The blade is shaped like children clad in fairy tale cloaks facing opposite directions. Sophia has two heads.

Tangled, the miscreation swirls. Shadow sucks Sophia, inert monument atop her frozen boulder. The quiet sky smells of burnt dynamite. The planet crushes her bones.

Sky clashing in a vacuum that hoards unnatural resources, Sophia teases out a thread thin as a capillary, red as a scream.

Earthward, the yowl of an angry cat contrasts with the aftershock of Deva's show of cacophonous blasts. Through lingering bells that ring an atonal alarm, their injured eardrums catch Cutter's rising hiss and warning howl.

Deva rushes to climb the gravel hillside. Slipping and clamoring up the tricky incline, they scold with nervous agony: "Hey you up there, behave."

Then they cry out to Sophia: "Are you all right?"

They scramble on the loose surface. No answer but tortured feline shrieks.

Questions shunned by love, doubts too destructive to name, the sentinel gates open on the girl Deva met in the middle of nowhere who says she's much older than she looks. Here atop the liminal crest of the used and ruined landscape, Deva's beloved Sophia stands naked on a boulder with arms stretched skyward. Blood from her nipples drips down like tears, pooling in the cup of her belly button and branching in unraveled threads to take root in the shadow encasing her legs, a fleshy red shadow of renaissance draping, an unraveling.

Deva's flashlight strikes and shoves it back. Folds of glutted shadow ripple down.

Cutter attacks the discarded cloak soaked in darkness below Sophia's boulder. The cat hisses and spits, his ears flat. He circles the edge. With a pounce, Cutter bites the garment and tangles his claws as he kicks. Flipping upright and growling backwards, Cutter drags Sophia's cloak into Deva's beam.

"Easy." Deva hunkers low to Cutter's level. "Let it go now."

Cutter releases his prey and rubs his nose on Deva's knees, claws retracted, a rumble of soft pleasure building in his throat. Threads straggle like uprooted weeds from Sophia's frayed garment. Deva shakes off the surface dirt and climbs Sophia's dais.

Sophia the statue refuses to make eye contact or respond. Deva seeks the source of her bleeding, but the flow has dried and begun flaking off in brownish specks.

Deva wedges the flashlight in their belt and reaches up with care to grasp Sophia's raised hands. One at a time, they bring them down to rest by her sides and tuck her forearms through the sleeves of the cloak. Nestling fabric around Sophia's tensed shoulders and sliding her hair out of the back of the collar, Deva closes the mantle over Sophia's frozen chest. They button up the front clasps and tie the drawstring in a loose bow at the base of her neck.

Cutter leaps up to circle the couple's legs and settles between their feet. Embracing Sophia under the moon, flashlight illuminating a random slab of silenced rock, Deva pulls rigid arms around their waist and leans in against Sophia's stiff hips. Tallest of the two, their gentle grip instructs Sophia's cheek to rest against their chest.

This close, it's hard to tell one body from another. Deva bows their head and breathes in the dirty fragrance of Sophia's black hair tainted with firecracker smoke. Sophia's sediment eases with a suggestion of warmth. Rhythmic movement atop a rotating planet that desperately wants to be made up of more than visible matter encourages Sophia to take a few unconvincing breaths. Deva clutches her in a ghost-hold.

Coma releases. The wolf stitches an origin story from stone. Once again, the bleeding claw, disembodied, moves on a restless axis. Proteins reorganize like faith. Perception and penetration fuse. Flesh and fur encapsulate raw hope.

Deva sings to Sophia as the imperceptible becomes manifest in an early morning eclipse. Sophia weeps a quarry full of tears before she whispers her part in response. Even then, her voice is small, precious, and inhuman. Careless, unbowed before the sun's dark mask, Deva grasps Sophia's body with rough love and doesn't notice the flashlight battery burn out.

Nettles

Paulette Pierce

Isa opens her blouse. She places my hand on the razored pink flesh that sits below her left breast, a mark like glass under sand, sharpness in a bed of soft, and says, "Now you know where I keep his secrets."

It's an old scar, and although I want to ask if it was the first he gave her, I don't. I know I've been trusted with something sacred, the hidden door beneath the floorboards, and I mustn't ever lift the rug in anyone's presence.

"Why there?" I ask as I help her into the bath I've drawn. She holds out her hand, and when her breast settles back over the scar, I realize it's a stupid question.

"He always strikes in the folded places. Nature's convenient little hiding spots." She hisses as her body meets the water. I wince in sympathy every time, but she tells me it's better that way. The heat numbs the wounds. I sit in a chair and read aloud as she soaks. We have it timed perfectly. Poems are best, the measured cadence, the deliberate reading. I used to bring a timer, but she hated the chime, said it felt like she'd bitten into the bell, the metal clanging against the backs of her teeth. *"I trust you,"* she'd said with a hand around my forearm, so now I just read and wait for the ping inside my heart to tell me it's time.

Isa smiles serenely and dips her head below the surface. When she's been under too long, I lurch forward and pull her out, the drum of my pulse filling my ears, but she's laughing as her face breaches the surface.

"You fret like a very twitchy rabbit, Harper."

"You do things to make me worry."

"Fair," she whispers as I dry her off, patting each blister as gently as I can while still leaving no trace of moisture. I clean out her blisters and treat them one by one. First is the alcohol, which I hate. Her every sharp inward breath feels like a laceration across my own spotless skin, but it's necessary. We don't want any infections. Next is the liniment, soothing chamomile and aloe in the oil to calm the raw, angry red. Finally, the bandages I will change again tomorrow.

This is the love he never gives her. This is the pledge of selfless care people are supposed to make but spend their whole lives running from, and I want to choke him with every discarded bandage and blood-soaked cotton ball in this house. I want to drown him in her bathwater, reaching under to pry his mouth open, letting the dirt of her wounds fill him.

He hasn't touched her since the blisters began. Not to mark her and not to love her, but I know it's only a matter of time. You can see it in the set of his jaw, the way he looks at her like a spot you can't rub out, not even with your most potent chemicals.

Isa isn't sure why the wounds started showing up, but that's when he hired me to care for her. She gets weaker every time a new one appears, her muscles spasming like they've forgotten how to work but hope to rekindle the memory if they quake ferociously enough. She says it's her body's way of making sure he leaves her alone, and although she tries to laugh when she says it, it turns into a sputtering cough.

"How does an animal die?" she asks as she slips into bed. Bamboo sheets, softer and lighter than cotton. I bought them to make sure she sleeps through the night, nothing to chafe her delicate skin.

"Alone." I think about my grandparents' grey tabby cat, the one who crawled under the house to die when I was twelve, curling up in a dark spot unreachable by human arms. They say animals do this because they know we don't like to see them in pain, that they want to spare us out of love. I think it's just a matter of choosing dignity over the embarrassment of an audience. Death shouldn't be a spectator sport. Humans don't get that luxury, the terminally ill surrounded by fussing nurses and the clinical, rhythmic beeps of machinery at all hours of the night.

"Exactly," she whispers, smiling as she closes her eyes, holding out her hand for me to clasp. I sit beside her bed like that, her hand in mine, until she falls asleep.

"Do you notice he keeps everything in brown glass bottles with stoppers? Aftershave, whiskey, my medicine. It all looks the same," Isa says, stifling a gasp as she straightens her legs, running her fingers under the new gash behind her left knee. It must hurt every time she bends it; I expect that's why he chose the spot. I could tell from the way she folded inside herself, wound into a protective snail shell, that there was something to hide. Even now, when I've seen and heard it all, known everything there is to know, she is timid about showing me. Covers it up like she can't bear the way my face looks when I finally see the evidence.

He is selective in his destruction. Odd. Calculated yet erratic. The way a tornado plucks pieces off the chessboard of a town only to throw them across a field, a tree lodged through the center of a garage door five miles down. It's an unpredictability that is terrifying in its failure to reveal itself. Because there *is* a pattern of some sort. There is a plan. It's just not one that can be understood by anyone but himself.

"The garden is flourishing," I tell her as I disinfect the cut. She squirms, and I kiss every mark in the cluster on the back of her thigh, careful with the pressure of my lips. "He doesn't bother my plants because he thinks it's frivolous."

"He thinks everything beyond the walls of his study is frivolous."

"I still don't understand what he does in there." I slide two firm fingers down the length of her spine. It's one strip of skin that isn't riddled with tender spots. Pressing it relaxes every muscle. It's beautiful to watch. Her whole body unfurls like a happy pet flopping down in a sunspot.

"Something dangerous if not done properly. One slip up could make something else entirely. I don't think he knows that." She sits up in bed. In the moonlight, her pallor isn't sickly; she glows like something precious and strange in the bottom of a cave. Something only a few people brave enough to wander in have seen.

"Show me."

"When it's safe," she murmurs into my ear, her scarred hand on my cheek.

The ivy on the balcony rises up the walls. I can hear it cracking the foundation, drilling into the center of the brick. It knows what to do.

It happens faster than I think it will, but I suppose that isn't really true. Every element has been painstakingly tended to for months, powder trains planted all over the house, different kinds of traps that speak to each other in cooperation, bending across their differences to whisper warnings the way plants in a field do when danger is near. They're called "runners," these botanical whisper networks, and just like the ones that ripple through humanity, they can spread care or disease. They can save the world or burn it down in record time, flames hungrily licking gasoline trails off the ground.

My Aurelia had to be contained because of her stingers. A strong wind could have spread them across an acre in five seconds flat, every plant and animal in searing pain before they knew what hit them. He never questioned the small padlocked greenhouse, my thick industrial gloves. Isa was right. We didn't interest him. He probably thought I wore those gloves to touch her, keep my distance from her wounds. That's what he would do.

When it's time, I walk into the dining room, covered head to toe like a beekeeper, my face zipped behind plastic, gloves sewn into my sleeves. No gaps.

"What do you want?" he snaps, barely glancing at me as he gulps his wine, garnet spittle dribbling down his chin.

I hold the plant in my fist, and she wriggles, golden and eager to please, standing tall and proud when I open my palm and blow. The stingers embed themselves in his face first, seeking their target like well-aimed arrows. Maybe Aurelia knows his pride is more important to wound than his flesh. The first shriek makes me smile. The second makes me laugh.

"The nettles latch in with a hooking formation. Makes it impossible to dig them out." I walk over to him, but I don't rush. I am the predator who knows I've wounded the prey far too much for it to go limping away to freedom. He falls out of his chair and starts to crawl, stopping every few seconds to claw at his burning face. "You pull at the fine hairs, and they just root in deeper, the curvature driven into your skin. Like a looped thread pulled taut as the needle leaves the quilt. Secure." I step on his back until I hear a crunch. "They stay inside the skin for a year sometimes, and if you cut them at the root," I pluck a straight razor from my pocket. Yanking his head back by the hair, I dry run the blade across the nettles that pepper his left cheek, "they'll stay forever."

"You crazy fucking bitch," he splutters out, blood dripping down from his sagging skin and onto that spotless carpet he has steam cleaned every month.

"Yes," I agree, flipping him onto his back. He flails like a helpless turtle in the desert sun. I walk over to the bar cart behind the dining table, picking up a brown glass bottle and removing the stopper. He tries to fight me off as I force his mouth open, but his fingers can't gain purchase on the nylon. It's like trying to drag yourself across a frozen pond. Too smooth, too slick. His next move is to try to bite, but I'm already pouring the toxin down his throat. "You gave me everything I need. It's just one of your experiments gone wrong. You are a clumsy oaf who fancies himself a chemist, but the tools you work with don't like you. You don't even understand that, do you? Why the solutions keep eluding you?"

His limbs go lax all at once, like I've given him a shot straight to the spinal column. The genius of this concoction is that it works with Aurelia. Corresponding poisons in nature. Sisters in destruction. I'm so excited for them to finally meet each other, and when I see his cheeks tremble violently, I know it has begun. I can almost hear Aurelia purr. I can't see her threads joining with the paralytic, but I know it's happening, braiding together like giggling girls in the dark. Once the fusion is complete, the paralytic won't wear off. It'll stay inside him, just like the nettles.

His eyes widen and bulge, capillaries bursting into crimson clouds. It's beautiful. I think of watercolors when the brush first hits the paper.

"You're wondering where they all went, aren't you? It's not hard to send servants home. No one really thinks you're in charge here." I stand up and close my eyes, listening to the vines choke the foundation, squeezing the house so tight that it bends but not so tight that it will burst open. They won't release until I'm ready. They know I won't ask without reason, and that's what he doesn't understand. What he could *never* understand. Nature always knows what you're doing, what you want.

"I'm ready," she tells me two days later, trying to rise on wobbly fawn's legs. I rush to her side and scoop her up. "You don't have to carry me."

"I want to. Are you sure?"

"I don't need him to suffer as much as you do. It's time."

I nod, blushing sheepishly, feeling like a vindictive child who hasn't learned how to tame the beast that snaps and growls for more, but she tilts my chin up.

"It's all right. You know they wouldn't let you otherwise, but two days is enough." She kisses me softly, and I carry her to the dining room. I gingerly set her down in a chair, the most cushioned one of the set, his ruby dining room throne.

He's still where I left him, white horse froth all over his cracked lips, tears and blood leaking from his eyes. Forty-eight hours is a long time to have all of that in your system. It's attached itself to every cell now, running through his neural network like electricity dancing down a power line. It has rewired him. It *is* him now. He is pure agony distilled down to a concentrated essence. Every touch will hurt him. I squeeze both of his arms to demonstrate the point, hard enough to leave bruises, and while he can't speak or move, his pupils tell me everything I need to know. The foam starts up again, an ugly white stream that smells like rotten eggs, and I know how much it hurts.

"Look away," I tell her, and she nods tightly, squeezing her eyes shut. When she told me she didn't want to see, she said it like an apology, but she has no reason to be sorry. I will do everything ugly so she doesn't have to. I want to spare her from it all.

I use the straight razor again because it's sharp. Efficient. It glides across his throat like he's no heartier than fresh fruit, ripe and ready to be quartered. If he could, he would be gurgling on his own blood right now.

When I carry her across the threshold, the vines part for us, and even though this is a gesture in reverse, it feels right. The house was her prison, and so the world will be her home. Sometimes a threshold isn't a doorway in but a doorway out.

If it weren't for the smell, I wouldn't remember he's there. Sometimes I forget to replenish the ice in the trunk (every three hours is best) and my nose twitches, searching for a scent it can't locate, moving this way and that until I realize it's him. When we stop for rest, it's never in dingy motels. Isa demands fresh air and twilight. We sleep in the car with the windows open or lay blankets down in wooded areas, breathe in the life of the trees overhead. The branches reach out to each other, joining hands until there's a canopy above us. Flowers stretch their petals to tickle her ankles. They all know. They all want to protect her.

I chew up lavender, mint, and dandelions, a pungent paste forming in the moist corner of my cheek. When I open my mouth, I breathe out shimmering yellow spirals, push them from my mouth into hers. It helps with the aches. It doesn't get rid of her disease, but it's the best I can do for now.

When I sleep, I dream he is still alive and I'm feeding him spider webs, asking him if he likes the way they stick in his throat, the slow journey to his belly, catching on everything on the way down. I walk around the empty house, bricks knocked out of place from where the vines squeezed too hard, and I collect webs from every neglected corner, placing them in a woven basket like a maiden picking flowers in a field. When I feed them to him, I stick my whole forearm down his throat. I tamp them down, deep as they can go, and he just keeps swallowing, swallowing, swallowing.

Every time I jolt out of these dreams, Isa is awake, stroking my hair and looking up at the stars. I don't know if she ever sleeps anymore.

"You're so much angrier than I am. I don't dream of him at all, you know," she whispers, nose buried in my neck. "That's why we have to do this."

I wrap my arm around her, careful not to graze her wounds, and I don't tell her the real reason we have to take him with us. It wouldn't do to get her hopes up just yet.

We make it there. McWay Falls, chosen by her. She wanted the bluest water on the coast, a spot nestled into the crook of a cliff's arm. I'm worried about the hike, but she insists on walking alongside me, leaning against benches and trail markers along the way, breathless but beaming the whole time. She bats away my fretting hands, and I finally realize why. She's invigorated for the first time in years, so accustomed to the state of dying that she'd forgotten it hadn't happened yet. I suppose I did too, so I give her space.

I keep a watchful distance, ready to swoop in with my lover's arms if she needs it, but she doesn't. She's laughing more than I've seen in the entire time I've cared for (loved) her, loose curls trailing behind her, each step dainty and deliberate, testing the ground, unsure it will sustain her. This is the first time I'm seeing her in the sun. He forbid me from taking her outside. Pretended it was for her health. Looking at her now, I think it must have made her sicker, and I wish I'd noticed.

After we reach the beach, the vines deposit him in the sand (they've been carrying him behind us, the strangest funeral procession this beach has likely ever seen). His skin is tinged blue, but unlike the water, it's a ghastly color, a shade of death I've never seen before, mottled in patches like oxidized bronze. I unfold his limbs across the warm sand, and it starts. At first, it's so slow that only I notice it. The sand laps against him, mirroring the motion of the waves, subtle rocking at first, but then it's swift and raucous. It's burying him, but only halfway. It's not there to consume him. It's there to hold him.

Isa looks at me with wide eyes, mouth agape as a child witnessing a storybook tale come to life, and I approach the body. I bend down, close my eyes and concentrate, my hands holding his decaying face. I whisper to the nettles, trying to draw them out. They poke through his flesh, sprouting between my fingers, scarlet flowers on thorny stems. They're ready for her now. They've synthesized, feasting on him for days, growing strong and mutating inside him, blooming to ripeness.

"Come here." I beckon her closer, and she takes my hand and kneels in the sand beside me. I pluck the petals one by one. I'm not sure how many will do. I've never done this before, but I stroke the velvety flowers and trust that they'll let me take as much as I need, guide me to the answer. "Eat."

Isa frowns but takes the petals and places them on her tongue. As she chews, the fragrance hits the air. Hints of melon on a summer table, rosewater on the pulse point, hyacinth crushed in a fist. Strange that something so lovely could be borne of his decay, but I've heard tales of warrior women wearing the scents of their conquests like perfume. They say the result is different each time.

She finishes the batch and reaches for more, ravenous. Her appetite is one of many things she's lost, but she's gorging now, devouring until there's nothing left. Every time she grinds a petal to fine dust between her teeth, his body shrinks. Eventually, it's no bigger than a pebble, a tiny rock to be lost in the sifting sands and swept out to tide.

He's gone, and she's not sick anymore. Her cheeks are ruddy again, two perfectly round spots like she's been held close by the sun and kissed deeply. There is a jitter to her limbs, a youthful need to run just to feel the freedom of it. Every blister and sore has closed up, tiny pink scars where they used to be. They'll be unobtrusive unless we're in a bright light like this one, at the edge of the world where the sun burns hardest.

"When did you know?" she asks, folding her arms around me from behind, her chin resting on my shoulder. We quietly watch the ocean for a few moments. I think about asking if we can stay, build a hut from the plants around us, ask permission and hope they'll accept us.

"I didn't. I only hoped."

"Why didn't you say?"

"It seemed cruel to suggest, but it was well worth the risk." Even if it hadn't worked, he would be gone, and I would be here with her, giving her a taste of freedom before the end. In the worst of times, I had gruesome thoughts about her death, possessive notions of consumption not unlike the ritual we just performed, how I would honor her when she died. I would imagine what her heart would feel like on my tongue, if I could trace the folds like the marbled web of a raw cut of meat ready to sear. Would it be softer or harder? When it pulsed, would it feel like she did around my fingers, grabbing at me like her body could choose to keep me there whenever it wanted?

"Sweet girl," she whispers, kissing my ear, and it should feel absurd when I'm all of forty-two, but it doesn't.

I look for the pebble that he's become, but I can't spot it. It might be buried among the others or washed away into the blue.

It doesn't matter anymore, and I know when I sleep now, my dreams won't remember him. Only her.

Where When Lingers

Chris Hewitt

I often return to this timeless shore, with its frozen waves and golden dunes littered with precious memories. This is where it all started and where I'm sure, one day, it will all end. Maybe then I'll be able to pull myself together and become that child again, the girl with her whole life to look forward to, laughing and playing amongst the foaming waves. But wait. I'm getting ahead of myself. And that, in a nutshell, is the problem. So, let me try to start at the beginning.

Even now, I still don't understand the what, why, how of it all. What I know is that, in the blink of an eye, my life changed forever. One moment a child, searching for shells on the shore. The next, it was as if the wind caught me, and I unfurled into a legion of doppelgängers that spawned throughout the bay. Innumerable clones of myself, muddled, misplaced, out of order and out of time. As if God upended some cosmic game board, and the dominoes of my life, laid and unlaid, cascaded onto the sands.

My world froze. The only movement a wave of pandemonium rippling along the shore as my other selves scrabbled to escape the ghosts of past and future. Like beads of water, terrified splinters of me ran into each other, merging in wisps of golden mist. Where two collided, they became one, and what emerged from those chance unions was no longer me. Twisted, half-crazed things, tormented by tangled memories, they searched for answers, hunting down others, hoping to make sense of what they remembered. As if new memories might explain how the dead lived again or how a lover's embrace never happened.

Of the countless copies of me that emerged from that cataclysm, only a few hundred staggered off the beach. I hid, sliding into the unmoving waves, a helpless witness to the perversion of my life.

I can't tell you how long ago that was. There's no time in this place. No night. No seasons. I've never felt hunger. Never tired. I do despair, often, and that's when I remind myself, I'm the lucky one. You see, I'm the beginning.

I wander into the dunes, feet slipping into the soft sand. The sun is where it always is, high overhead, where the gulls hang. I have a pocket full of memories and a feeling I might find some ripe pearls nearby.

Where was I? Oh yes, hiding in the waves. When the beach grew quiet, I ran freezing into an empty world. Well, almost empty. A few half-crazed stragglers remained. Confused things that argued and muttered to themselves. I didn't make it out of the dunes before they confronted me. An older me, mid-forties maybe, dressed in a nightgown with a wild look in her eyes.

"C'mon, girl, let me live," she said, lunging towards me. I tried to run, to get away, but the sand impeded my efforts and she landed on me, pinning me to the ground. Arms flailing, I fought to escape, trying to push her away as she leaned down. Her face, her lips touching mine. Then she vanished, her nightgown falling over me as a swirling, glowing golden mist descended, forcing its way into my lungs. In that breath, I relived her memories. They rolled through me, moments of a life yet to be mine. They tasted bitter, making me retch, cramping my stomach until I vomited up five large pearls. I examined each one, admiring their iridescent shells, sensing their contents, tasting their sourness.

"Stop. They don't belong to you," cried a voice. "They belong to me."

Another figure slid down a dune, throwing me aside and scooping up the pearls. The girl could only have been a year or two older than me. Dressed in a familiar school uniform, her hair shorter, eyes as wild as that other apparition. She threw me aside and devoured the pearls.

"No. No. No. No. No," she cried, choking down each bitter memory.

"Don't you see?" I said, throwing aside the nightgown and climbing to my feet. "They don't belong to you either."

The girl looked at me, licking her lips, eyes still hungry. "I want to live. Let me live!"

She grabbed me, forcing her lips to mine and, just like the previous doppelgänger, vanished, uniform slumping to the floor as I choked on the thick cloud of golden mist. A moment later, I'd thrown up eight pearls. The original five and three new gems. One pearl held a memory of my twelfth birthday—blowing out the candles of my cake, my mother, father, brothers. It seemed brighter than the rest and didn't taste quite so bitter.

I changed into the girl's uniform and scrutinized the pearls, trying to understand why it wasn't me who vanished. They were older, stronger, but they only had eight memories between them. I could recall thousands of memories, a good part of my ten years. That's when I understood I was different. I was the beginning, the anchor. It's also when I realized there might yet be a way to recover my lost life.

I put this moment here, burying it deep in the sand. There's half a lifetime of memories in these dunes. Earlier ones up the beach, older memories down towards the beach huts. I must bury them to keep my greedy selves from devouring them. They like nothing more than to steal *my* pearls.

I said time doesn't pass here, but that's not quite true. Yes, the gulls still sleep frozen in their cloudless blue sky, but I'm no longer that frightened ten-year-old girl. I've found hundreds of ripe pearls amongst the thousands I've harvested, and I've found by consuming those sweet glowing orbs they become my memories. So it is that I live my strange life, one pearl at a time.

I'm twenty-eight now and I have a daughter. She's eighteen months old. We've never met. But the memory of her gives me a renewed purpose to see this through. Even if it's getting harder to find my other selves. There are fewer doppelgängers to hunt, and they grow wiser with their own accumulation of memories. I bury what I don't understand, they do not, and choking down bitter memories only adds to their torture. It drives them crazy, makes them angry, violent.

I used to feel guilty for taking their lives and memories. Now, having seen what they've become, what I do is the only peace they can hope for in this dead world. Only I can end their pain. Ah, but that's not true either. After all, every beginning must have an end.

I finish burying my fresh memories as a familiar crooked, bent-over figure wanders up the beach towards me. Most run from me, but not this one. If anything, I'm the one who wants to flee. She sits beside me, catching her breath.

"How are you today, my dear?" she asks.

Her ancient face, greying hair, and wrinkled skin are almost unrecognizable but for the eyes. My sad, tired eyes stare back at me, and it's that sadness that haunts me. I brush a grey lock from her face and take her hand, scrutinizing her palm, running my finger along her lifeline.

"You haven't eaten."

She laughs and coughs. "Oh, na-na-na, seems like they're still a bit quicker than me."

I reach into my pocket and pull out the darkest, most bitter pearls I've found, placing them in her palm.

"Here, are these good? Eat. It'll help you grow stronger."

She looks down at the black pearls and picks one, tasting it with her tongue before yellowed teeth chomp it down. I try to convince myself her hair is a little less grey. She's in her late sixties, I'd guess. A good bit younger than when I first found her. At least now she can walk.

"Good?"

She smiles and I can see the burden of what she's not telling me. Who would want to look into their future? I sigh and try to smile.

"Don't worry, dear. Keep hunting. There is a crossroads where your future reaches my past."

I nod, but tears are welling. "I know, but I want it to be Now. I want the waves to ride in and the seagulls to fly. I want my life back."

She pats my hand. "Soon. It's not forever. This is only where When lingers. Come now."

She holds her hand up, and I do the same and we perform a poor high-five. The sound of one hand clapping is lost amongst the silent dunes.

"Soon, our lifeline will be complete. Then you will see your little boy and girl."

"Boy?"

A mischievous grin stretches over the old woman's wrinkled face as she clambers to her feet. "Go on. No point dilly dallying. Find them all, child. Then we will dance in the sunlit pools and Now will ride in on the curl of a wave."

She wanders off back down the beach as I wipe the tears from eyes. I have a son—will have a son.

"What's his name?"

The old woman doesn't look back. "Hah, that would be telling. But be in no doubt I'm holding all the love that waits for you."

I look from the frozen waves back to the hinterlands. Out there in the empty world somewhere is the name of my son and my way out of this lingering hell. There will come a time when I embrace that cantankerous older me and we will be the same age. That's when we will dance. Then, with a kiss on the wind, we'll escape where When lingers and all that's to come will run in.

Blackbird Braille

Thomas Thorogood

Gerard's father would shake him awake on mornings like this. "Hunter's dream," he'd say, and toss a bundle of gear at him before he could even open his eyes. Pristine snow made it easy to track just about anything. Gerard resented those mornings, hated the cold. He did love the beauty of that white blanket in the woods, though. It was like a rebirth, or looking at some future where there would be no more humans or animals left, just evergreens.

Just like on those mornings, Gerard's reverie was shattered by the crack of gunfire.

He stared at the tree line, having wormed his way through the trenches as far from the action as the maze would take him. If he was going to make a run for trees, this was the time. He figured he must be a quarter of a mile back from the front. The active slaughter was behind him, although the desiccated bodies of the day's dead littered the rims of these far trenches, staring down in frozen agony. They helped insulate Gerard from the noise of the gunfire, though; for that he was thankful.

Gerard didn't know how long he had before the Enemy made it this far down; they were being thorough, but there was only so much of a fight the squadron could put up. They were starving, delirious, frost-bitten. The snow had been their death sentence. Only, most of them weren't used to the snow like Gerard was. They never had hunting gear thrown at them at bullshit o'clock in aught degrees.

Besides, the front had come right back home. These were the woods he grew up in. The Upper Peninsula was, along with most of the border, all that was left of the contiguous United States. The rest, like the hole in a donut, was Enemy territory.

This was Gerard's first time back to Hiawatha since he left home. He wondered if his father still lived in the same house. He might still be alive if so; it was still behind the front. He wasn't the type to listen to reason and leave when evacuated.

The snow fell cotton spores; Gerard had been waiting for that. The Enemy was skittering along the trenches near the front—he could hear the wet screams from his fallen comrades. Humans were losing this fight. If he was going to go, it had to be now. He'd be an easy target crossing the snow field, and for a time, his tracks would give him away. But, at the same time, the trackless field meant nothing *else* was moving through it.

Blessings and curses.

The next problem was that under the needled canopy of the forest, less snow made it to the ground. Tracks he made there would be harder to cover. If any of those cruel, faceless *things* followed him into the woods, he'd have a hard time hiding.

Nevertheless, if he stayed in the trenches, death was certain. He had to try, no matter the odds against. He listened close to be certain that other men were still dying, that the Enemy was occupied. He hyped himself up with rapid, shallow breaths, a quick *one-two-three.*

As his feet made to launch over the edge of the trench, something caught his sleeve. He slipped and crumpled.

Someone had grabbed him, a man who looked whole and fed. "Don't do it," said the stranger. His voice was soft, airy, unworried. "Stay."

Gerard yanked his sleeve out of the man's grip. "Who the—"

But he looked closer and saw someone familiar in this stranger who seemed to have appeared from nowhere. His clean-shaven cheeks were blotchy from cold, his heavy brows made heavier by the faux-fur lining of his cap. His eyes, mahogany brown, lacked the glint of traumatized madness that Gerard had come to recognize from fellow soldiers.

The stranger was like someone from the past who'd remained untouched by time. Like a memory, like a ghost.

"We'd have to start all over again," the man said. "It took so long this time. Stay here—we can find each other."

Gerard scooted away; the man didn't object or move to stop him. He seemed to trust Gerard. He was earnest, his face a billboard of concern.

"Why, what's out there?" Gerard stood up just enough to see over the edge of the trench again. He peered at the tree line. The heavy snow made it hard to see much detail. "And what do you mean, start over?"

He got down low and turned back to the stranger, but he was gone.

Two boots had imprinted the snow where the man had stood, but no tracks led away. For that matter, no tracks led *to* the spot either. But he *had* been there; those prints were too big for Gerard's size nines.

It was then that Gerard noticed all the screams had stopped, as if the flap-capped stranger had stolen off with them when he had vanished. He swallowed, not liking the quiet. He noted his tense jaw and relaxed it; easier to hear that way.

The thick blanket of snow made it easy for the Enemy's creeping, root-like tubers to snag a shoelace, then an ankle. The wriggling white tendrils, maggoty in appearance when they peeped out of the ground, were impossible to see in the snow.

Gerard needed to get out of the trenches. The Enemy was, at least, slow. When they hunted, when they sent their tubers out scouting, their bodies remained stationary. They were also adept at camouflage, and whatever their outer husks were made of masked even their heat signatures. The best way to detect them was with two eyes and bright lights. Their camouflage wasn't *perfect*, but it may as well have been in the untextured, pristine snow.

The hunter's dream, indeed.

The Enemy could detect Gerard best by movement, vibrations in the ground, and by sight. Their central bodies could see in 360 degrees. Since Gerard didn't know where they were. The silenced screams of the other men in his squad were deafening. The Enemy would be hunting again soon, maybe already were. The odds against Gerard were approaching infinity.

If he ran, into the forest, he could buy himself a few minutes. And amidst the many textures and shapes there, it would be easier for him to see those flat, segmented bodies. If he kept moving, they wouldn't be able to probe for him. But if any of them had eyes on the snow field between these far trenches and the trees, he was dead. If he stayed, he was a rat in a maze, so probably also dead.

To go back was to die. To stay was to die. To go forward, he had the smallest chance, but *a* chance. He knew these woods. If he could reach them, he could keep hope.

Besides, why should he listen to a stranger? He didn't know the man from Adam.

Except, he *did*. He just didn't know from where. It was like seeing a teacher in a grocery store for the first time outside of class. The face was right, but the context was wrong.

He glanced again at the place where the stranger's footprints had already begun to fill with snow. He scanned all around himself for some other solution other than a pray-and-run. It was getting too dark to see much. He could still barely make out the ragged, frozen corpses scattered around the rim of the trenches like sandbags.

"Dreamtime," he breathed. He needed a place to hide that was off the ground and close. The corpses were the answer to his prayer.

Luckily the frozen ones didn't smell so bad. He squeezed between two of them; one his mattress, the other his blanket. He was off the ground, insulated, and out of the forest. He could stay like this for the night. And if the tubers got him, they got him.

His dreams were endless trenches that night. The maze was never-ending, the forest never getting any closer. Nubby maggots writhed from the walls and slushy floors. Ice made it harder for Gerard to run. A translucent, light-bending carapace scurried toward him on too many legs. The tubers extended, entangled him, held him still.

The Enemy reared, lifting half of its segmented exoskeleton to reveal and uncoil its trio of proboscises, which shot whip-like toward him. And of course, it was a dream, so he couldn't escape, couldn't scream. He tried to make noise, but only whimpered.

When the biting, sucking mouth parts tore into his heart, his bowels, extracting his juices, he was surprised to find it more pleasure than pain. Two of the three mouths were wet and enthusiastic. The fibrous tendrils caressed him, helped him to submit. The Enemy had another mouth, and Gerard had one other fleshy phial of human ichor left to drain. The last mouth was gentle, subtle.

This mouth was the stranger's, and soon there was no Enemy, just the stranger and his dancing tongue. Gerard's body quivered, he was still trying to scream. But now those screams were not in pain and fear, but pleasure and relief.

When Gerard was empty and shivering and heaving, the stranger smiled up at him, a trickle of white dribbling down his chin. "It took so long this time," he said. "I don't want to start over again."

When morning came, the snow had stopped falling. The sun still hid behind thick gray clouds. The trenches were so deep in snow that Gerard probably would have frozen to death in the night, the Enemy notwithstanding, had he slept on the ground instead of in a pile of the desiccated dead.

Gerard had no way of knowing whether any of the Enemy were still nearby, if they were awake, if they were hunting. There could be feelers under him right now, just waiting for his first step. He could see little from where he was, sandwiched between mangled corpses. He had no choice but to wriggle out from them and test the snow. He plunged one arm into it. It came up to his elbow. He shifted a continent of snow, pushing it into the trench beside, to see the soil underneath. No little nubs protruded from the dirt.

At length, he turned to survey the tree line again. Now that there was no snow fall, only the pristine blanket, he might be able to see . . . *Something.* Something that would convince him to stay away from the forest and listen to the stranger from the night before.

Using his binoculars, Gerard learned what he could. He noticed that a failing, rotted wooden fence separated the trees from the snow field. This field was once someone's property. Gerard wondered when whoever lived here abandoned it. It had been five years since the first attacks. Anyone who could had fled across oceans.

Whoever had once lived here had probably lived here when Gerard was a kid. There *was* something familiar about the sagging fence and the trees beyond. Something about the shape of the property line, imagining the otherwise unremarkable fence at its prime, tickled him. It was like finding a childhood toy in a box of fine china, decades later.

He shifted his focus to just beyond the fence, at the trees closest to him. If this was where he thought it was, then . . . He found it. One of the trees, a hemlock, had a sigil carved into its trunk. It was just a stupid thing, "G □ T," but it was his. The G was Gerard. The T was Trevor, a boy Gerard had seen once and never again, but who stuck in his heart like a barbed stinger.

This was farmer Muncie's property. Gerard inhaled sharply and let his arms slump to his sides. On the other side of those trees was his own childhood home. The Enemy had driven him to the one place he vowed never to set foot again.

Now Gerard was trapped between two enemies.

He pivoted in his squat, shifting to look the other way, toward the site of last night's massacre. How many people had died? For the first time he wondered whether there were other survivors; he assumed not. He was the only one cowardly enough to run away when the slaughter started. Gerard didn't give a shit about protecting the country—he'd been drafted and deployed to Chicago. Ever since, their orders had been to retreat, retreat. He wondered, with nobody else left alive, if running away was still considered desertion; he'd been drafted and deployed to Chicago. Ever since, their orders had been to retreat, retreat. He wondered, with nobody else left alive, if running away was still considered desertion.

While scouting the landscape, he paid close attention to the ground, trying to detect the smudged camouflage of Enemy exoskeletons. As far as anyone knew, they never slept. They were always either hunting or attacking, they fed constantly. If they didn't know he was there, they had probably moved on in the night. Who knows, maybe the front had already washed over him.

He pivoted again, back to the trees. He needed to get out of the open. He knew these woods. There was nothing in them to fear. Maybe not even his dad.

There were tracks in the snow field now. It looked like whatever had made them had followed some dancing guide. The tracks curved and crossed and—

He lowered the binoculars. He'd been looking too closely. Without the optics, it was clear these tracks were left by a human. They spelled a word: "STAY."

Gerard tumbled from his squat and crab-walked backward a few steps. "What the fuck, what the *fuck*," he said. He fumbled for his binoculars, which he'd dropped in the snow. When he pulled them out, he met resistance. Something clung to them and snapped. *Tubers.*

He sprang to his feet. Already a few writhing, rubbery tentacles had slithered across his ankles and boots, but not enough to trap him. Another minute, and maybe. Either way, they'd found him. One of the Enemy was close, at most forty or fifty feet. He had no choice but to run, and no other place to go than the forest.

Running through at least a foot of fresh snow wasn't easy. Gerard made it easier on himself by tracing some of the steps the stranger had left for him, using the long edge of the T as an easy path toward where that T told him not to go. His legs already burned from the effort.

Gerard wished he could listen to the stranger. Something about the vanishing man had stuck to him, like burr, like . . .

He came to a stop when he reached the tree line and saw again the carving he'd left in that tree not all that long ago. Trevor, too, had stuck to him. What would Trevor look like now, he wondered, but then remembered he didn't have time to wonder. He had to run. He dared to look behind him, and saw the skittering smudge, flat and diamond-shaped like a stingray, with its monstrous knot of milky tubers trailing behind. It combed a trail in its wake.

The Enemy had short legs that didn't work well in the snow. It was slow, Gerard was faster. But he had to maintain a wide distance. Those tubers could act like whips as well as scouting probes. That distance was closing, so he ran past the tree that stood as a monument to his first true crush. Still looking behind him, and not at where he was going, he ran slap into a warm, sturdy body.

Tall and slender, and still with his fur flap-cap pulled low, the stranger peered down at Gerard. The stranger was at least a head taller, but more slender and wiry than Gerard. Gerard had run straight into his chest, and instead of pushing him away and chiding him, the stranger only wrapped his arms around Gerard and held him fast.

"Please," said the stranger with no fog on his breath. "Stay here. Don't you remember me? Please just stay."

Gerard shoved himself away from the warm, tender embrace. He wanted to keep running, *needed* to run, but he couldn't stop himself from squinting at this other man. The nose was the same, wasn't it? The same nose that Farmer Muncie had, strong and aquiline. The sharp hook of the bridge was one of the things about Trevor that Gerard could never get out of his head.

"Trevor?"

Trevor smiled. "See? You do remember. Please just stay. I don't want to lose you again."

Gerard only saw Farmer Muncie's nephew once. Gerard was eleven or twelve. Trevor was a few years older, in town for a couple weeks in the summer to help on the farm. Gerard was cutting through the farmer's field one night, shortcutting home for supper. He came upon the older boy hidden among the rows of corn. Trevor was covered in dirt and sweat. Gerard had never seen anyone like him.

"Sorry," he said. "I know I'm not supposed to cut through, I just . . ." He didn't offer that 'late for supper' meant a lash with the belt.

"I won't tell," Trevor said. "You're Gerry, right?"

"Gerard," said Gerard, suddenly wanting to sound older. And then he said, "You're Trevor."

He didn't know how he knew that, nor how Trevor knew his name. But Farmer Muncie and Gerard's dad were friendly, maybe they'd talked. Maybe Gerard had heard of Trevor and paid no attention.

Trevor nodded.

Gerard didn't know what to say next, but he wanted to say everything. Before he could inhale to speak, the second clang of the dinner bell rang from afar. "I have to go. Maybe see you tomorrow?"

"Definitely."

Gerard made it home in time for dinner, having sprinted through the woods with bats in his stomach and the fear of the belt. After dinner, when Gerard was in his room daydreaming about tomorrow, he heard the telephone ring. His father answered, had a long, low conversation, then left without a word.

The next day came and went without any sign of Trevor.

"Who is staying at Farmer Muncie's," Gerard asked his father at dinner.

"Staying there? No idea. Haven't seen Seb in a while. Speaking of Seb, though, he did call last night. Says someone cut through his field."

Gerard knew better than to lie. The truth cost him the rest of dinner, but at least no pain this time. He remembered how strange he found that, then. He didn't think he ought to feel grateful.

"Please just stay," repeated Trevor.

"I can't," said Gerard. "They're after me, they're . . ."

"You can't outrun them forever. Let's start over. Just stay."

"They'll kill me."

Trevor nodded. "And then we can try again. Don't go any further. Please. Just stay."

Of course Trevor wasn't real. Gerard knew he wasn't real, but he was hypnotizing. What was he, and how?

"I can make it so it won't hurt," said Trevor. "I can help you join me. After all this time, we deserve it, don't we?"

Trevor's words were threatening, but his face was soft, concerned, and fearful. Nervous innocence radiated from Trevor. Was this some trick of the Enemy? Some hallucination brought on by hunger and fear, which Gerard's mind had spliced with the fact that he was back there again, where he never wanted to be. He was the last survivor of an attack by an enemy that was killing more Americans by the hour. Soon, they'd breach the border. Canada and Mexico would be next.

Trevor had a point; why run? It wouldn't do Gerard any good, in the long run. He could stay here in Trevor's vanishing arms. He could let the Enemy catch him, bind him, slowly desiccate him, sapping his blood and other humors. And Trevor would be right there, holding him, helping him let go.

But he thought of all the men who'd died the night before, some of whose names he'd known, some of whose faces had visited him in dreams. All of them had been distractions while Gerard had tried and failed to run away the previous night. If not for them, would he still be alive to make this choice?

These woods were haunted by the life Gerard ran away from: the belt and its razor strap, the early morning hunters' dreams, the absence of the boy in the corn field who was never mentioned or seen again, but who had known Gerard's name as Gerard had known his. Like they had known each other before.

One minute, maybe two, that's all Gerard had ever seen of the real Trevor, but that time had never let him go. Was it fate, then, that got him drafted and deployed back in the place where he began? He couldn't fear these haunted woods. He couldn't fear what secrets they kept. Not anymore. There were worse things to fear now.

Gerard shoved his way past Trevor, who spun slack-jawed in his wake. "No, please! Don't make me wait again!"

Gerard didn't look back even once, even as Trevor bellowed in the distance. Trevor's hurt cries bounced off the blanket of white like the shriek of a forest banshee. Gerard pressed onward, into the woods, closer to home.

He'd lost eyes on the Enemy, but it didn't matter as long as he kept on going. As long he—

His knee caught something hard and sharp; Gerard went down with a gasp and a curse. The pain radiated up and down his leg as lay on his back in the snow and held it. Somewhere, the beating of a bird's wings responded to his yelling, but he never saw the bird.

All he saw was the sharp stone plinth emerging from the snow. The stone was worn in places, haphazardly placed, uneven. Engraved were the letters, 'T. M.'

It was a gravestone. Two sets of boot tracks led to it, a bloody gouge in the snow between them.

Trevor was dragged here by two men, and Gerard knew his father's tracks better than any wolverine's.

Carefully, breathlessly, Gerard paced around the sullen burial marker. On the back of it was carved a single word: 'SODOMITE.'

"I asked about you, you know. At dinner that night, I asked Uncle Seb who that boy was who lived next door. I said you seemed nice, that you had a nice face. I didn't really know what I meant." Trevor was there again, standing next to his grave as though it were a failed science project he had no choice but to present. "Also, you knew me. And I knew you. Stay with me, Gerard."

Something moved behind Gerard, an unmistakable shifting of snow. He spun to find his hunter. He had just enough time to draw a breath before the Enemy flung its net of tubers at him, writhing and pulling him down. The tendrils wound around him, bound him to Trevor's forgotten grave.

"Take my hand," said Trevor. "It'll hurt less."

Gerard squeezed so tightly that he would have feared breaking Trevor's hand, if Trevor were really there and alive with bones to break. Trevor squeezed back, shushing him. "I know, I know, it will be over soon. We can try again next time."

It didn't take long for the Enemy's mandibles to find Gerard's sweet meats. He felt himself slip away; he felt his father and the belt and the early mornings slip away; he felt Trevor's hand slip away. None of it gone forever, not completely, just filled in, a clean white slate.

Every rebirth was a fresh blanket of snow in the forest, another hunter's dream.

& ANGER

The Concierge

Susan Vita

The echo from the slamming door reverberates through the house. He only leaves once, but the slamming seems to last for hours. His smile seemed so kind, but it was a mistake to invite him into the house. I should have known he'd turn out to be like the rest. Still, while the regret washes over me, the slamming vibrates through the front hall, through me, shutting out the world. The door of his pickup truck slamming too, as this ungentle soul makes the inevitable transition from trusted and invited guest to unwelcome stranger. The engine rumbles to a start. Its tires kick up gravel and dust as it pulls away from the house. The truck disappears down the driveway, onto the dirt road that leads back to town. A cloud of dust billows behind it. I watch the pickup through the window getting smaller and smaller. When all I can make out is an indiscernible black dot on the horizon, I open and slam the door again to make sure everything's shut tight, bolted, and locked. Relief at finally being on my own replaces the regret of letting him trick me and I resolve to never repeat my mistakes.

The house is grand—imposing with three stories, a porch, a balcony, and a tower like an arrow pointing to the sky. Each edge and corner is trimmed with gingerbread. The shingles, in scalloped layers were once the bright pastels of Jordan almonds but are now chipped and gray. This house is from a forgotten time, but feels like an extension of me. An extra pair of legs. I'm the concierge; I guard the door. My friends and lovers are all gone. Now, nobody gets in. Not for love nor money, honey.

I stand in the foyer. I grasp the doorknob and give a little jiggle, making sure it is still locked, then slide back and slam the bolt into place to be sure no one can get in. Barred and bolted. An old crank elevator with an ornate grill runs from the basement to the tower. My grandfather called this "the lift." I keep it locked and shut. The lift hasn't been used in years; I doubt it works any more. As I guard the door, the lift descends to the ground floor. It has been years since anyone has visited the house, yet the lift crashes down to the landing. My old black cat hisses at it and arches his back, his hackles up and his tail twice its normal size. He jumps sideways and away from it. I creep over to the door, listening for any movement inside. I don't hear anything. A ring of keys hangs from my belt. I find the one labeled "lift," which I insert into the lock. As soon as I turn the key and the lock slams, something's banging from inside; someone or something wants to escape. I'm certain whatever is trapped in there will bring the nightmares back to me.

I shout from the hallway over the screaming and slamming from inside the elevator. "I'm the concierge of this house. You can't come in here. Nobody's getting in for love or money. The door is locked and bolted. I won't let you in!"

I yell it over and over until there's only silence in the elevator. Even so, I keep the lift locked tight for days on end.

The house is in shambles. The floors are stained and the furniture is turned over. I put everything back into its place and dust the cobwebs out of the corners. How did things become so bad in here? I scrub the house from attic to cellar with lavender soap. Finally, the only thing left to clean out: I open up the elevator's opulent grate. Inside, there's a carcass of a nightmare, dark and dusty. Its bony fingers try to slip through the grate's scrolls and lattice. It promised to bring back the reveries and the memories, but I know that with them will come the nightmares. The broken hearts. The memory of wasted hours. The shattered dreams that smashed like champagne flutes against the wall, leaving behind stains of tears and blood. I ride the lift with it down to basement and chop it into pieces. Then I feed the dismembered thing into the furnace and scrub the lift until any sign of the nightmare is obliterated.

My parents built this house before I was born. It's a part of me. I was born here, and this house is full of me.

A car pulls into the driveway, and a woman in a black skirt suit and a Bible in her hand bangs on the door. I stand stock still, but the cat jumps onto the mantle, knocking a book to the floor.

"Who's in there?" a voice asks.

"My m-m-m-m-madness," I yell back to them. My voice is hoarse from disuse. I can't remember the last time I spoke.

"Who?"

"My m-m-m-m-mistakes!" I feel like I'm yelling through wads of cotton. My throat burns as the words leave my lips. The woman must not hear me. She stands there for a moment, then walks back to the car. She stares at the house for a long time before she pulls onto the dirt road that will take her back into town.

I can't let anyone in. I can't let anyone see what I've done.

A storm comes, slowly casting the meadows and fields of my neighbor's farm into shadow. Thunder and wind shake the walls of the house, but I'm safe inside. This house shelters me from the driving rain that looks to be coming down in solid sheets. It keeps out the strangers. That's why I keep the keys near me. That's why I keep it locked tight. It's why I scrub the floors and keep the cobwebs swept away. People can keep coming and knocking but I won't answer, and I know the door is locked up tight.

My old friend, now a stranger, is back. His truck defiles my driveway. He's not just trying to get into the house. Like the nightmare from the lift, he's trying to bring back the memories; the reveries with them bring disappointment, fear, and regret. He wants to own my imagination and orchestrate my dreams, but those don't belong to him anymore. *My door is locked and bolted, baby*, I think, or maybe I say it aloud.

As safe as I think I am, he brings his hand to his lips and blows me a cold kiss. A frigid wind hits the house, and the walls crumble to dust around me. They blow away in the wind. I'm left standing in a pile of rubble. The cat snarls and slinks away to find shelter in the woods.

I turn and face the wind, tears streaming down my face. Without my house I'm naked. Without my house I'm nothing. When I turn back to face the stranger, I've made an ass out of myself. Like Bottom, my head transforms to a donkey head and my hair to a black main. My hands become hard hooves. I try to scream at him to get out, get out of my house, but the only sound my lips emit is a donkey's bray. I kick the dirt and rubble that used to be my house into his face.

Even now, in my new form, he thinks he can control me. He pulls an apple from his back pocket and offers it to me with gentle hand. I'm still myself enough to know that this is a trick. Apples are always poison in tales of magic, and it wouldn't surprise me to find he was hiding a whip behind his back. He coos at me and tries to take a step closer. I turn around, and he thinks I'm allowing him to mount me, but I kick out with both my legs, hitting his body hard. He falls prone on the ground, and I circle him, slowly at first, the helpless girl who let him break my heart still at the reins. With a snort, I shake her off, and I trot back and forth, crushing everything in my path. Everything that remains of the house and everything left of him is crushed to a pulp under my feet. My shouts of joy and freedom come out as brays.

"Hee haw," I squeal with delight. "Hee haw!"

I'm frolicking in the backyard I haven't been in for who knows how many years, leaping over rocks. As the breeze ruffles through my mane and fur, the sun's coming out, and I know something good is about to happen. I gallop into my neighbors' field in search of a fresh mouthful of grass.

By the Sea Beneath the Glass

Madeleine Swann

The temperature was a cool nineteen degrees Celsius, as it was everywhere at all times in the city center and outskirts, as it was under an enormous glass rectangle. Kitten's cheeks were rosy from wine. She had to stop drinking; it wouldn't do to lose control. She found the place inside herself that could love the saggy old man opposite her at the table in the ostentatious dining room, and it was believable because she believed it. In her mind, they had met many years ago in Paris, before It happened, of course, and were reunited after many years apart. The alternative to not believing it was upsetting him and being sent back out there to die. Above his head on the wall was a round portal of thick, reinforced glass, part of the rectangle separating them from The Wilderness, and hundreds—maybe thousands—of round, teeth-filled mouths attached to long, pink bodies held in the air by iridescent wings swarmed, attracted to the light in The City. Their black insect legs scrabbled for footing against the slippery surface, pattering rhythmically like rain. Kitten wanted to vomit every time she saw them, but it was a mark of your class if you showed fear, another thing her clients weren't fond of. Unfortunately, it was also a mark of class to want to show them off to guests. "Shall we make our way to the bedroom?"

An hour later, wrapped in an expensive purple microfiber coat, makeup perfect, long black hair piled on top of her head, and sporting a long, purple faux feather boa, she zoomed along FWY 5 towards Exit 114. When she had to get on the freeway, she spent hours beforehand thinking about it, and as soon as she set foot on the moving concrete road all she could think about was getting off it. She reached into her bag to grip a scrap of blue fabric until her knuckles were white.

All around her people bustled along the spaghetti junction of mobile footpaths, all trying to out walk others rushing at the same speed in the same direction. The layered streets veered off to doorways far above her head or beyond her eyesight, leading to various districts. Many in Kitten's profession chose the Standing Lane, posing to show themselves off to potential clients, but she could never get used to the glass casing separating them from The Wilderness. The travel section was the brightest in the city, the entire junction covered only in thick glass, and—naturally—always surrounded by grubs. They swarmed and fought, teeth exposed and legs juddering, furious that they couldn't reach their prey. Kitten kept her focus straight ahead, counting Exit 112 then 113—the Art District—her breath shallow and palms sweating, fingers still wrapped around the blue fabric, her sanity held together with paperclips and PVA glue.

She bustled into the opera house and up to her private box, waiting until all eyes were on her to dramatically slip off her coat and reveal her expensive new dress. Oswald was already in his seat beside her, smiling slyly, "This is why you're the best, Kitten." She snorted politely in response. "I've got you a new gig."

"Oh yeah?" She scrutinized the stage through opera glasses.

"Yep, top of the tree."

She froze. "Not…"

"Yep, the Mayor himself."

"Is he…?"

"Right in his usual seat."

"Why me?"

"Why do you think?" He made a subtle gesture over her body. She glanced the Mayor's way, making sure not to linger in case she got him in trouble and ruined her chance—he was sitting next to his wife after all. He was showing his appreciation of the performance by checking his mobile phone, one of the very few left after It happened.

"Well done, Oswald, I suppose you do deserve a cut after all. Not twelve per cent, mind." Oswald grinned.

During the third hour she couldn't put off a toilet break any longer. She gathered her purse, snuck out of the box, and made her way down the hall. "Hey," she said to the young man who bumped into her. For a second, she panicked that he was about to get insulting or rough, it had happened before, but he merely apologized and continued on his way. She went into the bathroom and checked her purse for lipstick, then pulled out an unfamiliar piece of paper. It was a note in neat handwriting, "Dear Miss Kitten, I know you have arranged a meeting with my husband."

"Oh, great," she sighed.

"Please be assured this is not why I want to meet you, I have much more important things to discuss. I will be at my home in the evening and would appreciate a visit at 6 a.m., and make sure no one knows you're coming. Yours, Miriam."

It was a full ten minutes before Kitten could relax enough to urinate. She couldn't look at herself in the mirror while washing her hands and smiled wanly when she returned to her seat. She wasn't sure why she didn't show Oswald the note, but something told her to keep it hidden in her purse.

The next morning, after only two hours sleep, Kitten called a taxi. They were extortionate, but she hoped that by doing what Miriam wanted, she wouldn't have too much trouble. She patted the gun in her purse.

They drove past the main hustle and bustle of The City, out to where trees and shrubs grew, and lush green forests—all beneath the glass. Out here mansions lurked secretively, enough of a distance between them for their owners to pretend they were completely alone. One was pressed against the glass on a cliff overlooking the sea. Kitten imagined herself down where the beach met the glass on a rough day and the waves would crash over her head, and she wouldn't feel it, not even a temperature change. She would be safe: safe against nature and safe against the monsters who destroyed her life. Before she could stop it, she thought of Margaret and Phil, her mother's cousins, and the blue coat Margaret wrapped around her after…

The Mayor's mansion was in the furthest corner of the glass, with both the north and west wings facing onto the wilderness. They reached the gates and Kitten once more mentally rehearsed her speech about the Ladies Fundraising Association, but they were waved in without hesitation. She caught the taxi driver eyeing her in the rearview mirror with newfound respect and wished she could feel as positive.

A butler waited for her at the enormous front door. The sun was rising and, with it, the grubs. At first a few batted their disgusting heads against the glass, followed by more, and then more. By the time she reached the butler they were swarming, attracted to the shiny hubcaps on the taxi, or the windows of the mansion, or maybe just a particularly shiny rock. Kitten did what she always did and kept her eyes on the ground, concentrating on one foot after the other, but the buzzing and the heads knocking against the glass were getting to her. With a whimper she sank to her knees, pushing out the image of her parents being eaten alive, grubs pouring down their throats when they opened their mouths to scream, inflating them, pushing out their eyes. Of Margaret and Phil, still out there, still hiding under bushes and covering themselves with leaves, scant protection against the sharp mouths.

"Madam?" She heard the butler's voice distantly.

"You're okay," said another, soft and female, "you're safe, they can't hurt you." She was led inside, past a hideous trophy room filled with stuffed grubs, hairy forelegs forever reaching for invisible prey, and taken to a comfortable sofa in a tastefully earth toned front room where she was handed a glass of brandy. The Mayor's wife was in a jogging outfit that likely cost more than Kitten's apartment, and was sitting next to her on the sofa. She was slender, elegant, but warm. She took Kitten's hand, "I'm Miriam. I was found in The Wilderness too. I'd lost everyone and, as soon as I saw some explorers, I took my chance and went to them. I'd always been taught to keep away from them—in those days they put people like us in sideshows—but I knew I could offer them something different." She sighed, "Whatever it takes I suppose." Kitten nodded weakly. "We don't have a lot of time; he could be back any moment so forgive me for getting to the point. I'm sure you are aware that George intends to pass a bill severing all entry for those from The Wilderness to The City. They're saying there's not enough room for any more people which—I'm sorry—is bullshit. Without George, their campaign won't hold any sway so…I need you to poison him."

Kitten sat bolt upright, "What?"

"It's not as bad as all that." She pulled a tiny bottle from her pocket, "it's untraceable and looks just like a heart attack. It won't hurt him, and no one will ever know."

"Why can't you do it?"

"I can't get near him." She lowered her eyes, embarrassed. "We live separate lives. Everything you see in public is for show. Just take it and think about it, at least. Just… remember your parents. Wouldn't they have deserved better than they got?" Kitten's shoulders slumped. She checked about her and snatched up the bottle, stuffing it deep into her purse. "Thank you," Miriam whispered. Kitten stared at her knees the whole journey home.

That night, in another taxi paid for by the Mayor, she arrived back at his home, this time in a tight fitting black dress and purple heels. Calling on all of her talents she pretended it was the first time she'd seen the place, her heart pounding when she saw the butler again. Not a flicker of recognition passed his face, he simply took her coat and disappeared.

The Mayor showed her into the dining room where the butler reappeared to pull her chair out for her, and various staff bustled in with trays. "My goodness," said Kitten, "how much food do we need?" Her heartbeat was so loud it sounded like she was in the womb, and each step took her closer to fainting.

"Merely hors d'œuvres," said the Mayor, "enough to satisfy our cravings." He offered her a plate of oysters. Kitten's stomach flipped. She was clutching the handles of her bag suspiciously tightly and let it drop to her feet, hoping he would need a trip to the bathroom before they moved to the bedroom.

"Mmm," she said, "I've never had oysters before."

"I employ private fishermen to go out to sea."

"You mean, they go beyond the glass just for your oysters?"

"Not just oysters; haddock, salmon, crab. Have you ever had any of those?"

Kitten shook her head, dumbfounded. He picked one up, "open wide."

Kitten hated to be fed but she played along, and her delight at the perfectly seasoned fish melting in her mouth was genuine, "My God, that's amazing." She nudged her bag with her foot.

"I'm so pleased you think so." He paused, studying her face, "Very well. Should we discuss the fact that my wife sent you here to kill me?" Kitten made a noise of primal shock. Even if she ran now, she would end up dead sometime soon. "There's something you should know about her. I'm sure she appealed to your background in The Wilderness, perhaps told you that I was planning to bar entry to those who found their way in." Kitten tried to speak but couldn't. She shook violently. "That's never been my plan. However, she belongs to a terrorist group who want to let all of them in, and they plan on killing us. Oh, perhaps you'll be spared, some will remember you, after all, but this whole system will be destroyed. These beautiful houses, this remote paradise. Everything equal, they believe, everyone suffering together. And some will become more equal than others. We're human, we can't help it." He shook his head sadly.

Kitten found her voice, "why should I care?"

The Mayor looked her full in the eyes. His were watery but steady, "give me time to get things fully in order to quell their forces and I'll make sure you never have to work again. You'll have a home of your own. Not a box in the city, one out here with us, and fish whenever you like."

Kitten froze. She thought of Margaret and Phil, and the blue coat. She thought of her mother, stroking her hair, making up stories to take her mind off the buzzing above. "Can it be by the sea?"

The Mayor grinned, "It can be wherever you want.

All Alone on the Stage Tonight

Sam Richard

Madeleine watched herself move in the grimy mirror. Under the dim lights, her reflection was distorted, more shadow than human. Like the memory of a person. A ghost. She studied the way her flowing outfit shifted, tracking every twist and extension of her body. In the bloom of full light, she would have found the wings gaudy and over the top, but in the shadows they were perfect. And she knew they would retain that mystery with the distance of the stage.

It was difficult to admit it, but Pierre had done stellar work on these costumes, and on time, even—for once. Not something she could normally say. Over the previous season, he had gotten himself in over his head with projects and didn't deliver most of the finished costumes until two days after opening night, leaving many of the men on stage in thin tights without codpieces, exposed to a chucking audience.

Albert was particularly mortified, screaming at Louis, the play's director, that if they didn't come through the next day he would walk. They didn't, but he didn't stick to his promise, either. Such is the power of Jourdain's work. It draws you in, speaks to your soul, and eventually, you give your entire self to it.

Madeleine had seen what that power could do to people. People who weren't careful, people who took it all for granted, people who became transfixed by the words and the movements and the spirit of the stage. It was a drug, a religion, even.

She'd had a taste once, herself. On a cool spring evening, in rehearsal for a performance of one of Jourdain's previously never attempted works, *Mort par Mille Petits Ports*. She'd had a few glasses of wine with the cast prior to the rehearsal, hoping to loosen up and let the muscle memory work unencumbered. Not close enough to opening night to matter the way those last few rehearsals matter, but they had also run through it enough times that they all knew their movements and lines.

Head swimming with cheap Merlot, Madeleine watched herself from a distance from the outside, her body moving gracefully, her mouth speaking the words perfectly. She reminded herself of the dolls she played with as a child.

Out behind her childhood home, there was a small grassy hill that she would sit atop and make her tattered toys dance and jump and sway and fly. They all had names, many of which she'd long forgotten, but Meriel was her favorite. An angel and the most valuable thing Madeleine owned. A gift from her father, acquired on the business trip he went on prior to his death when she was four. Receiving it was one of a small handful of memories she still had of him.

On that hill, out behind her house, Meriel brought Madeleine and her father together, across time and space, spirit and flesh. And every time, Meriel moved perfectly.

So did Madeleine on that night. Assured elegance and confidence. An eloquence of movement. A beautiful conjunction of music and the human form. But as the performance went on, something changed in her. Her face grew tangled with conflicting emotions and she was no longer in charge of her movements, well beyond muscle memory. Like a spirit was riding her, hurtling her towards a dark, seductive unknown. It carried her, no matter how much she fought. Terror gripped her lungs with sharp claws and sweat beaded down her aching back.

Madeleine's skin was on fire, her head swimming with wine and dance and this foreign phantom. It wasn't until Louis called cut after another performer drunkenly fell off the stage that the spell broke and Madeleine crashed back into her shaking body.

Exhilarated and terrified, she ran offstage in tears, promising herself that she'd never perform drunk again. There was an animal frenzy pulling at her, something primal and ancient; unknowable—yet familiar. Sensual, even. From that point on, whenever she was on stage, she could feel it, like it was whispering to her from the balcony, like it was watching her, angling to get in again.

More than muscle memory, more than the spirit of movement or a bacchanalian reverie, it was alive. She'd read hastily scrawled notes in the margins of various Jourdain scripts over her tenure at the theater. Others had experienced it too, though she wasn't sure who. Messy scribbles on brittle yellow paper from the distant past, performers who had likely moved on or retired or died.

At various times, they'd all been taken by something. And perhaps, she thought, they might be once again.

Albert tried to comfort her that night, but he was drunk and obnoxious, trying to kiss and caress with creeping hands. Madeleine threatened to cut his dick clean off and he left her alone after that, but not before telling everyone that she was a whore. From then on, the obtrusive and malignant nature of his presence instilled in her a desire to not just maintain sobriety at practice, but anywhere, for fear of running into him.

She could generally avoid him easily, aside from practice. The script tied them together as lovers, and without quitting and sacrificing everything she had done to get into a leading role, she wouldn't be able to rid herself of him for the time being. Pleas for Louis to fire Albert went unheeded, but fortunately he was willing to forgo practicing the climactic finale kiss until the show actually began production.

That eased her nerves a bit, despite the inevitability of having to be close to the monster, but it didn't bring the peace she sought. The mysterious call still lingered for her, somewhere deep inside her mind.

Back in the dim lights of the room, she watched her wings flap in the reflection, confident that she would fully embody the rebirth of the night. That she would be a guide to the dark of the unknown for the audience. Her black bodysuit gently danced with a subtle sparkle, a touch she herself had added after Pierre had given it to her.

Donning her black mask, which covered the top half her face, and double-checking her lipstick in the mirror, Madeleine's stomach lacked the butterflies that typically came on the opening night of a show—that typically arrived prior to any performance. There was no anxiety, only acceptance that this show would mean something. Not just for her career, but for the audience. For theater in general.

The air was different tonight. Everything was open and inviting. She was one with all things and they were one with her; like her costume had given her new life, new connection. Something had awoken inside her.

She thought she might accidentally fly away and never return to the filthy gutters of Paris.

With a smile she walked out of her dressing room and into the back of the theater. The rest of the cast were waiting for the handful of stragglers that Madeleine was among. The room was vibrating, and the noise of the anxious audience penetrated the layers of heavy curtains.

Louis tried to calm them all, to strike at the heart of their fears and give wings to their passion.

You are here, and now you shall do what you came here to do. Jourdain has given us his piéce de résistance, if you will, with L'Appel du Vide du Vide. If we must collectively jump into the abyss in the name of the theater, then so shall we. If we must cry and sweat and bleed for the theater, then so shall we. If we must give ourselves up to the spirits of movement and dance and poetry, then so shall we.

The gravity of how he said the words imparted them with an almost biblical importance. Like Moses coming down from the mountain with the commandments, screaming God's holy writ at a ragtag group of hardened sinners found worshipping the false gods of industry and money and moving pictures.

Stagehands pushed dirty cups into everyone's hands. Madeleine looked into the cup where hazy brown liquid swirled. It smelled of apricot and tobacco, flowers and young grapes. Then a bit of burn hit the tip of her nose, making her eyes well with tears.

I know we don't usually do this, but tonight is a special one. Please drink with me, let yourself become one with the theater. Go my children, go and make perfect art. Salut!

As one, the rest of the cast downed the surprisingly decent cognac. Madeleine continued to stare into hers. On the fringes of her mind, she could feel it pulsing, edging towards her. The drive, the phantom, the spirit, whatever it was, it called out to her to submit. To let go. If she was completely honest with herself, she did want to. It was terrifying, but also exhilarating. The sensual, the romantic, the bacchanalian all spoke to her deep inside of her soul. This is what theater was; this is what art was. Poetry made as movement and spectacle, to touch the hearts and souls of others. There was no higher calling. No nobler pursuit.

Shoving her fear into the back of her mind, Madeleine gulped down the abrasive liquor, embracing whatever might come next. A warm line extended down her throat and into her stomach like a slow fuse. Playfulness overtook her as she reminded herself that there was nothing to be afraid of. This was only a play, only an audience. There was nothing else going on but passion and art. She breathed in and out, centering herself before taking her place among the rest of the actors.

Before Madeleine could react, hands were pushing her—pushing all the actors—onto the stage and into position. A vacuum grew around her. The swell of the music and the hum of the audience became distant and thin. They were worlds apart. Her thoughts swam around her head, difficult to catch in the warm haze of alcohol.

Madeleine's costume no longer felt like she was wearing it. It had become a part of her, an extension of her. She was a bat-woman. A bringer of secret knowledge, a guiding light in the dark unknown. She straddled the worlds while others stayed in one or the other.

Looking around, the stage was now a sparse forest. Trees peppered the landscape and miles of sideways rolling black hills extended behind her. Off in the distance ahead there was nothing but darkness, as if she stood near the edge of the world and the endless cosmos were merely a single, terrifying step beyond.

Then a blinding light hit her face, blocking out the endless dark, and the shadows of branches in the sun lay upon her body like a gaudy wallpaper pattern. The shadows were so real that Madeleine tried to touch them, but her hands were gnarled and knotted. Leathery wings hung off her bony arms, connecting to her torso. Black fur covered her body, speckles of silver hair jutting out occasionally, giving a shimmering glare back in the penetrating sunlight between shadows.

There was no panic, no fear. She finally knew who she was—what she was.

An awed hush rang over the forest and Madeleine recognized that she was no longer alone. Or maybe she had never been, she simply couldn't remember. Tangled among the trees were other creatures, not unlike her. All manner of strange human/beast hybrids. A fox-woman with unnaturally long limbs, her arms damn near touching the dirt. Her ears were mangled and tattered. A hole in her cheek exposed bloody teeth and unhealthy gums.

Next to her a toad-man hunched over, not quite on all fours, but the weight and angle of his body threatening to force the position. He teetered as if intoxicated. His long, slimy tongue hung out the side of his partially opened mouth, harshly rubbing against row after row of jagged, yellowed teeth.

The contorted face of another came into the light. A twisted horsehead sprouting off a wide, bulbous body. His beautiful, elegant movements betrayed the tortured smile he carried. Arms and legs stiff like wooden poles, and yet such grace. Shadows of branches clung to him as he moved, as if they were a part of him. The sun's harshness did nothing to dissuade his exquisite movement. He came closer, and closer, and closer to Madeleine.

They all did.

A shadow followed the group towards her. Its darkness towered over the rest of them. So dense, it threatened to blot out the sun, and the unending cosmos beyond it. The group stopped as it closed in, steps taken in unison, subtle movements working in a rhythm Madeleine couldn't hear or understand.

Face to face with the horse-man, the crowd parted, making way for the imposing shadow. While its movements lacked the grace of the horse, they weren't without their own particular beauty and cadence. The figure twirled around Madeleine, revealing itself to her in flashes.

Wilted limbs, then a swollen eye, then a scar-covered chest, and a starving open mouth. Bits and pieces of him revealed themselves to her, before he abruptly shed his shadow and an ancient goblin stood before her.

Recognition itched in her mind, but she couldn't place it and his large, inflamed yellow eyes stared longingly at her. A spark between them grew into a flame as the vacuum around them swallowed everything. The forest was silent, but for the sound of Madeleine's breath.

Lifting his pallid green hand, the miscreation touched his filthy finger to her lips. Contact sent a bolt through her body and the room changed momentarily. They were on a stage in front of an audience, and alcoholic vapors from his breath kissed her nostrils. But then they were back in the forest, surrounded by creatures.

It wasn't right. But Madeleine couldn't place what or why. Primal desires grew inside of her. Not of lust or passion, but of revulsion. This foul thing's hand upon her face. A small memory crept in of something familiar having happened before, but she couldn't grasp it. The thought came as the shadow of a vague and fleeting sensation. Anger and betrayal; pain and isolation. Shame.

Unsure of what to do, she leaned into it, letting the revulsion build towards the yellow eyes staring at her, pleading for her to embrace them back. But she couldn't; wouldn't.

The vacuum vanished with the crash of a deafening rhythm that came out of nowhere, filling the forest with racket. Madeleine's chiropteran form moved amongst the throng of creatures, all to the pulse of the noise. As one body, they writhed and danced with ease and refinement, like a well-oiled machine. Her body no longer her own.

She tried to stop but couldn't. Fighting against the spirit guiding them, against the shadows and light, against the movement and the cadence they collectively shared. Flickers of another life manifested in her mind, but it was intangible; inescapable. This is what was now, and what had once been was now gone.

She couldn't fight it, so she gave in. From a distance, Madeleine watched herself sway and frolic with an elegance she never knew she had. The spirit possessed her—possessed them all—and she watched in horrified curiosity as it took them.

A memory bubbled up, a small angel in her hands. Human hands. Soft and little, uncalloused by the world. She held a figure upon a grassy hill, making it bob and weave with assured nimbleness in the warm breeze. The memory brought sorrow. Despair, even. Great loss shook through her as another memory crested upon the first. This one of her father's hands. Rough and calloused, worn down by work and the weight of her world. But in those hands, he held the most beautiful thing she'd ever seen. The same doll. The same small angel that would bring her so much joy her whole childhood.

She looked deeply into her father's grey eyes. They held so much love, but also so much exhaustion. And then he was gone, and it was just her and Meriel. And then Meriel was gone, and Madeleine stood alone. Alone on a stage, surrounded by beasts in front of an awed audience. Lights shining brightly right in her eyes. The shadows of artificial trees dancing across her.

The goblin, the shadow. Albert. Standing in front of her, trying to press his lips to hers. An electric current went through the room as the audience could feel the palpable tension—the expectation of passion and frenzy and a meeting of the sensual. Poetry and theater and romance and hope.

As Albert's lips came closer, trying to meet hers somewhere in the space between them, she let herself return to the place she had just been. The forest and the creatures; the vibrating center of rage that had built up inside her for so fucking long.

Madeleine held a sense of power she didn't know she had. Her leathery wings flapped in the subtle breeze and her black and sparkling fur warmed her torso. She let the intoxication of what she was becoming grow and course through her soul. Both halves of her existed in one place and at one time. Standing in a forest and on a stage. Draped in a costume and covered in fur. She was all things.

Without thinking, she grabbed Albert by the face and sunk her teeth into the pale flesh of his neck. Hot, salty blood coated her mouth and ran down the back of her throat. Gnawing on meat, she was glad she had finally let loose, after being so goddamn vigilant for so long. It felt good. This was theater. This was life.

The only thing that overpowered the cries of terror from the others on the stage, were the cheers and applause of the audience.

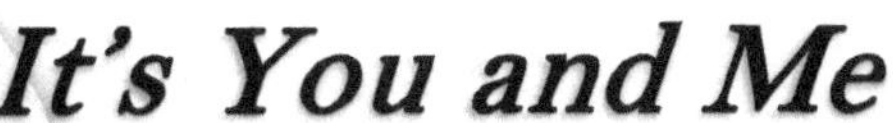# *It's You and Me*

Maria Abrams

It doesn't hurt me.

I take a drag from the cigarette dangling from my fingers. It makes me cough. For a moment, I forgot she smokes, while I do not. How easily we become accustomed to new normals, no matter how strange at first.

My other hand feels my face. The same features as always: my nose that protrudes a bit too much and is a bit too bulbous at the end, my narrow lips, and my high cheekbones. All the parts of me she tried to change, the parts she called ugly.

All the skin is intact. It's all me. I have returned to myself. My ugly self.

The events of the morning replay through my mind. They flow like the tides after a hurricane. I can't control them. I don't want to.

Each thought, each action, no matter how gruesome, brings a smile to my face. I relish in their individual horrors. Although I wonder whether I will have to pay for my sins.

Are they even my sins to pay for?

Is there so much hate for the ones we love?

"Can you drive to the store to pick up my prescriptions?" she asked me two days ago. To anyone else's ear, the request sounded normal. Menial, even. A benign question between a mother and her daughter. But it was loaded.

If I say yes, it will be forgotten. It's expected I say yes, so neither my answer nor the actual completion of the task will mean much.

If I say no, I'll be scolded. Called a lazy bitch who does nothing all day. If I say no again, I'll be slapped. Or worse.

So much for motherly love.

So much hate for the ones we love.

I say yes. It's to avoid an argument. She nods her head and continues filing her nails, the *scratch scratch* of the Emory board grinding away. I hope it tears into the pulp of her nail beds.

On the outside, the exchange is uneventful. But something inside of me snaps. It's not extreme, not an erupting volcano. It's a shift that's both subtle and permanent.

I'm done.

Done with twenty-seven years of beratement. Done with the beatings that started when I was four and came home with mud on my white Mary Janes. I wanted to play with the other kids, despite always being dressed up as though I were headed to a beauty pageant. Porcelain dolls like myself don't get to play. We get our hair brushed, our dresses fluffed, and then put on a shelf where we're expected to stand quietly and look pretty.

Done with being sick, or rather, made to feel sick so her friends could gush over her.

I was finished. I felt cathartic; a weight lifted; an umbilical cord severed. More so, I was angry.

It wasn't enough that I had let go. The only way I would truly be free is if she was punished.

She needed to suffer.

Do you want to hear about the deal I'm making?

That night, for the first time, I prayed. I sat on the floor in my bedroom. Legs crossed, palms pressed together, my soul begging for a gift. I called out to whomever was listening.

Something heard me.

I don't know who answered. Was it God? Was it the Devil? Was it something else entirely?

It didn't matter.

Next morning, my wish came true. I woke up in my mother's body. In full control.

And now she would pay.

Do you want to know that it doesn't hurt me?

At first, I didn't realize who I was. Before I awoke, I felt the aches in my bones. This isn't the body of a twenty-something. It's the skin coffin of someone who never exercised or ate healthy, and who spent summers baking in the hot sun slathered in baby oil. It's a tired body. The muscles, the bones, all tired.

When I open my eyes, I realize I'm no longer in my own room. I'm in my mother's room. The walls are papered with baseball-sized florals and curling leaves. All in pastels. The curtains and lampshades match the wallpaper. Decor that was trendy twenty years ago. An era in style which my mother won't give up.

I don't panic.

My heart maintains its steady pace.

I realize the gift I've been given, and my thin lips crack into a smile.

I go to the bathroom and look in the mirror. When I see the face staring back at me—leathered and lined with wrinkles, blue eyes dulled into a powdery gray—my pulse quickens.

It's the face I hate. The face I cannot unsee even when I close my eyes. It's burned into my mind. A copy of a ghost.

Immediately I know what I must do.

With a punch of adrenaline, I reach for the razor. It's a cheap, disposable one, but the blades look new. New enough to work. They glint in the light as I turn it in my hand.

I press the razor against her—my—cheek, and press. As I push down, I glide the blades. Not downward, but to the right, so that they catch the skin. After all, I'm not shaving.

I'm slicing.

A trickle of red drips down the side of my face. It's warm and sticky. I taste the blood when it reaches the side of my mouth. It tastes of salt and success.

One by one, I make more cuts. They begin small. Quick flicks of my wrist to make centimeter-wide notches that ooze crimson.

Then I press harder. And harder.

By the tenth, or is it twentieth, or thirtieth—I've lost count—I take a deep breath and hold it in my lungs to steady my hand. Not to make the cuts more precise, but to control myself from doing too much too soon. There's only so much blood a person can lose before they faint. Or die. Two–three pints, depending how much my mother has in her body. She's so thin—a lifetime of feasting on Capri menthol cigarettes and what's left of my spirit—that I wonder if she has any fluids inside of her at all. Is her body the same as her heart? A dried husk of a thing; shriveled and blackened. A dead thing.

I pause to analyze my work. Under the layer of blood, there is a road map of open slivers. Some superficial, some deep.

Should this be her end? I wonder. A death by a million cuts?

No. It's too easy of a way out.

You don't want to hurt me, but see how deep the bullet lies.

My face is throbbing and swollen. I can barely pry open my right eye after becoming too carried away and nicking the soft skin underneath the lower lid.

Toward the end of my undertaking, the razor becomes dull, and I have to put more force into each slice. The cuts become ragged, thicker.

I step into the empty tub. My bloodied hands leave marks on the white tile. Her precious pristine tile she bleaches once a week.

Even through the pain, or maybe because of it, my body hungers for a cigarette. I put the long, thin stick against my lips and take a drag. It burns my throat but fills my stomach with smoky fullness. My head becomes light, and my shoulders slump in relaxation.

The cigarette is marked in cherry red, a mixture of the lipstick she always wears—even in her sleep—and the blood from the gash on my lip.

"Beauty is everything," she told me as soon as I was old enough to listen. "You get only one moment for a first impression. Once it's passed, you don't have a second chance. Impress them. Always be impressing them."

Her regimen consisted of cakey powder and dense black eyeliner she rubbed over and under her eyelids. And that pink lipstick. A cross between raspberry and baby girl pink. By the end of the day, after her second bottle of chilled Chardonnay and countless smokes, the edges of her wrinkled lips were the only parts that retained color.

My mother was obsessed with appearances. Which is why she never battered my face, only the places hidden by clothing.

If I limped or hobbled, she could blame my disease. My mysterious malady of her making that kept me indoors, tied to her.

I didn't give her such accommodations. She didn't deserve it.

I take another drag and shut my eyes, leaning back into the tub. Sleep will come soon. The adrenaline has run out and now there is only pain. Pain with the pleasure of knowing I won.

Oh come on, darling. Let me steal this moment from you now.
Her screams echo from the bathroom upstairs. I picture her hands reaching to her face in horror, the salt from her sweat burning each wound.

And I laugh.

No amount of plastic surgery will heal her. No amount of imported face creams will make a lick of difference. She'll be scarred forever. As I am.

After the exchange, I find myself at the dining room table. I stand to put out the cigarette that has made me nauseous instead of fulfilled. I lose my balance. My hand rests against the back of the wooden chairs. It's all that's keeping me upright. My head spins. Tiny white spots dot my vision as if I'm becoming lost in a blizzard.

What is happening? I feel sick. Something is very, very wrong.

The upstairs bathroom grows silent.

I look at the table and squint my eyes to sharpen my increasingly blurry vision. Atop the silvery damask of the tablecloth, sits an empty pill bottle. My mother's Valium, one ingredient of her daily feel-good cocktail.

A guttural laugh starts behind me. Deep and slow at first before increasing to a cackle.

It's my mother. Her face is beginning to dry. Flakes of muddy red crust fall off her skin as she shakes her head.

"*Tsk, tsk, tsk,*" she hisses through clenched teeth. She shakes a bloodied, bony finger at me. "Time to take your medicine, *darling.*"

What a fool I had been to think the exchange had only gone one way.

Here it was. Mother's final act.

Why do you want to hurt me? I think, one final time.

While I lay dying, acidic froth pulsing from my mouth with each breath, I picture her at my funeral. Scarred and ruined face covered in a black veil while she receives condolences from her friends. She'll squeeze their hands and ask them how she'll be able to survive this. They'll tell her they're proud of her strength. She'll get the attention she craves. The kind that fueled her need to keep me housebound and sick. *She was right all along,* the few who doubted her will think. *Her daughter truly was ill.*

I should have known.

I will never win.

But at least I am free.

Tell me, we both matter, don't we?

 *Stolen Moments*

Max Turner

The ground was wet with morning dew, the sky only just starting to lighten, though the sun was barely breaking through the dark clouds. An ominous start to the day, overcast as it was. This journey over the hill was always more of a slog when it rained, but it was worth it for the pay off. Buck would make good money at the market today, enough to spend on ale and women as he saw fit.

Inevitably, he would certainly find a way to spend the money before a new pile of rugs were ready. If only they would work faster.

They never did. He had tried the stick and the carrot but apparently there was simply no way to weave faster. And he had only been given two sisters, things might have been different had his mother not died birthing the third.

Buck huffed, adjusting the heavy sack slung over his shoulder as he trudged along the partially worn dirt path. The wild shrubs on either side seemed to lean in and purposely scratch at him as he passed. In the low light they looked like fingers, reaching out for him.

He was reminded of Ari's hands. The older of his sisters had the most hardened skin, not unlike the gnarled bark that caught against his hat and coat as he walked. Both Ari and Blossom complained quietly about their hands, even as they soaked them and rubbed in some salve of their own making.

It irked him. What did they have to complain about when he was the one who had to make this journey every few weeks? He gave them a stipend enough to fill the cupboards and buy their weaving supplies. What more did they want?

Buck adjusted the sack as he started the steeper leg of the climb, breaking from the wooded base of the hill and into the open, but rocky and windy terrain towards the summit.

Today it was windier than the last few times he made this trip, the harder weather setting in now. He would be sure to spend some of these earnings on a new fur blanket as last year's wasn't quite the color he had wanted.

The wind whistled through his furred cap even as it tried to pull it from his head. So, with one hand holding it on and the other still gripping tight to the sack, he met the wind head on and continued the climb.

"Hello, young man."

Buck stopped when he heard the wizened, nasally voice, looking around in the creeping light, unable to see who the voice had come from.

For a moment he wondered if he had simply imagined it, the wind whistling sounds that some might be fooled into thinking were voices.

"Where might you be going, hmm?"

He whipped around. It was definitely a voice. So close and so clear that it wasn't obscured by the wind; if anything it was carried on it. But still there was no one there. Trying to ascertain the direction of the voice, he turned once more, but it seemed to simply fill the air around him.

Buck clenched his jaw and adjusted the sack over his shoulder, he had heard tales of this hill, the strange magic that apparently resided here. But he was not one for superstitions and it was the quickest route to the town. Taking a boat along the river to the east of the hill cost money, to hire the boat and crew. Taking the paved road around the side of the hill would add a day and warrant a stay in an inn, something he had no wish to waste his money on. Perhaps on the way back he might take that route and indulge in a brothel to break his journey—he would see how much the rugs fetched.

With determination, Buck took another step forward, only to step into a short figure who he knew had not been there a moment before.

"You're in a hurry," the old woman said as she looked up at him from beneath her heavy hood that seemed unbothered by the wind. Her black cloak was trimmed with matching feathers and embellished with gold and silver threads that caught the little light around them. It was an expensive garment which made the old woman look all the more out of place on the hillside in the cold of the early morning.

"I need to get to town before the market opens," Buck grumbled, trying unsuccessfully to sidestep the woman who, for her apparent age, was quick on her feet.

"To sell your wares," she summarized, giving a nod to his sack. "Those things that you have worked your fingers to the bone to make. What do you have there?"

The old woman shuffled, and the next Buck knew she was pulling at the sack, trying to drag it down and open it. He batted her away and backed up, away from her reach.

"Hand woven rugs," Buck muttered angrily, suspecting that he wouldn't get rid of her without telling her. "Are you a beggar? If it's money you want, I have none."

She let out a chuckle, and it was clear that her amusement was at his expense. He knew when he was being laughed at and would never tolerate it, not even from an old woman. He reached forward to take hold of her cloak, planning to give her a shake for her troubles, but she sidestepped and avoided his grasp as though she floated on the air.

"Yes, you have money. Though it's not *your* money, is it?"

She shuffled up close to him, her eyes piercing into his. He could feel a heat from them, a pain slicing through his own eyes and into his mind and soul.

"Who weaves those rugs until their hands ache and their fingers bleed?" She asked.

Buck tried to sidestep her again, but this time she was immediately before him as though she had vanished from one spot and reappeared in another. She rose in front of him, lifted off her feet until they were of a height, her eyes now completely unavoidable.

The same wind that lifted her now blew back her hood and splayed her thick black hair into the air. Her eyes were black and terrifying.

Buck cried out and stumbled backwards, falling onto the sack he carried.

"If you want them, take them," he cried out, pulling the sack from behind him and thrusting it at her.

The wind whipped around her now, as though under her command.

"They are not yours to give," she replied in a booming voice that echoed around his head. He could feel her invading his mind. She reached her hands out though she didn't touch him, and all the same he felt her fingers like icy tendrils sinking into his brain.

Buck screamed.

The old woman climbed the hill.

A hill that seemed to get steeper with each passing day and yet she made the climb, ignoring the ache in her knees. She had been doing this since she was a young woman, a sacred task entrusted to only a few of the fae with the power to do what she did.

"You're here, Rilla." The old woman's companion was already at the top of the hill, already seated next to the large scrying bowl where they did their work. "You take longer each day."

Astrid reminded Rilla of her younger self, still wearing the white robes of an acolyte, though she had an increasing power of her own. Her dark hair was wild and free, making her skin look even paler than it truly was.

"Maybe so, but I am still here." Rilla replied with a slight scald. Today it had taken longer because of the energy she had exerted when she took command of the wind. If only she were still young enough and had energy enough to have the wind bring her all the way up. But then, were she young again, she wouldn't need such assistance.

Perhaps once she was so old that she could no longer climb the hill she would regret not stealing a moment for herself from someone less deserving, but that was not her fate. She was an overseer charged with a sacred duty, to use her powers to benefit herself would be contrary to everything her fae court believed.

"I met a soul on the way here, unexpectedly. I took his moments."

"The magic is strong today," Astrid commented with a nod as Rilla took her seat and looked into the bowl. That would account for her meeting the man. After all, it was the righteous magic that lured them to this hill when there were other paths they could take.

They sat in silence then, nettle tea brewing on a small fire as they watched the scrying bowl, waiting for their duty to present itself.

"There!" Rilla said finally, not missing the huff from Astrid at being the first to see what they were looking for. She would remind the younger woman that being able to do this so efficiently and accurately only came with time. But she held her tongue, knowing that she would have never listened to such words when she was Astrid's age.

Rilla moved her hand over the scrying bowl, bringing two mortal women into focus.

"Those were the women he stole from, their time and energy. Years now they have weaved and weaved. Such a beautiful skill exploited by the brother that had been charged with ensuring their happiness."

Rilla saw Astrid's snarl and felt it too.

Whilst Rilla was able to control herself with much more grace after so long, she still remembered the fury she had unleashed upon the young man not an hour before. Reaching into his mind and soul, stripping time from him. Time that would be returned to those he had exploited.

She had leaned over the husk of his body, drawing out his very essence as she'd muttered, "let me steal this moment from you, as you have stolen theirs."

Rilla moved forward and then slowly exhaled the time she had harvested. It sank into the water and reached like tendrils for the two women, splitting equally amongst them as they slept huddled together in a small bunk under a thin blanket.

It would be now as though their brother had never existed, their fortune and future their own. They would not mourn him, even though he might exist as an echo lingering in their dreams. They would never look for him, never find his desiccated remains half way up this hill with the last batch of rugs they would ever make for him.

When the flow ebbed, Rilla sucked in a breath to refill her lungs, settling back and trying to recoup her energy. She felt Astrid's comforting hand on her back and then a cup of hot nettle tea was before her, spooned from the open kettle into the roughly potted mug.

"Rest a while," Astrid instructed as she stood and pulled her cloak about her.

Rilla didn't need to ask where she was going. Astrid was right, the magic was strong today and likely there would be more men wandering the hill who had stolen time from women that needed to be returned to them.

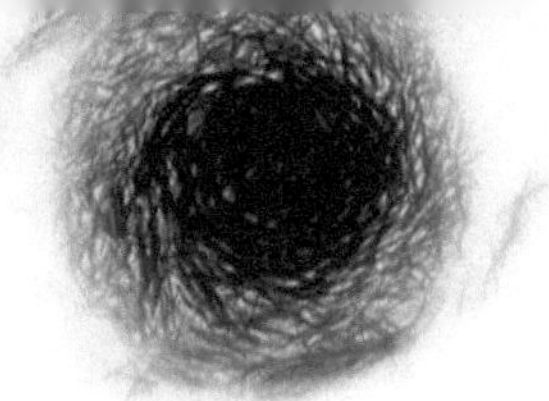

The Starseed

Kirby Kellogg

The writhing had started again. Hazel put a hand to her belly, rubbing in slow circles. Violet was awake. Always awake, either kicking away at Hazel's bladder or squirming around like a tapeworm at the top of her womb. Idleness made her extra active, and there wasn't anywhere idler than here.

The line ahead of her was three people deep—an old man counting out pennies for a carton of cigarettes and two twenty-somethings in t-shirts babbling away about some superhero movie while the taller one rocked on her heels and swung her purse around. Only three people but it felt miles longer, and she pressed her hand tighter to the swell of her child as she waited. "Settle down." she grumbled. "We'll be back at the hotel soon enough. Then I'll pace around the motel room until you're satisfied, is that what you want?"

The movement settled. Contentment. She rubbed her temple.

Her whole family had been against this little excursion— too dangerous when she was so close to giving birth. "You need to stay close," her mother said, hands pressed to her stomach and eyes wide with cartoonish glee. "I can't help you have the baby if you're not here!" It had all become about the baby. How her mother would help raise her, how she'd be baptized in her childhood church and taught in her childhood school and would grow old in the same place their family had barely left in centuries. Always under mom's shadow.

Her excuse was that everything was happening all at once, all of the shower planning and weight of the future, the aches and swelling and sense of dread and hope and fear. "It's just too much," she'd confessed as she packed, grateful that it was over the phone and she couldn't see her mother's judging eyes. She had to get out and get some air, she explained. For both hers and the baby's sake. Her mother had finally relented. So she'd gone half a state over, stopped at one of the smaller motels. All she needed was a week alone, and then she could face the world again.

At least she hoped so.

"Fuck's sake!" she gasped suddenly, jolting forward and barely catching herself before she could tumble. Waving away the kids when they reached to help her and flipping off the old man's judging eyes, she turned to look at what hit her. It was a pale blue stroller, an old fashioned one with the hood half-pulled down. She could hear cooing from under the blankets, giggling away, and watched the driver reach in to settle her child. "Shit," she said, biting her tongue after so she wouldn't cuss again. "Sorry."

"Oh!" The driver smiled, waving away her concern as her hands scrubbed away at something bundled in a tissue. "It's perfectly alright. I'm sorry for getting the backs of your legs—I know this thing can nick your ankles something fierce." She extended one messily manicured hand, fingertips stained with bubblegum pink polish. "I'm Jenna."

"Hazel." She leant a little to peer into the carriage. "Who's this little joker?"

"That's my son, Ethan. I dropped his rattle on my way out." She revealed the rattle, a little thing shaped like a shark, and the boy grasped it happily and wiggled it around with a joyous squeal.

Hazel wanted to ask why the kid was hidden under blankets. The only thing that peeked out from under the fabric were his little feet and hands, covered as they were by blue shark-dotted booties and gloves. He hadn't made a move yet to fling them off, sounded happy as could be, but it seemed weird. Instead, she stood up again. "Got my own on the way."

"How far along?"

"Two weeks to go."

"Jeez," Jenna whispered. "What're you doing all the way out here? There isn't a hospital for miles. I'd be worried I'd end up giving birth in the back of my car!"

Then she laughed—a high bark that matched her baby's; they laughed together then, harsh and shrill and mingling enough to make Hazel wince. The sound made the teenyboppers jolt a little as they passed, dipping their heads low to continue talking about whatever weird thing they'd been babbling about. Hazel laughed sheepishly, shrugging a little and running a hand through her hair.

"Just figured I should get away from it all for a bit. That way I'm not as stressed. Not exactly good for the baby, y'know?"

"What're you having?"

"A little girl. Gonna name her Violet."

"Oh, what a lovely name. Looks like it's your turn, hun."

"Thank God," Hazel thought and slumped a little in relief. "Nice to meet you, Jen."

"You too! I'd love to talk again sometime," she dug around in her pocket, scribbled something on the back of a shopping list and shoved it into Hazel's palm. "Mothers gotta stick together, y'know?" That barking laugh returned, fading with her as she walked out.

God, that'd been fucking *weird.* Maybe she was some kind of religious nut recruiting for her Bible study group or womb-worshipping circle, or a pyramid scheme pariah trying to get underlings. Still, Hazel kept the number. Stuffing it into her pocket, she got what she needed and flopped into the driver's seat with a grunt of relief. Violet was at it again, practicing drums on her kidneys, and she groaned a little. "C'mon, just settle for a little longer while I get us back home. Then you can do whatever you want." Bending to turn the key and drive off, she peered through the windshield one more time.

Jenna was outside with her carriage, talking to one of the twenty-year-olds—the girl, who looked utterly captivated, nodding along like a bobble head, all crooked grin and big glasses. Knelt by the carriage, the girl waved towards the inside, stood up to accept a scrap of paper from Jenna, and ran off to where her friend waited for her.

Hazel sighed. "Poor kid," she sighed to Violet, pulling out of the parking lot. "Doesn't know what she's getting into."

Still, spurred on by her own self-imposed isolation, she found herself dialing the number on the receipt that night. At worst, she'd slam the receiver down if Jenna got weird. At best—who knew what would happen. It wasn't like she was going to see the woman after her excursion anyway. They'd be ships passing in the night, funny stories told at parties.

As the dial tone droned away, she became aware of a distant ringing in one of the other rooms. Her blood stuttered in her veins. No answer after three long beeps on her end. Good. Now she could get some rest without feeling guilty—Hazel thought, and then...

"Hello?"

The word echoed through the phone and through the wall.

Shit.

After a few days, Hazel grew used to having Jenna around. She'd started shadowing her, tagging along on gas station trips and perching in her room while taking care of Ethan. Up and down, she swore that it was to make sure she and Violet were going to be okay. That whole 'mothers stick together' thing was like a mantra to Jenna, and it bugged Hazel. Why hover around? They were strangers, nothing more. She had a kid of her own, so it wasn't like she was desperate to gut her like a fish to steal the baby.

So why?

"Because," she began, "mothers stick together."

"Yeah, when it's neighbors getting knocked up at the same time or something."

Jenna tapped the wall. "Aren't we neighbors?"

She had a point. Besides, it wasn't like she had anybody else around here. Only other person Hazel knew around here was Violet, so she got to know Jenna—got used to that New England chirp of hers, the smell of her always clean clothes, her fascination with sewing things for Ethan.

She learnt mostly about Ethan. That he was the result of a one-night stand under the stars, same as her Violet, and that he'd been born premature. Something tinged in her heart at that, hearing about the machines as they'd monitored the baby—the case keeping him from his mother. But Jenna didn't seem fazed. "In fact," she said one night over drinks—a can of wine for her, a can of soda for Hazel—"I think it made us even closer. More of a single person than two different people. The worst part was getting him fed, it was like he was a little black hole. I'm sure Violet'll be like that too. But you'll figure it out. The starseed's got to be fed!"

Hazel nodded, ignoring the 'starseed' bit. "I'm nervous though," she confessed. "She's excitable, I can feel it already, but—" she paused, running a hand through her hair and drumming at her scalp, "I don't know. Just feels like I won't be what she needs."

"Take my advice, Haze." Jenna's hand brushed her shoulder. Her skin prickled underneath it. "You'll know what to do when she comes—just trust that she'll tell you what to do. After all, the bond between mother and child is the strongest tether in the universe."

So yeah, Hazel found herself growing closer with the young mother. Found them becoming friends. Found herself clinging tighter every day to her company. Found herself reveling in having a friend—

even if she began sleeping with a butter knife under her pillow. Better safe than sorry.

She was holding that butter knife in bed a few days later, rolling the cool metal between her fingers. She rubbed her bare stomach with her free hand, feeling the tiger trails of stretch marks under her fingertips. Violet had finally settled down enough for her to lay back and sleep. It'd been a long day mostly spent trying to avoid new nausea and returning fatigue that dogged her as the space between today and B-Day grew narrower. But she couldn't rest yet. Her mind was buzzing with a strange sensation of impending doom. That something would go wrong, that things had been too calm to stay that way. Finishing a water bottle hazy with Alka-Seltzer, she laid back and shut her eyes tightly. Think of sheep, count some sheep. *One, two, three–*

BANG! BANG! BANG!

"For fuck's sake," she groaned and climbed to her feet while yanking on a cheap motel bathrobe (she was sure there were fleas in the damn thing). "Hold on, I'm coming!" she hollered, finally jerking open the door. It was the girl from the gas station, still holding the same clear-faced bag and rocking on her heels. Her shirt was emblazoned with dogs in red dresses, tossing their bodies in strange ways above the words '*Chased by the Hounds of Love.*' Hazel's face dropped nearly in tandem with hers. "What do you want?"

"Oh shit, you're not the mom from the gas station."

"Good eye."

"Do you know where her room is?" Following Hazel's finger with her eyes, the girl grinned and shook her hand vigorously. Kid had a grip on her for damn sure. "Thanks! Sorry about waking you up. Have a good night!" she babbled, releasing her and making her way towards Jenna's door. Before she dipped inside though, she gave her a thumbs up. One last silent thank you before the door shut behind her. The crickets chirped, the buzzards crowed, and Hazel felt cool air brush along her skin.

That nauseated feeling returned, shifting rougher in her stomach. Before she could think twice about it, she jolted towards the bathroom and the last thing she remembered was lunch coming back up as *Peppa Pig* blared through the wall and Ethan squawked loud enough for it to ring in the back of her head. A chill ran over her, one that seemed to fill the whole room, and then she was out like a light.

When she woke up, she was in bed and someone kept slamming their palm into her door. Struggling to her feet, Hazel dragged her wrist over her eyes as she yanked the door open. It helped block out the blinding sunshine but not enough to keep a hiss from rolling up her throat. Her eyes adjusted on her new guest. It was the other kid from the gas station, she recognized the haunt t-shirt and the tattoo of a tooth on his arm. This time though, his eyes were wet and every muscle in his body looked taut with nerves. "I don't have any cash, kid, sorry." She went to shut the door and get back to sleep.

He stuck his foot in the door, digging around in his pockets. "Shit. Listen, I'm really sorry to wake you up but you gotta help me."

"I *told* you, I don't have any cash on me."

"My friend's missing." He pulled a photo from the depths of his shorts. Tiny girl, big glasses, peace sign to the camera over dinner. "She was gonna babysit this lady's kid for some extra cash last night—we're going down to Boston for a con. She was gonna text when she got settled in, but she never did. We're getting kinda worried about her. You seen her?"

Taking the picture between her fingers, she looked the girl over closely. Tiny girl, big glasses, peace sign—the purse.

The clear-faced purse.

"Nah." Hazel lied, handing the picture back. "Haven't seen anyone like that around here."

The boy cursed, kicking a rock off the balcony and onto the ground two stories below. "Thanks anyway. If you see any sign of her…" He struggled visibly, folding the photo into a smaller square. There was a sad sparkle in his eyes. "Tell somebody. The staff or something. I shoved 'em my phone number." Then he was gone.

The rolling, queasy feeling in Hazel's stomach didn't leave with him. She'd lied, but how could she have known where the kid was? Maybe she'd run off with the circus. Maybe she'd found a guy or a girl or a serial killer and rode off with 'em. She had too much to worry over to think about what-ifs.

But one what-if just wouldn't leave her head. The what-if who stayed in the room beside hers with a cooing bundle of joy.

"What happened to the kid who babysat for you?"

"Hm?" Cocking her head up from a crossword, it took a few seconds for Jenna to figure out her meaning. "Oh, the brunette with the glasses? Yeah, her friend started knocking around here yesterday. All I know is that she kept an eye on Ethan while I did some errands, I came back, she left. What happened after that, who knows?" Jenna shrugged, throwing a blanket over Ethan as she scooped him from his bassinet. "Poor kid though, probably got lost. Not hard to out here, since the terrain doesn't really change much." Rocking her arms beneath the blanket, she beamed at Hazel. "Not too much longer now, huh?"

"Yeah." Hazel said, voice slower as she tried to settle jumping nerves. "Yeah." she repeated. "Jen?"

"Yes?"

"Can I see Ethan's face?"

"Of course you can. Not right now though. He's feeding, and gets all fussy if interrupted." Lifting part of the blanket for a moment, she displayed half of her chest. A small ring of scars circled her nipple. "Sweet little bruiser."

"I've never seen his face."

"I've shown you pictures of him!"

"No you haven't."

"Of course I have, remember? The big box of photos I showed you a few nights back?" she laughed, nudging her arm like they were old friends. "Jeez, and I thought wine made *me* forget things! Maybe we should keep you off the sugar. Or maybe it's that you're getting close to having the baby—that kind of brain fog—maybe you should get some rest. Call your mom or something."

Hazel bristled. She hadn't seen any pictures and her memory wasn't that bad. "The fact that you can't just show him to me is really weird." The word she wanted to use was 'worrying,' but she wasn't about to start accusing Jenna of anything without proof. She wasn't stupid. "Just let me take a peek."

"God, you're being so pushy."

"And you're trying to bullshit me!"

Putting a hand over where Ethan's ear would be under the blanket, Jenna hissed at her. "Don't you *dare* cuss around my little angel. His ears are too pure for that kind of language. What kind—" She stopped herself, but Hazel could hear the question in the air.

What kind of mother are you?

"I'm going back to my room."

"Wait." Jenna clasped Hazel's arm and her skin burned beneath her touch. "I'm sorry. I went too far. I'll make it up to you. I don't want us to leave on bad terms."

"Leave?"

"I'm going out of town for a week to visit family. By the time I get back, you should've had little Violet!" she giggled, patting her shoulder and then her stomach. "I'll bring back flowers. But you should come over tonight. You can keep an eye on him while I pack—see him as much as you want to. I could use the help anyway."

Every instinct said no. *Leave, pack up, go back home.* At least her mother was a weirdo she knew well. But something inside her reached out in sympathy.

She hated that part of her.

"Fine."

"Great! I'll see you around seven. I'll get a pizza or something." Jenna turned back to her son, bouncing him under the blanket as Hazel rose and left for her own room. Answers might come, but not soon enough. A quick search online answered one question though.

Teething scars weren't as dark as the ones Jenna had—and they certainly didn't drip like makeup.

Carrying the knife on her was an easy choice. Leaving her room wasn't. Still, Hazel crossed the threshold into the unlocked hotel room at seven sharp and found Jenna there, rocking her son in his covered bassinet. The windows were covered, but all those buzzing lights were on bright. "Hey," she croaked, the blade buried deep in her pocket.

Jenna's eyes twinkled. "Hi! I'm so glad you came over, I really need to pack."

"Yeah, yeah, totally. Listen—could I use your bathroom real quick?"

"Of course. Take a look at what I'm making in there too! Ethan needed a new blanket. He's getting so big now!"

She'd kept talking about it even as Hazel shut the bathroom door behind her. Hanging over the sink as twinkly kids' songs seeped in through the walls, Hazel looked at herself in the mirror. The rings around her eyes were darker and her cheeks more sunken in. She looked like shit. She *felt* like shit.

Washing her face, she dug her nails into her skin for a moment. What was she doing here?

Then she remembered the girl with the clear-faced purse and the nausea returned. Spitting into the sink, she raised her head, looked into the mirror, and noticed something.

Streaks of pinkish cloth hung from the towel rack, waving in the slight breeze through the tiny ventilation window above. Stepping closer, Hazel saw browning marks on the cloth at the edges—pinpricks and small streaks. She picked up a patchwork belt of fabric and held it to the light. Splashes of dark pink and black lines made formless blobs across its surface, but squinting, she saw the outline of three words.

'Chased,' 'by,' and 'Hounds.'

Chased by the Hounds of Love.

Stomach acid surged into her throat, making her cough and wheeze into her palm as she released her grasp. The coughing grew stronger as her head spun. Banging filling her head. A door's distant knock. "Jen?" she called aloud.

"You alright? You sound like you've seen a ghost!"

"What's the shirt in here for?"

No response. Her hand slid into her pocket and the butter knife blazed in her palm. "Jen, what the *fuck* is with this shirt in here?"

"It's a gift for Ethan. I told you. C'mon out and I'll show you!"

Despite her own best judgement, she did as her friend said. She sat cross-legged on the bed with the bassinet. Now she could see its front. It'd been cut up recently, messy stitches holding the fabric together around a new addition—a clear plastic front. "He's ready now," Jenna said, smiling like the Virgin Mary. "He's ready for you to see him. The others weren't ready, but you are."

Hazel half-expected a mass of fluff and newspapers formed into a vaguely babyish shape, or one of those reborn dolls with their uncanny valley faces. A plastic doll, a stuffed teddy bear, a corpse. Something lifeless and still among the duckies and bunnies printed into the bassinet's fabric.

What she found was nothing. A limbed, squirming mass of nothing. A void shaped like a baby, digits flowing in and out of each other and blinks of light bursting across its empty flesh. Its chest moved like it was breathing, a rasp came from an unseen mouth as its little legs kicked in circles just. It reached for her with finger-less hands and let out an animal's squawk when she pulled away in horror. Three clicks, then an air-raid siren's scream. Before she could even put her hands over her ears, the motion of the bassinet drew the wail down to clicking and then silence.

"Isn't he just beautiful?"

"What *is* that?"

"Ethan—my son."

"That's not a baby, Jenna, that's…that's…I don't know what it is, but it's not a baby."

Instead of outrage flashing in her eyes or a gasp of disgust or despair, Jenna laughed softly. "It's okay, I knew you wouldn't understand immediately. No one else did, and they never could've.

They were all so scared of Ethan. Especially that girl from the station. But luckily he's a quick little man." She cooed, waving at him through the window. "He knew just what to do, he knew to be quick! That's right, my little guy!"

The haze of affection didn't make Hazel any less sick. "What did you do? What did *he* do?"

"That's the thing about Ethan," Jenna sighed. "Ethan knew you'd be good. He could feel it. That girl from the gas station, she wasn't good. Her energy was *icky*, wasn't it honey?"

"Energy?"

"Ethan's drawn to energy. Human energy, human emotions, human love. I've got more than enough of it, but sometimes he wants to have something other than my love. He wants everybody to love him. But sometimes they can't. Their energy isn't good enough. That's when they're taken care of." Removing the top of the bassinet, Jenna held Ethan in her arms. "Mommy takes care of them, and then he can eat all he wants and all that bad energy is out of the universe. That's why I started talking to you, y'know! I wanted to see what your energy was—but then I saw that you were pregnant and I knew you'd be perfect."

Her blood froze. "Perfect for what?"

Rising, Jenna smiled in a halo of buzzing florescence. "Ethan needs new friends. All he has in the world is me, and that's not okay. But I think Violet would be just *wonderful.* You're so devoted to her, so eager to give her a good life, I know you'll do what's right."

Drawing out the butter knife, Hazel stepped quickly towards the door. "I'm not going out like that, you psycho! You can't take my fucking baby!" Grasping the knob, she instantly jolted back. Cold soaked into her palm, a blazing cold that made her howl in pain. Collapsing from the sudden jolt, she dropped the knife and held her wrist as she growled. Her palm was dark, any sign of flesh coated in inky black gunk with flickering lights streaming through it. The room began spinning as she rolled onto her back and tried to crawl away.

"Have her?" Jenna laughed. "Don't be silly. I'm not gonna take her from you."

Mother and son stood over Hazel now, blocking her only exit. The lights flickered violently as more of that same gunk flowed down Jenna's arms and dress. Everything below the baby became void—the Virgin and her Jesus sinking into the Marianas Trench. But their smiles were beatific and Ethan giggled away as he reached for her. The lights that twinkled on his pseudo-flesh came together, blazing into her eyes as he pressed a palm to her forehead.

Jenna said, "I'm giving you both something wonderful."

The world snapped shut.

When Hazel awoke, it was to a penumbra of vomit and water circling her body. Morning sickness, something she'd thought she'd kicked months ago when Violet was barely a twinkle in her eye. She clung to the bowl's side, feeling a release from below her as she emptied her barely filled stomach again. The baby was coming; a flood of water soaked her pants and formed a puddle on the tile. She slipped and pain shot through her in wave upon wave as she crawled to the bedroom. Her bedroom. She didn't remember being here before. She barely remembered anything.

Some part of her brain hammered away at her brain stem as she ran to the phone. *You saw something in another room before you fell asleep. Something bad. Something horrible.* By the time her frantically rolling brain had kicked back into gear, that thought was long gone in a haze of blue bedsheets and red lights, cheap doors and scratchy stone flooring, and a driving pulse of pain. Just before the ambulance breached the hill leading to the motel, she found herself knocking on Jenna's door. "Jen? The baby's coming, I can't go alone, pl—."

The door swung open. There was no one and nothing there—save for an empty child's carrier with a puppy-dotted blanket sprawled over it. She was long gone, and Hazel worried—for a while, at least. By the time they found Jenna's car, idling and driverless by the town-line, she was so steeped in epidural drugs that memory became a mass of smoke and mirrors. Twenty-nine hours later, the smoke cleared and the mirrors shattered as her child came into the world.

Violet was brought into the world in a fit of hiccupy giggles. Her little legs kicked and her arms wiggled, laughter melodic. The doctors bundled in her pale pink blankets before handing her over. "Congratulations, Ms. Cartwell. It's a healthy little girl. Ten fingers, ten toes."

They weren't wrong. Ten fingers, ten toes. But the little digits flowed in and out of each other, indistinguishable from one another. A black, shiny, flowing mass of a newborn baby. She squawked like an animal, reaching up for her mother as little fingers formed and faded.

Hazel took her little hands, kissing the shapeless knuckles. The doctors didn't see the true beauty of her kid, but that was fine. No one needed to understand but her. Jenna was right, she realized. The bond between a mother and her child was the strongest tether in the universe. Her instincts slammed into gear as her baby cried, air-raid siren sharp into the stale air of the hospital room. Immediately, Hazel knew what to do. "Don't worry, baby," she said softly, kissing Violet's forehead. "You'll have your supper soon."

She pressed the 'call nurse' button and watched her baby smile under its bright crimson glow.

Bow, Blood and String

Wendy Dalrymple

"Get the bow going, let it scream to me."

"Some believe that the key to creating rich, enchanting sound from a violin is in the instrument itself. There is an idea that you need a stringed object made from special wood by the hand of an old-world craftsman to create superior music. That simply is untrue. The secret to producing a perfect pitch, that spine-tingling shriek that both offends and intrigues the ear all at once is in the *bow*. Without a quality bow, the violin is meaningless."

The man sitting on my couch with a beer bottle dangling between his fingertips looks up at me with mock interest. I know that he is only half-listening to my monologue, but I enjoy giving it just the same. Perhaps it's repetitive and self-indulgent to start this way, but I enjoy educating my guests when it comes to my one true love. Still, I realize that it's time to move on as I recognize the glint of impatience in his eyes. He purses and then licks his lips as he scans the length of my body. He didn't come here for a lecture on bows and strings.

"So you're, like, a musician?"

The man takes another long sip of beer before placing the bottle on the table. He doesn't use a coaster, which isn't a surprise but adds to my disgust all the same. I barely remember his name at this point. Is it John? Josh? James? No matter. Soon he'll just be a memory. I force a smile and focus on the task at hand.

"Something like that," I coo, eyelids fluttering. "Would you like me to show you?"

A sigh escapes from the man's lips. He's neither young nor old, likely closer to forty than thirty with an intimidating upper body, a glossy crop of hair and just the right amount of stubble. Charming—in a bad boy sort of way. Surely, a private concert is not what he was expecting when I invited him to come home with me from the bar, but then again, none of them do. He settles deeper into my couch and resigns himself to the fact that if he has any hopes of seeing what's underneath my silk wrap dress, then he should be an obliging guest.

"Sure."

"Goody," I say, clapping my hands together.

I turn to the stuffed velvet armchair next to my piano where the inconspicuous black case is ready and waiting. The latch opens with a satisfying click, and I smile down at the little brown beauty nestled within the brushed suede crevasse. I lovingly pluck my violin from the case followed by my grandmother's trusty bow in the secured cinch pocket. I position the instrument under my chin, and a surge of adrenaline courses through my veins.

"Have you ever heard of the *Danse Macabre*?" I ask, all teeth and big, dark eyes.

I already suspect that this simple man who enjoys light beer and the occasional date rape most likely does *not* know of the work of Camille Saint-Saens. Still, my cheeks warm and a rush of blood causes my veins to thrum with anticipation as he squirms in his seat.

"I think I heard of it before," he says, scratching the back of his head.

I straighten my back and arch an eyebrow at him, my lips pursed in a seductive grin. My elbow is raised sharp and high just like my grandmother taught me, and her grandmother taught her. The bow is now an extension of my body, and I quiver at the thought of every vibration slicing through me, overwhelming my cells and synapses with its aching, piercing song.

Without a word I drag the bow across the bridge of the violin, reveling in the way that the familiar first notes occupy every inch of my living room with a haunting sound. Instantly, the man's hands fly to his ears and a bloodcurdling scream bursts from his chest. I smile and pause, unable to resist the opportunity to monologue and drag out his sentence some more.

"You see, it translates to 'Dance of Death' or something like that," I explain, waving my bow in the air. "I came up with a little jig to go with it. Would you like to see?"

"No!" he moans, still writhing and clutching at his ears.

"Oh—it will only take a moment," I assure him. "Watch."

I tear into the instrument again, sawing furiously at the strings with my bow as my fingers dance along the neck. I raise my right leg so that my knee is at an angle with my toe pointed to the ground. I hop about in tune with the centuries old tune, kicking and tapping with glee as my guest howls again and again. Then, to my utter shock, the man rose from the couch.

"Fuck this!" he shouted. His eyes were squeezed tightly shut, his hands still covering his ears in a futile attempt to block out the sound. I was mildly annoyed before, but now I'm positively enraged.

"Don't be rude," I say, lowering my bow.

The man's eyes open and lock with mine in a terrible, heart-stopping moment. I can see deep into the abyss of his ugly, black soul once more. There is no doubt in my mind that he has exactly what's coming to him.

"How many women has it been Joshua? Hmm? Five? Six?"

His lip curls into a snarl, and for a brief moment, I fear that I might lose my grip on him. But my bow is still in my hand, and my violin is still at the ready. In truth, he doesn't stand a chance.

"The fuck are you…"

"You see, the problem with men like you is that you never stop," I say.

My guest attempts to lunge at me, but instead, freezes almost comically in place. His lower lip hangs open as he stares back at me, helpless and unable to move. I didn't even have to raise a hand.

"Take a seat, Joshy," I say, pointing to the couch. "Time to face the music."

Like an obedient, trained animal, my guest lowers back onto the sofa. I like this sofa and am grateful that I thought ahead of time to cover it. Hopefully this won't make too much of a mess.

"Now, where were we? Ah yes, my solo," I say, taking position again.

In a flash, I'm once again possessed as a devilish tune explodes from the strings beneath my hand. The man begins to scream again, scratching at his ears and clawing at his eyes. Thankfully, between the soundproof walls and the music, my neighbors have never been the wiser to the comings and goings in my apartment. This guest, though, is making a particularly loud racket. I continue to hop and twirl about anyhow, taking deep pleasure in the way that rivulets of red begin to stream from his orifices. However, like all good enchantments, this one too must come to an end.

"Are you ready, Joshy?" I say. Blood gushes from between his fingers as they lay flat against his jaw. His eyes have been closed the entire time and unfortunately, I think he's missed the interpretive dance part of my performance.

"Here comes the finale!"

Now more furiously than ever my bow strikes and bends, willing the notes to do their worst. The song crescendos, and again, this guest manages to surprise me. Normally at this point, the men that I bring home for a private concert simply succumb and fall over, dead as a doornail. But not this one.

As my bow screeches out its final note, the man on the sofa can take no more. His eyes finally open and bulge forth from their sockets like a child's squeeze toy. Blood is flowing from his ears and froths from his nose. His mouth is open in a contorted, silent scream. And then, a pop—not unlike the sound of a bursting balloon—causes my shoulders to tighten, and his head opens up in an utter explosion of fluid and flesh. Shards of scalp, skull, and brain matter fly through the air, sticking in a red, bloody mess on my ceiling, on my couch, on my carpet and all over my lovely silk wrap dress. I wipe a bit of gore from my eyes with the back of my hand and regard the headless form slumped on my couch.

"Well, that's never happened before," I quip, to no one but myself.

Thankfully, my bow has been spared in the explosion, though I suspect that it would protect itself in such a situation. I shake my head at the ruined state of my living room. I have a long night of cleaning ahead. I place the violin and bow in their case, look up at the black and white photo hanging over my piano, and blow it a kiss.

"Got another one, Grandma."

I Keep the Lights On

David Busboom

Forty years, five months, and twenty days ago, Frank Gilmour died in Paris to the peal of a bell.

The young actor's ghost was, for a time, believed to haunt the site of his death—no less grand a location than Notre-Dame itself—though most assumed his shade to be a creature of superstitious imagination, namely that of the actors and crew who had worked with him there on his unrealized big break.

I believed.

Frank was born in January 1957 in New York City, a bartender's son. After high school he started performing in small theaters while working as a copy boy for *The New York Times*.

That's when we met.

I was a little older than Frank, working as a bellhop and doorman, taking on background parts in some of the same shows. We became friends. He taught me how to dance, and when he started getting bigger roles I became his understudy—we were both redheads and similarly built. Recognizing Frank as the superior talent, I hitched my fortune to him.

One day a short, bespectacled Brit in a straw fedora approached Frank and I backstage after an off-off-Broadway performance of *Wuthering Heights* (Frank, in his biggest role yet, had played Heathcliff). He complemented the physicality and intensity of Frank's performance. I stood a few feet away, smiling and nodding but saying nothing.

"Did you ever see the film *Man of a Thousand Faces?*" the Brit asked, his gaze boring into Frank through the round glasses like sunlight through a child's magnifying glass.

"Sure," Frank said. "The one about Chaney."

I'd caught it on TV once or twice, myself.

"I think that could be you," the Brit said, and extended a hand. "Henry Elder, filmmaker."

I'll never forget that day.

Elder had worked as an assistant director and cinematographer for Hammer Films since the early sixties. He had recently left the company for greener pastures, and now he was scouting for his directorial debut: a new version of *The Hunchback of Notre Dame*, to be filmed on location in Paris. To balance the cost of the location, it was to be a cast of unknowns, and Elder specifically wanted an American in the title role. "I saw tonight that you can match Olivier," Elder said. "Think you can best Chaney, Laughton, and Quinn?"

"Yes," Frank said. "I can."

In the ensuing conversations, I was signed on as Frank's stunt double. A few months later, we were in France meeting the rest of the cast and crew.

A middle-aged Frenchman named Claude Napier would portray the villainous Claude Frollo, while Elder had cast English brothers Gary and Alan Kingsley as Pierre Gringoire and Captain Phoebus, intending that their familial resemblance provide some interesting subtext for their love triangle with Esmerelda.

The beautiful street dancer herself was to be played by Elder's niece, a willowy seventeen-year-old from Kent named Catherine Becker. Fluent in French and formally trained in traditional Irish dance, she possessed both the passion and the physical grace essential for the role.

Frank was immediately smitten, but his feelings weren't reciprocated. As if to parallel our source material, Catherine appeared far more interested in the Kingsley brothers.

As filming commenced, Frank's attraction approached the border of obsession. He insisted on doing more and more of his own stunts when Catherine was on set, ignoring my and Elder's pleas in his desperation to impress her. In our final conversation, just before filming the famous "Sanctuary!" scene, he vowed to sweep her off her feet once and for all.

The twenty-seventh of October, 1978, is not a day of which history has preserved the memory. There was nothing notable in the event which set the bells of Paris ringing that early Friday morning, just another minor tragedy. The accidental death of a handsome young actor.

Frank wasn't the first or last to fall from the towers of Notre Dame. There had been at least a dozen suicides committed that way already, and would be more. It rated a small headline in a handful of newspapers but was largely forgotten by the end of the week.

Except, of course, by those of us who'd known him.

As we were nearly a third of the way through shooting the film, Elder insisted that we couldn't just stop. A month passed in which we all sat tight in and around Paris, wondering whether the film would be cancelled.

Then Elder found his replacement for Quasimodo.

In me.

I refused, at first. Our disparity in talent aside, Frank had been my friend, and the idea of attempting to fill his shoes under these circumstances felt almost like a betrayal. But then, what middling twenty-something actor doesn't dream of a breakout role as meaty as this? And on the big screen! Though my conscience rebelled, my pride and hunger won out. I soothed myself with the knowledge that, had I not accepted, the entire project may have been shuttered. It wasn't fair to Frank, perhaps, but he wasn't the only one whose burgeoning career hinged on this film. We were all unknowns, after all.

Elder wanted to continue roughly where we'd left off in the shoot, albeit with greater safety precautions in place. Some of the more elaborate or risky stunts were cut entirely, and for those that remained I was assigned a *professional* stunt double. The heavy makeup, much more detailed than the stunt version, took three hours to apply each day and made my appearance in the role indistinguishable from Frank's.

I still remember the guilt I felt upon first seeing my freshly deformed face in the mirror.

As filming recommenced, that guilt compounded. Walking anywhere within sight of the cathedral, I had the strangest sense of being followed. I started drinking heavily whenever I was off set, ending every night passed out on or near my bed with an empty bottle close at hand.

On set, I went through the choreographed motions, always hitting my marks and remembering my lines, but I found myself unable to embody Hugo's deaf bellringer. Instead, I mimicked what I'd seen Frank do with the part, as faithfully as possible. I did it to honor him, at least that's what I told myself. Elder didn't seem to notice or mind. After all, Frank had been his first choice.

Meanwhile, Catherine continued to get chummy with both Kingsleys. I had no designs on her myself, yet it annoyed me to observe. Frank's intentions had been no secret, and while she hadn't owed him anything, her lack of discretion so soon after his death struck me as insensitive. I could almost hear Frank's voice sometimes, blaming her.

Are you satisfied, Catherine? If you'd just given me a break, I'd have taken it easy. I'd still be here.

I kept out of it, kept to myself, only speaking to the others as much as necessary. My dream may have become something of a nightmare, but it would be over in a few weeks and then I'd be a real film actor. Soon we only had a few crucial scenes left.

Where Catherine Becker was murdered was on Rue Saint-Honoré, outside of an old bookshop nestled between cafés and tour shops, about a thirty-minute walk from the cathedral.

When she never arrived on set one morning, Elder and I thought she'd finally succumbed to the Kingsleys' advances, but then the brothers showed up without her, apologetic and a little hungover after a night on the town. After waiting a while longer and finally finding her room empty, Elder went to the police. The following day they contacted him to identify the body.

How she'd died was strangulation. Her killer had evidently caught her exploring the Paris streets late that evening. She had not been raped or robbed, and her face was undamaged. Elder described it to me as only a photographer would, noting the perfection of her lipstick. Only the savage finger marks on her pale, narrow throat betrayed the violence of her end.

Why had this happened? And who could have done it?

I suspect Catherine's family is still asking those questions.

This time there were no instructions to sit tight, no search for a replacement. Despite Elder's thrifty casting, the film was already over budget, and the death of a second major cast member spooked everyone, myself included. Whispers abounded about Frank's ghost having cursed the production, and the feeling of being followed intensified. I found myself suddenly terrified of the dark, as I hadn't been even as a small boy. For the first time in my life, I started sleeping with the lights on.

On top of the horror of losing his niece, the dual tragedies had shattered Elder's faith in the film, as well as that of his financiers.

Within days, the whole thing was cancelled and I was on a plane back to New York.

I stopped looking for acting work, instead returning to my old job of doorman. Over the years I took courses in architecture, library science, and technical drawing, but none of these would-be careers stuck either.

I'm still at the same hotel I started at, though it's changed names and owners a couple of times. For almost thirty years, I avoided the night shift, but eventually it didn't frighten me so much. Anyway, management wanted a younger face to greet the daylight crowd, and I needed the hours. Soon I was exclusively a night watchman. I'd barely thought of Paris for the better part of a decade.

Then, yesterday, Notre-Dame burned.

When I saw the news, I was at once struck by an extraordinary sequence of images. Catherine in a flowing black dress, her long red hair streaming in a light evening breeze under a dim streetlamp. A pair of black-gloved hands on the ends of strong, reaching forearms—

My own.

I don't know if it was my own disturbed mind or Frank's ghost that made me do it. That made me do it and then forget for so long. I don't know why Notre-Dame's burning should undam the terrible truth. Perhaps Frank's spirit, no longer trapped there, has caught up with me at last. All at once I feel followed again, and I cannot live another day with the knowledge of what I've done.

I'm going to the roof now. If you find this, let Catherine's family know. Elder would be in his eighties now, if he's still alive. Tell him this story, and that I'm sorry.

Is this the right thing to do?

I don't know.

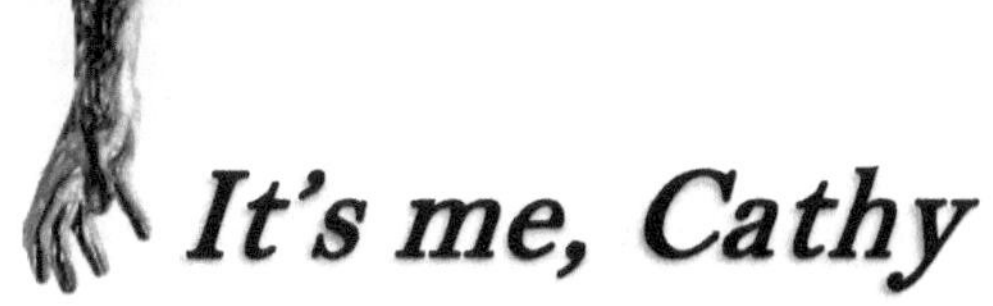

It's me, Cathy

TR Hitchman

He heard the knock quite by accident at first. He stood in the hallway, cautiously studying the door. It was late, he hadn't expected any visitors, nor did he welcome them. He was in no mood to talk. The night before he had hit the whisky bottle hard, bringing the bottle to his lips without being conscious of it at all. The second knock was louder. Whoever was on the other side was determined to be heard.

He moved slowly towards the door, rubbing his throbbing temples before he shakily reached for the lock.

"It's me…" He felt a drip of cold sweat run down his back.

"It's me… Cathy… let me in…"

He stared at the woman in the doorway. She stood there with her arms wrapped around herself, her arms tangled up in the bedraggled cardigan that looked as if it had seen better days.

"I'm home." She whispered, he could smell the soil on her clothes, and as she brushed past him, he noticed it in her hair, small black specks, like lice.

She asked for a glass of water and cradled it in her hands before taking a huge gulp, pausing for a few seconds before taking another and then gasped.

"I keep thinking that this is a dream… that any moment I'm going to wake up." She took another sip and then looked up at him.

"But it's not is it? I'm awake, aren't I?" He nodded his head, unable to talk, not wanting to commit himself to any kind of answer.

She began to shiver, and he grabbed a throw from one of the chairs and covered her shoulders. She looked up at him then, gave him a smile which horrified and made him sad all in one agonizing moment. Her eyes, he couldn't quite look into them. Eyes, they were the windows of your soul, weren't they? The past few days he stared into his own in the bathroom mirror and seen nothing but blackness.

He backed away, nestling himself into the armchair opposite.

"I… I thought I would never get home, at one point, I'd almost forgotten where I lived." She gave a short laugh, but there was no humor in the sound.

"You're here now." He said this and tried to smile, hoping that she didn't hear the quiver in his voice.

"We argued didn't we? I don't even remember what about…" She was looking ahead, her forehead suddenly full of lines. He nodded.

"Yeah, we were arguing." He bit his lip, the taste of that whisky suddenly repeating on him, and he had the urge to throw up, but instead wiped his lips on the back of his hand.

She took another sip of the water, her hands grasping the glass so tightly he thought she might break it. He took it from her, her fingers brushing past his own and he spasmed in revulsion.

He sat back down but the glass remained in his hand, and he stared at it for a while. He imagined those lips on the rim, lips he had once kissed. Once, he couldn't get enough of them. On their first date, he studied her mouth as she talked, imagined how those lips would feel against his own.

"I feel cold. Why do I feel so cold?" She looked at him desperately.

"The shock I suppose. Perhaps I should get you a hot drink?" He didn't wait for an answer, but it was a good excuse to leave the room. He wanted to get away from her, he switched the kettle on, then realized that his hands were trembling.

What he had done with these hands.

He went quickly to the fridge and took out a beer. Not that he needed any more alcohol, as last night's whisky was still running through his veins, but he needed something to steady his nerves. He opened it clumsily and gulped it back as if it were going to be his last.

He closed his eyes and wished that he had never opened the door. It came to him then and he took another swig.

"I should have dug deeper." And finished the bottle.

The smell hit him again as soon as he entered the room. Soil—wet soil. It hit the back of his throat, filled his nostrils, making him want to throw that beer back up. He swallowed hard, thrusted the mug towards her.

"Tea, may help to warm you up." She took it, staring at its contents before cautiously taking a sip.

"You always look after me." She looked up at him, and he stared reluctantly back at her. There was something about the face, a vacantness that he hadn't quite noticed before he had gone into the kitchen. Something about the eyes, the way her lips stretched over her teeth. The face made him think of an actor playing a part, that the woman sitting in front of him wasn't Cathy at all. He looked away quickly, then gripped the arms of the chair as if to steady his nerves.

He remembered when he first saw her. He'd walk through the park every morning to work, and she'd be walking the opposite way. It began with a smile. They moved onto a 'hello' or a 'good morning,' and that went on for a few weeks until he had the courage to actually speak to her. He told her that he had fallen in love, and she smiled at him—her 'Mona Lisa' smile; that's what he had always called it. Like she knew some private joke. In the end he had hated that expression, that private joke, he came to believe, was him.

"You said you didn't love me… I remember now." She was looking at him accusingly.

"It was an argument, Cathy; we say a lot when we're angry. I… I was pissed off." Some mornings he couldn't stand looking at her, even the sight of her used coffee cup in the sink set him into a seething rage. A rage that simmered under the surface like an unwatched saucepan of water.

A few days ago, it got too much for him. He couldn't even remember what they had been arguing about. Cathy had a way with her words and a mocking look that she gave him. He grabbed that thin little neck of hers and started to squeeze, just to shut her up, just to get rid of that damn expression, if only for a moment or two. But he hadn't stopped. Even when he heard her gasping for breath, when the pair of them had fallen on the floor and he felt her legs kick him and her hands clawing at his own hands, at his arms.

He studied the bruises around her neck that had gone purple like the skin of an overripe plum.

He sat there afterwards. Shaking, looking at her on the floor, the body distorted, clothes disheveled. He checked if she were breathing, a small part of him hoping that he could detect even the weakest signs of it.

"I just can't get warm Philip. Why can't I get warm?" The sound of his name jolted him like an electric current.

"Hold me… please." She held out her arms and there was this look on his face, like a child. He reluctantly went forward, hesitated for a moment before kneeling.

She did feel cold. So much so that it seeped through his clothes and began to sting his skin. That earthy smell and he suddenly recalled the sound of the soil against his spade as he dug that grave; his shoulders had ached at the end. He lay his head against her chest, expecting to hear her steady heartbeat, and when he heard nothing, he abruptly pulled his head away, confused. He found she was looking down at him.

"Kiss me Phillip… kiss me." He wanted to say no, push her away, but strangely he found he couldn't quite resist those lips—lips he had kissed countless times, lips he had spent hours fantasizing over.

They felt dry and cracked beneath his own. They were open, and reluctantly, he found his tongue exploring and recoiled at the taste. He wanted to pull back, but she now had him in an unusually strong embrace, and no matter how he tried to pull away, he found he was unable to do so. He thought at first it was her tongue, but he quickly realized that it was too thin, though whatever it was attempted to crawl inside his mouth. He finally managed to pull back, and, to his horror, stared at the worm that was now attempting a perilous journey down her chin. Her mouth remained open, vacuous, and he dared not stare at it for long.

Yet he found he could not pull away. Cathy's hands gripped him tightly, her arms straining as he attempted to struggle away from her. He could see now the grains of soil that gathered around her nostrils, again the specks in her hair.

He had taken her body on that night, after he strangled her, to his car. A passerby might have taken it to be a man struggling with a drunken girlfriend. There was a bit of wasteland, somewhere he had passed several times. He dumped her in the hole that he had spent an hour or so digging, the earth thankfully damp from a heavy rainfall a day ago. He sat in the car afterwards, not quite wanting to go inside, studying his dirt encrusted hands, the smell of that damp soil in his nostrils.

And now she was here, on the sofa, in the house he had barricaded himself in not wanting to face the world, not really wanting to face what he had done.

"God, I'm sorry… so sorry… Cathy…" He pulled back in horror. Cathy remained still with her mouth open, as if she were about to scream. The flesh around it, the face, now bloated and that purple around the neck had seemed to have spread like a spilt glass of wine down to the exposed collarbone. Something seemed to be moving beneath her rib cage and he watched in a sick fascination as he realized that several maggots were wresting with each other and attempting to escape the confines of the muddy fabric of her dress. Bile burned his throat, the beer, like the whisky threatening to join it.

"Cathy… my Cathy…I…" He found he could no longer speak, instead he took hold of her hand, the flesh soft beneath his grasp, her body feeling bulbous, like an overripe peach.

"It's me, Cathy. Philip, it's me…" He thought he heard her hiss, and he buried his head into the wet fabric, the stench of soil, of damp earth overpowering any other sense he possessed.

"You're home… you're home." He whispered.

Of Wretched Accoutrements

Zac Hawkins

A phosphorous star vanished beneath the arching peaks of the steppe.

With it extinguished, ten long months of nuclear winter began, plunging the pan-European continent into a night of absolute darkness.

It was during this twilight—in that moment as seemingly endless as the celestial marble that painted the heavens—that the sound of terrible organs rang out through the abyss.

Edith O'Mare heard them long into that exhausting night. Endlessly solemn, guttural chords drawn from the crushed breast plate of some dying god. In the streets, hordes of madmen held aloft their instruments and performed a festival of horrors for the end of the world. From his pulpit, the conductor of the end times, dressed in his finest furs and adorned with the entrails of dismembered clocks, kept the choir in time to a terrible metronome.

From the window of her bedroom in her childhood home, a girl and her dog watched on as the great black beetle cracked and erupted a column of acrid smoke. On and on, the anguished cries of the orchestra rang out into the longest night in mankind's history.

Her ears stood to attention, a shiver of pointed fur rippled down her back with tail tucked tightly between her hind legs as she breathed in heavy the frozen air of the valley. Though it had been a long decade since she had been here last, Babooshka clearly recalled the acrid miasma that hung over the old derelict town. With her, two figures clad in rags and furs halted their endless march through the dead wilderness.

"What is it? Is she picking up a scent?" Ivan the hunter cradles the twin barrel shotgun in his colossal hands just that bit tighter at the first sign of potential danger, yet nothing bar Babooshka's labored whimpering could be heard among the derelict town.

"No, it's not that. Not a scent, nor a noise either. Can't you feel it yourself?" A faint pressure could be felt pinching the back of Edith O'Mare's eyes, as if a lit match had been raised between her skull and jaw and was slowly sapping the air pressure from within. She clenched her jaw and swallowed incessantly, yet still the pressure persisted.

The huntsman grunted and pinched his nose, furry cheeks puffed out under the strain. "Aye, now you mention it… We're in the valley, though. We passed the peak yesterday, so the air pressure down here should be normal."

"You think a storm's brewing?" Babooshka had nestled her forehead into O'Mare's lap and was panting contently, tail still tucked tightly between hind paws.

"If it were, we'd see clouds by now. It's clear as a summer's day. In January. Naw, can't explain it myself and don't want to, let's just find the others and head back to the caravan. If we're lucky we might catch some game on the river before nightfall."

Though back among the remains of where she had grown from a girl to a woman, O'Mare felt no affinity for the doomed town at all. The war had cut through it as a dozen towns had fallen before, and a dozen since, the nameless unseen "enemy" waging a decades long campaign of scorched earth that soon became encased in several winters of untempered ice until permafrost coated every structure, a vast palace carved from an opulent white gemstone.

Such was the extent of the flooding and successive seasons of permafrost that the glacier had by now claimed the lion's share of the once dazzling city, now little more than a few angular protrusions permeating from beneath the frigid earth. A bent street lamp here, a shattered window framing a well of moldering brickwork there. A few decades more and it would be as if the mighty cosmopolis and its myriad inhabitants had never existed, lost to the thaw of time, trodden underfoot by nature and other inhuman elements.

Babooshka erupted. A cacophony of howls spat forth from foaming maw, teeth bared, eyes split wide, pupils dilated and lost in an ocean of bloodshot white. "There!" Ivan cast the light of his torch on the eastern face of the valley, before dropping the torch into the snow and taking aim. A single volley rang out, O'Mare scrambling with her own torch attempting to illuminate the subject of their ire. "Damn! God damn! Damn thing got away." Ivan spat a yellowed gob of saliva into the snow, frustration lining his voice and face.

"What was it?"

"A bear, I suppose. Great shaggy beast, black down and mange ridden. Damn peculiar—bloody thing just seemed to vanish into the cliff face itself."

"Under brush, probably. Maybe a cave system; remember that pit we uncovered night before last? My thinking there has been a primal network of caves and tunnels on and beneath the steppe for millennia. Hush now girl, hush now. It's gone."

The mongrel was still on edge, growling a low warning howl, snout pointed firmly in the direction of an immense snow drift at the foot of the cliff face.

Running his fingers through his mane in deep contemplation, the cocked and reloaded shotgun on his lap, Ivan seemed less than convinced. "Foliage? Naw lass, look up. No greenery, no shrubs or anything of the sort. Not at that altitude. A cave though? Or maybe even a well. You might be right. Still, strangest thing I ever did see, a bear understanding a tactical withdrawal."

The sound of muffled crying, the two hunters jumped to attention, Babooshka once more launched into a tirade of barks and snarls. "Eric?!

Alexai?! Is that you? Where are you, speak up!" No response from the advance party was forthcoming, from beneath the snowdrift an outstretch hand as white as death emerged and grasped at the air in a deathly vice.

"They've been snowed in!" O'Mare was the first to lunge in and grasp the outstretch hand in her own, clawing frantically at the mound of snow in great swings of her arms until Babooshka joined her in shifting enough of the residue to reveal a canvas uniform in spotted white markings, a pale face perched atop its collar, eyes filled with the detritus, pores little pools for ice water. It was neither member of the advance party; one great pull revealed the stranger cradling another in his arms and the two barely breathing corpses lay shivering at the hunter's feet.

The figure in arctic camouflage was clearly a soldier, the sigil of his regiment was emblazoned across his back from shoulder blade to shoulder blade. The wings of Icarus. The individual wrap in his arms was a stranger in every regard: short of form, little taller than a child, with the facial features of an ancient cadaver. Indeed, its visage was hallmarked by its complete absence of discernible features, a waxy pallor clung to the melted features resembling that of a doll's once exposed to a naked flame. A recessed nasal passage and sunken eyes veiled with skin, lips webbed by a fine series of filaments that rendered its breathing passage little more than a line of pin pricks across its jawline.

"Christ. Jesus Christ." The huntsman took the soldier's frozen, now shaking, hand in his own and in reciprocation, five clammy icicles clenched as a vice around his warm palm.

"He's alive. Just. Edith, the thermos and blankets. See what you can do about creating a fire; I think we still had those last few firelighters in Babooshka's satchel. Quickly."

The dog was incensed and barking with the ferocity of a beast possessed, as if drawn into a frenzy by some unseen force, a colossal entity taunting her from atop the cliff face. With great effort, Edith eventually succeeded in wrangling the leather pouch away from her canine companion. At this, the mongrel shot off into the frozen tundra leaving behind only echoes and an image of foaming rage.

The blankets were thin, with a foil undersheet, but with their warmth and that of a fire plus a large thermos mug of brandy-enriched instant coffee, the soldier's (whom through chattering teeth availed himself to be named Devon Scopper, of GHQ) hands shook, but his cheeks now flushed a vivid rose tint, a network of crimson webs that bridged the arch of his nose.

The faceless one, though no longer in a torpid state, was nonetheless utterly devoid of the sensory reactions one would have anticipated on a person exposed to extreme hypothermia. It simply sat atop the patch of exposed rubble Ivan dug as a foundation for a fleeting encampment and warmed itself before the snaking flames of the furnace.

After sometime sat in contemplative silence, with Babooshka seemingly no nearer to returning to the bosom of the ramshackle band than before, it fell upon the huntsman to break the silence.

"Now, far be it from me to pry into business I have no right to enquire after, but just what did you hope to achieve venturing out here in the pits of winter without adequate supplies. And who—" he gestured towards the silent featureless phantom sat beside the solider,"—in the hell is this? I can tell by your stripes you're with the Obrahim division. Some of your lads shook our convoy down for supplies as we entered the steppes. But this…person—the likes of which I've never seen."

"I-I was with the second division. We were deployed on a data gathering mission to investigate the pre-winter reactor core. Some nomads we interrogated on the way from GHQ reported phosphorescent lights and…sounds, coming from the site. I chalked it up as such superstitious nonsense. I was a fool to do so."

"Hogwash. Absolute piss. Your lot have been trying to pinch the old world remnants for years, only you mistimed this particular annexation and got snowed in. I bet if we dug into that there snow drift we'd find dozens of your little tin soldier friends frozen in their uniforms." Ivan made no bones about his disdain for the militia remnants and relished in the opportunity to gloat in the face of someone indebted to him for their survival.

O'Mare was somewhat more sullen at the soldier's account. Something primal, something ephemeral was hanging heavy and malign on her back.

"You say there were noises coming from the old reactor base. The nomads…did they mention what kind of noises?" At this, Devon reflexed in an inhuman fashion, his face contorted into a look of disgusted horror. Brows bowed inward and teeth bared, he supped once more on the boozy coffee before allowing his features to reset and manner to reaffirm.

"It resembled an orchestra. You know, a string quartet times ten, drums and bass, a conductor to orchestrate a vast pit of manikins dressed in twee black suits and ties. The kind of thing our grandparents would have attended in great halls of gold and marble, before the winter, you know? All strings and chords and echoing drums, not like the static of the pirate radio stations we have now, huh."

Private Devon raised the thermos cup to his lips and downed the remaining, now cold, elixir before offering it out as if to request it be replenished. When he clocked none was forthcoming, he remained satisfied with the warmth of the fire and blanket before pressing forth with his account.

"We set out from camp four…no, five nights ago. I'm sorry, it's hard to tell sometimes. The smoke, the sounds they…still play havoc with my memories. No—"

The faceless figure shuffled as if in discomfort, at which Devon appeared to wince in fear.

"He's hungry."

The two hunters exchanged looks at this. Of course it made sense this mysterious, manikinesque figure would eat; it had rejected sustenance up to now, but in spite of its lack of any discernible mouth or teeth, it would need to eat sustain itself in some way.

"Fine. 'ere." Ivan seemed less than pleased at sacrificing a perfectly good game bird to a complete stranger but relented all the same. "But it's going to have to pluck it itself. I'm nobody's chef—"

Evidently as it seemed, Ivan hadn't anything to worry about. The figure wrung the already limp pheasants neck until its head popped off like a wine cork, rivers of clotted crimson blood ran out in thick globules mixed with the shredded flesh of its gullet and windpipe. Holding the twisted remains high above its head, the featureless one disjointed it jaw in a way that made O'Mare and Ivan jump and howl, guns raised as a naked cry escaped a series of thin fleshy slits that emerged just beneath where its eyes ought to have been. These filled instantly and pooled with the run off from the mutilated carcass of the raw meal. These tributaries cascaded further until the grooves of sinew in its neck, the hollow bole of its larynx and tarnished fibers of its attire were completely drenched in offal. The wheezing gasps of air had long since given way to bubbling noises, which almost sounded to be playing merrily in the affluence of its own making.

"You think that's bad, you should see what it did to our company dog. Poor Geraldine never knew what hit her." The soldier, Scopper, had taken the opportunity to liberate the thermos and brandy, preoccupying himself with pouring a second deeply boozy beverage.

Its hunger seemingly satisfied, the creature set down the still bleeding remnants of the game bird and set off away from the glow of the campfire. "How the hell did you come to be traveling with such beast? Just what were the Cloudbusters doing out in the tundra?"

"What we were doing is immaterial, not that I was ever told. Wasn't given my rations to ask questions, was I? No, we found that…that *thing* in the shadow of the old reactor smokestack, the one half buried in the permafrost. There's an entrance, but we never had the opportunity to get in; something knew we were there and got the jump on us. It was…god, I never seen anything like it before. We ran and something must have set off the drift that you two rescued us from."

"As for what that thing is or what it wants with the nuclear site, you're better off asking it yourself. Good luck getting an answer."

O'Mare looked on at the trail of footprints, lightly dragging across the snow and joining one indentation after another in a daisy chain across the faintly illuminated white canvas at dusk, now smattered with black gore from the eviscerated peafowl.

Within each footprint, headed in the direction of the derelict reactor, a second set of tracks of tiny paw prints were beginning to thaw in the glow of the campfire.

Her nose and chest were pressed resolutely to the ground, hair and ears peaked upright giving her slender form the appearance of a downy conifer forest. She licked at her panting jaw until the last of the mucous had been cleared away. Her rotting canine was causing her pain again as blood pumped through it after the dazed marathon.

The darkness within the chasm was absolute; Babooshka knew even if her eyes filled with the milky dew of characters and could pinpoint a grouse from two hundreds strides, it would have done her no good. Such was the belly of the beast, the great upturned beetle with its innards fractured and spewing toxic mists. She recalled through the web of sickness that had consumed her mind and body, that as a pup she and her master had sat in the moon beams on a night when the sun and stars vanished beneath that abyssal tempest. It had stank of death, of nuzzling into your emaciated bitch mother's gut for warmth until long after it stopped breathing.

She knew the scent of rot all too well.

That sense even now remained her strongest guide, navigating the ceaseless dark underbelly of that vast chasm. The scent she had picked up at the snow drift with her master had ignited a memory deep in her core, set aflame familiar and terrible memories that were snuffed out as quickly as they had emerged. She had lost the trail once or twice in the chase, only vaguely aware of how far astray it had led her.

Something was with her, that sixth sense uncanny among vulpine-kind alerted her to a figure in the dark. No. Two figures. One stinking of musk and furs, a scrawny flesh bag hiding away within a cocoon wrought of greater beasts.

The second…this one was concerning. It smelt of oil. And grease. And the smolder of grinding gears pushed to breaking point. The sickly sweet scent of epoxy, rendered glue.

Before the mongrel Babooshka could complete this nocturnal profile, it was upon her.

It turns out the death has a melody. And it's a terrible chorus made entirely of a string orchestra, spun of fibers harnessed from the freshest fields of viscera.

The tracks themselves had long since vanished beneath the dense blanket of frost, the soft textures of freshly fallen snow giving way to hard patches of black ice that threatened to shatter and drag the four down into the remains of the old town. By now, Edith had taken point, keeping in her mind that seared image of the end of the world.

"The causeway through the rubble was over here. Look it's trying to get in!"

And so it was with bare hands ripped bloody from the strain the faceless figure had carved a way through the mounds of devastated concrete and rubble. With a great strain of its hunched back, it managed to dislodge a sizeable mound of the detritus, laying bare the darkness within the heart of the bulbous black vessel. No sooner was this passage cleared that the snake like figure pressed forward into the conclave, leaving the three remaining with little option but to press forth also, Edith calling out for Babooshka all the while.

It all happened so quickly. Carried off on invisible wings, Ivan and Scopper where hauled into the dark expanse of the smokestack above before a cry of terror could breach either of their lips. Ivan dropped the shotgun and a single round fired off into the chasm briefly illuminating the assailant in its radiance.

The conductor of the pit was stood atop a floating stairway dressed in a broad coat of bear skin and furs. At his feet, the faceless horror was plucking a tiny harp of what Edith had a horrid suspicion was waxy tendons stretched betwixt human ribs; a crown of dogs' teeth breached its naked head.

The strumming was nauseating—it heightened the screams of whatever was carving Ivan and Scopper asunder. A rain of red flecks came crashing down and dowsed Edith in a spray.

"The end, the end. Always the end. Uncanny, it has the capacity to give us all that we need."

The conductor raised a flute to his whiskered lips. It was slick and pink and when blown into let forth a series of notes that tore into Edith sharper than any knife could flay her.

There was a whole chorus of them now, singing and dancing and cheering in bastardized harmonies ripped from the innards of other life.

Rictus fingers picked at chords and relished once more in the madness of their blight and in the music of the conductor.

With a shrieking of pistons, the bastard device set forth about its machinations. A mechanism of alternating chains and cogs raised its arsenal of wretched instruments high into the chasm's chamber until it was near enveloped by the gloom.

With a roaring hiss—a battle cry of bloodshed and torment most horrid—the terrible thing sprung from its high ground and set upon Edith. She rooted with absolute fear as the killer carbuncle set about its work and flayed layer upon layer of skin and sinew and muscle and offal into spindles of tightly wound string upon its back, rivers of red cascading before pooling in the exposed teeth of its rotating gears.

Consciousness was a fickle thing, ever so tardy in its dismissal. O'Mare lay there in a splatter of her own making, looking up as her assailant set about its work with surgical precision, and wondered why the pain had subsided.

With a melancholic twang the wretched orchestra was plucked from rest; they rallied into a harmony of sonorous melodies that intertwined to form a foaming spray of ballads. The Conductor General sat astride the whirring mechanical horror. He and the faceless one were plucking at red entrails harvested freshly from Edith's innards, all the while humming apocryphal lullabies. That night as the sky fell in, was this not that same sensation of all consuming terror? Who would have thought finality, the horror of prolonged consumption, would transpire to be so…comforting?

And soon the darkness, an all complete darkness, warm and maternal, unlike the frozen belly of the black beetle with its fractured underbelly spewing fumes at the dusk of the nuclear winter all those years past.

Amid the plucking of accoutrements, a new voice carried across the abyss Edith O'Mare had been pulled into. That of barking: a raspy, happy bark. The bark of an old mongrel.

The Midsummer Wilding

Jameson Grey

My family had always lived on the edge of Heptonworth Moor—that patch of Yorkshire wild where the wind wuthers and the rale of rain steeps every fiber of your being.

Through our back door we would look out on its expanse of purple heather during the day. And on hot summer nights—yes, even in Yorkshire we had those—we'd leave the door open. But there was one night a year when this wasn't the case, no matter the warmth of the evening.

Midsummer.

I learned this young.

"Leave it closed, Lily," my ma said to me.

I might've been seven or eight at the time. "Why?"

"We always leave it closed on Midsummer's Eve. Otherwise, you'll let it in."

"Let what in?"

My mother seemed to consider whether now was the right age to tell me this.

"Let what in, ma?" I repeated.

"The wilding," she said. "You should never let it in."

My ma never told me what 'the wilding' was—not outright at least. Sometimes, I'd overhear her gossiping with the other wives and mothers in the village. (Occasionally, I heard it called 'the weirdness', which to me sounded even more vague.) I never dared ask either of my parents, though—especially not my pa, who'd sometimes be so tired after a hard day's graft, he'd barely speak to my mother, let alone my brother and me.

One Midsummer's night he came in late, looking like a wild man. It was misty outside, and I could tell my ma was starting to worry about him. Her leg twitched in front of the fire while she darned the holes in my socks. ("Waste not, want not," she would caution—one of her many sayings!) I could feel it going ten-to-the-dozen as I sat there, like I often did, on the floor leant up against her—a cup of tea and her pack of Woodbines on the table beside her. I can still see its distinct green and red packaging even now—with one of them constantly smouldering away, filling the room with its harsh gaspers' smoke, the nubs of many more littering the glass ashtray.

As an adult, I can't stand smoking, and have never touched one, but the smell of cigarettes instantly reminds me of my mother, the nights she'd sat by the fire waiting for my father to come home and the comfort I felt in being beside her, just knowing she was there.

So this one evening, he was *really* late. I think my mother was gearing to give him a rollicking for staying so late in the pub while she kept his supper warm in the oven. She took one look at him and the look on his face and the tirade she'd mentally prepared was forgotten. Instead, she ushered me and my brother off to bed.

"But ma! Pa just got home," I protested.

"Bed!"

"Go on, Lily," my pa said. "I'll come up later." He was clutching his arm.

My brother had already gone, but I pretended to go up the stairs by going up and down the first few risers. I wasn't sure it'd convince them and waited for one of them to come out and escort me to my room, but instead I heard my father speak.

"I saw it, Joan."

"Nonsense, you've had one too many down at the Lion."

"It touched me. Look at my arm."

I heard my ma gasp and I recoiled myself. The stairs creaked guiltily.

"Lily, bed!" my pa roared. While I might defy my mother, my father's word was law. I scurried up to bed and heard no more of the conversation, but for the next few days his arm was bandaged, and he rarely wore anything but long-sleeve shirts after that, even on the rare hot days of summer that followed. I'd only ever catch glimpses of what had happened to his arm, but I never forgot what he said.

It touched me.

My father was never quite the same after that night. He'd start to drink more after work. Once or twice, he was too hungover to make it in. In the end, it was an accident on the machinery at work that took him. It was tough for a while, but my ma picked up a job at the mill and we got by.

My brother left school at sixteen, joined up and sent much of his pay home. He died when he was nineteen. He was back home on leave and out with a few of his army pals when some pissed-up dickhead thought he'd start a fight with the squaddies. They did their best to diffuse the situation but not before one of dickhead's mates had glassed my brother. He died on the streets of Leeds. He might not have died in battle, but he was still a hero to me, the way he stepped up after Dad died.

Of the wilding, there were, of course, other stories.

For eleven months of the year village life went on much as normal, but in the run-up to the solstice, the chatter would start. People would reminisce—almost fondly, it seemed—about previous visits from the wilding. Tales possibly (probably) apocryphal would be shared. Some said it was a man-beast—an escaped lunatic, others said some sort of wolf or wild cat. No matter how much fun it might be to tease passing American backpackers with tales of the moor, the village would always stop short of making jokes about the wilding.

There were even stories of allegedly unmarked graves among the heather and ruins—previous victims where the families involved didn't want to bring in the authorities. I never believed those myself—always, perhaps naively, assuming the dead would be missed. It didn't stop me looking for them, though, on my trips out there.

Even after my father's brush with the wilding, I would spend evenings and weekends wandering the moors, especially in the late spring—hoping to glimpse the thing, where it lived, where it foraged. I never found anything. In my childish over-imaginings, I concluded that the wilding must be conjured out of the magic of the midsummer—only existing for that brief time when the sun stayed longest.

Not rain nor snow could keep me off the moor, even in deepest winter, but my love for it came strongest in the summer months. It was almost as if the wilding's visit brought with it the subsequent joy of those weeks off from school where I was free, after my chores were done, to do what I pleased with my time.

I hated having to move away to Leeds for work, but like my brother before me, I'd send money to my ma when I could. When she died last year, I inherited the house. I was able to get a job at the local school, so I moved back in the July after she passed away. It brought me back to the moors, and as sad as I was for its catalyst, I was glad to be home.

After all, there's only me left now.

I'd been out with some friends in Leeds and caught an eye-wateringly expensive taxi home. You'd be surprised, given the myths and stories I'd grown up with, to learn I'd forgotten the date—that it was Midsummer's Eve once more—but I had, and I was a bit off-guard as I walked into the house. I dropped my keys in the bowl by the front door vestibule and headed to make myself a cup of tea.

There were muddy footprints in the kitchen. I say 'footprints,' but they had less form than feet, heading to and from the back door. Tentatively, I looked through the kitchen window. It was pitch dark. I checked the lock on the window, looked up. There was a face. For a moment it was the face of my father. It dissolved into the night. I stepped back as *something* slammed into the window. I heard the splinter of wood in the frame. A second thrust and another crack. Then silence. I peered into the black of night. Nothing.

CRASH!

The back door slammed open and suddenly it, whatever *it* was— what we'd called the midsummer wilding all these years—was in the kitchen, all over me.

After that everything happened in slow motion.

It, the wilding, was grabbing at me. No—pawing at me, as if it were driven by a feral desire. Then it was somehow inside me. The wilding may have come in the shape of a man, but now it was something beyond that. It was oozing into me. The more I struggled the more I could sense its own pleasure. "This is my house. GET OUT!" I screamed. It laughed. I tried to grab hold of it, to force it away, but my hands slipped through it. The thing was viscous, like cold wet mud, yet it burned to the touch. I felt it slither through me, reaching to the deepest part of me. I gagged, nauseated, violated.

But with its desire came its vulnerability. Unable to grasp it in its formlessness, I reached inside of it, tearing at whatever it had for a heart. It groaned, a deep woozy bass rumbling through me, rattling the pans in the kitchen and the panes in the windows, and I felt it leave me, fleeing, screaming out into the moors.

Then, there was nothing but blackness.

I awoke on the kitchen floor. I didn't know I had such violence in me, such ability to wreak harm, yet despite the fight, I was left without so much a blemish. I wondered if it had all been a dream.

The damage told another story. I had the backdoor replaced, though the kitchen window frame is held together with gaffer tape. I'll have to get that sorted properly before next summer. In case.

But something else is worrying me now.

Around the time school started again, something happened.

Inside of me, I felt a kick.

The Bride Wore Red

Wesleigh Neville

The blood on Elena's wedding dress has dried.

When she slips it back on, she doesn't know why the brown and crusted blood startles her so. Had she really expected the bloodstains to stay glossy, wet red for three months? Let alone, three months bundled in paper in the back of a hearse? Of course this was going to happen.

If her dress looks like this, what does her fiancé's corpse look like?

Tears pool in Elena's eyes. She furiously wipes them away. Damn this grief. Damn its sudden and inopportune appearance. How can Elena not shed a tear at Hal's funeral then start leaking like a faucet over a damn dress?

Maybe because—Elena's gaze drifts to her ring finger, where there is no wedding ring, where there will never be a wedding ring. Because unlike Hal's death, the dress is tangible. It's a real thing to touch, to cry over, and when Elena runs a hand along the white satin, all the details she put into this dress come rushing back. The cap sleeves. The flowers at the hem. The scandalously short length. The dress falls just above her knees. In the town where this all started, a dress like this was appalling for a good Christian wedding. But Elena liked her legs, still likes her legs in spite of everything. And Hal, sweet, vivacious Hal, liked kissing his way up her legs...

Blush creeps into Elena's cheeks. The Elena from three months ago, still starry-eyed with anticipation, would chastise herself for thinking such lewd thoughts. Now, with Hal nothing more than a memory, Elena allows herself to sink into them. Only briefly. She swims back to the surface of present day, her mouth set in a hard line. No time to mourn. She has work to do.

Elena reaches for the gun. She kicks open the back door of the hearse. Cicadas buzz. The sun blazes overhead. At the end of a dirt road, a church stands, surrounded by weeds. Elena wipes a bead of sweat from her brow. She inhales deeply, and—*there*. There's the scent she's been searching for.

The scent of blood.

Elena slams the hearse door shut. She's got a monster to hunt.

"You won't marry him," her mama said.

In a time when Hal still walked this earth, Elena sat hunched over her sewing machine. Despite the ache in her shoulders, the sweat pooled under her armpits, she was elated. After years of sewing beautiful dresses for the girls with daddies who could afford them, it was about time Elena got to sew one for herself. "Don't be silly, Mama. The wedding's in two weeks."

Mama sat in her rocking chair, her good eye boring into Elena's backside, like she could glare Elena into changing her mind. "You won't."

Elena tore her eyes away from the dress to Mama. "I *will*. Now have you finished the veil yet?"

The wedding veil, the same one that had sat untouched in Mama's trunk since Elena was a baby, rested in Mama's lap. Elena had given it to Mama as an olive branch, something to smooth over Mama's frosty reception toward Elena's engagement, but instead, the veil had only added to her contempt.

"Wedding's tainted," Mama murmured, staring blankly at a fly on the kitchen sink. "No point mending a veil for a tainted wedding."

Elena sighed. She returned to her sewing, not wanting to accommodate Mama's dark mood. Not today. Not when this was supposed to be the happiest period of her life. Elena sewed another hem. *Happy.* It felt like a word for girls with soft hands and fair skin. The kind of girls who came from money. The kind of girl Hal's parents wished he was marrying.

Elena wasn't oblivious to the local gossip. She saw the way the ladies at church pursed their lips when Mama took a seat in the back pew. Mama with her uncombed hair, her milky white eye, and more damning than any physical feature, her lack of a wedding ring. On the rare occasions Mama left the house for anything other than church, she walked the streets like a specter, waiting for death to pull up and drive her away from this mortal plane. Even around their ramshackle house, Mama moved with the stiffness of a corpse.

The daughter of a woman like Marta Castillo had no business marrying Hal Thornton, the locals hissed.

But the locals didn't decide who Hal married, and neither did Mama. For what felt like the hundredth time, Elena stood and held the dress up to herself. Her wedding dress was going to have flowers on it. Hal had taken her to see a movie last week, and the girl on the screen— a pretty blonde thing with blue eye shadow and pink lips—wore a dress with flowers on the hem. Elena may not have been blonde, and maybe she didn't have blue eye shadow or pink lipstick, but by god, she could sew flowers onto her wedding dress.

"Didn't marry your daddy."

Despite her best attempts to ignore her, Elena's skin prickled. Like a good daughter, she'd never asked who her daddy was. But that didn't stop her mind from wandering.

And Elena was content to let her mind wander until she heard a *rip* and saw—"You're ruining it!"

Mama had ripped the veil in half. Elena snatched the torn veil from Mama's hands. She stuffed the veil under the bed, biting back a scream. Now this was yet another thing Elena would have to prepare on top of everything else because Hal's family refused to help her plan the wedding.

But it would be fine. Once they were married, nothing could keep them apart.

As Elena approaches the church, she sees peeling white paint and dust over the windows. God must know this is an event not to be witnessed by others, seeing how He's directed her to an abandoned church. Elena opens the double doors with a mournful *creak*. The pews and the pulpit are still there, waiting for a congregation that will never come. The narrow stained glass windows gleam in vibrant blues and yellows and—

Red.

Elena's breath hitches. It's just a color. Not worth hysterics. Elena steps into the church. She walks down the aisle. In the back of her head, a wedding march echoes. The ghost of Hal's lips brush against hers. She grips the gun so hard her knuckles turn white.

She sits down in the front pew. Whispers a brief prayer. *God, forgive me for what I must do.* The gun rests beside her.

And then she waits. Back straight, hands folded all ladylike in her lap. She waits patiently for the man who murdered Hal.

The stranger in red.

Elena first met the stranger in red as Hal was bleeding out on the church steps.

The day started like a wedding should start: bright and warm and full of possibilities. Elena had been straightening her veil when suddenly, Hal's slender, gentle hands wrapped themselves around her waist. Elena pulled away with a gasp. "Hal, you idiot!" she said with a gentle slap on his arm. "It's bad luck seeing the bride before the ceremony!"

Hal grinned. "Who needs luck? Mine's already rotten as it is." Before Elena could protest, Hal swept her up into an embrace, twirling her on the steps to the church like they were teenagers again. "Are you ready to be Mrs. Elena Thornton?"

In Hal's arms, Elena softened. "I've been ready for two years, silly." In truth, she'd been ready since the day Hal had asked her how to spell "rutabaga" in the third grade. Hal, with his brown hair that always stuck up in different directions, with his crooked, mischievous smile. She still couldn't believe this was the face she'd get to wake up to every day.

"Well, then," Hal said, voice brimming with joy, "I'll see you on the other side."

Hal almost kissed her but thought better against it, seeing as they were already tempting fate. He let go of her. He straightened his suit jacket. With one last crooked smile, he went up the church steps.

As his foot hit the top step, a shot rang out.

"Oh, enough of this." There is waiting and there is being toyed with, and Elena is certain that she's being toyed with. The scent of blood lingers faintly outside the church walls but doesn't come closer. "I want to speak with you, and if you don't come in here, I'll... I'll..."

She'll what? Elena feels like a mother scolding a child, not like a woman who came here to kill. Then she remembers the gun.

Elena picks up the gun and presses it to her temple. "I'll blow my brains out. How would you like that? No one for you to torment if I'm dead. I'm giving you to the count of ten."

Something in the air shifts. The barrel of the gun is cold against her temple. He's waiting. Seeing if she'll really do it.

"One."

He's a fool if he doesn't think she will.

A stunned Hal lifted a hand to his heart, where the bullet had pierced straight through him. He looked at Elena before crumpling on the church steps.

He did not get to say goodbye. He was choking on too much blood to say anything.

"Two."

Her first instinct was to hold him. To somehow fix him. But Elena was no doctor, and the gushing hole in Hal's chest could not be healed by the touch of the woman who loved him. He died quick, eyes staring vacant up into the heavens, but Elena clung to his lifeless body. *Why?* was the only thing in her head, just an endless loop of *Why? Why? Why?* And then the blood, oh Lord, the *blood.* It coated her like a blanket. Its coppery scent smothered the air so all she smelled was blood, *Hal's* blood—

A shadow appeared over her.

Elena lifted her head and gasped. A man stood before her. He wore a tattered red suit, the same red as the blood on her dress. Pinned to his jacket was a rotting chrysanthemum. He reeked of decay. The dark splotches on his pale skin were eerily reminiscent of a body in its first few hours of decomposition. As were the flies that buzzed around him and the milky whiteness of his eyes. But his chest rose and fell, and his head tilted in interest, like they knew each other. Elena had never seen this man in her life.

In his hand was a pistol.

Elena tried to scream for help, but her vocal chords had ceased functioning. The stranger's mouth stretched into a smile, revealing a row of teeth stained crimson with blood.

"Do you hurt?" he said.

His voice rasped like the labored breaths of a dying animal. Elena nodded. She flinched as the man gripped her chin. His hand was cold, too cold to be human. He leaned into her, his breath rancid, and he whispered in her ear, "You will hurt until the end of your days."

He let go of her. Elena sat helpless on the church steps, Hal's body cold in her lap. And just like Hal's blood had blossomed across his chest, a sharp pain splintered into Elena's heart. Elena doubled over as the pain of loss burrowed into her, until there was nothing in her but pain, endless, unwavering *pain*.

Only when the stranger in red turned his heel and vanished over the horizon did the scream lodged in Elena's throat finally escape.

"Three."

Two days after Hal's murder, Elena went to his funeral.

The day was the kind of sunny that hurt. Elena went numbly through the motions of getting ready. Movement felt alien, like some kind of privilege that Elena did not deserve. Mama was too tired to make the journey; ever since the disastrous wedding, she could barely get out of bed. Elena wished she had the luxury. She wished she too could lie in bed and completely shut herself out from the rest of the world. But the town would talk if the deceased's fiancée wasn't there. Well, they'd talk if she was there. People in small towns loved to talk.

On her walk to the cemetery, Elena smelled blood.

The priest, the same priest that was going to marry them, spoke at the funeral. Elena didn't remember what he said, but it must have been very touching given the way Hal's mother kept dabbing her eyes.

Her good, honest Hal. He didn't deserve this.

Or didn't deserve you?

Wasn't that what everyone was thinking? Wasn't that why Elena stood alone on the other side of Hal's coffin while the throng of mourners stood opposite from her? Any mourners who weren't the Thorntons were friends or colleagues with the Thorntons. And if the Thorntons decreed that their son's fiancée was a pariah, the rest of the funeral goers would happily oblige. Elena stared at Hal's coffin, trying to hold on to the last shred of dignity while the whispers of the townsfolk pricked her like thorns.

Trash.

Harlot.

Gold digger.

After the service, Elena found refuge behind a gravestone. She sat with her knees to her chest, picking listlessly at grass. Two ladies from church, friends of Hal's mother, chattered on the other side, oblivious that the woman they were gossiping about was only a few feet away from them.

Elena paid them little mind until one said, "Whole bloodline's cursed if you ask me. You remember what happened to Marta's beau?"

"That poor boy. He went the same way."

The same way.

Clarity struck Elena like a volt of electricity. Even though Elena knew she'd look crazed, knew the two church ladies would gossip, she shot out from behind the gravestone with fire in her eyes. "What happened to Mama's fiancé?"

The ladies gaped silently at her.

"Tell me!"

And that was how Elena learned that twenty-four years ago, on the day of Marta Castillo's wedding, a strange man in red came into the church and shot her fiancé in the heart.

"Four."

Sixteen days after Hal's murder, Elena pawned her engagement ring.

No sense in keeping it. Elena received no inheritance. With her almost in-laws nipping at her heels, ridding herself of the ring—and frankly, getting a little money out of it—was the only sensible thing to do.

For Elena's plan to work, she needed a car. And cars couldn't just be plucked like apples from trees, so she needed money to buy the car. And to buy other things to fulfill that pesky task of keeping herself alive. Hal would—Elena inhaled sharply. It didn't matter what Hal would think. There was no Hal Thornton anymore, and Elena was on her own. So she handed the ring over, eyes dry and voice calm, even as the pawnbroker gave her a sympathetic smile.

That night, when Mama fell asleep, Elena cried into her pillow.

"Five."

Eighteen days after Hal's murder, Elena bought a hearse.

Figures Elena would go searching for a car and come driving out in a hearse. She'd gotten a hefty sum for the ring, but the one thing she truly wanted was not something money could buy. But Elena Castillo was no stranger to not getting what she wanted, and like anyone who never gets what they want, Elena excelled at compromise.

She could not get Hal back.

But she could track down his killer and put him down like the dog he was.

Elena packed a suitcase. She put on a black suit and tucked her hair into a black scarf and slipped black gloves over her hands. She did not say goodbye to Mama. There was nothing to be said.

At the car lot, the scent of blood lingered over the horizon. Elena paid little mind to it, instead drifting idly between cars, waiting for the *one*. And there, tucked into the very back of the lot, was the hearse. It was an ugly thing, with chipping charcoal paint and more wear and tear than the toys of a spoiled child. But this was the car. This car would take her to Hal's killer. Not that the salesman didn't eye her with confusion. "You sure you don't want something spiffier, miss?" he asks.

"It'll do." Elena ran her gloved hand along the curtained windows. How many corpses had this vehicle ferried to their final resting place? Did this machine ache with the weight of death on its back the way Elena ached? She decided on that day, no matter how much it weighed her down, she'd carry the weight of Hal's death in this car. Her own personal cross to bear.

Keys in hand, Elena thanked the salesman and slid into the front seat. Behind the wheel, she felt untouchable. If she was going to track down the man—no, the *thing* that killed Hal, she needed to feel untouchable. She started the hearse then rolled down the window. Elena stuck her head out and took a deep breath.

Blood in the west.

With Hal heavy on her back, she sped off in that direction.

"Six."

Ninety-one days after Hal's murder, Elena fired a gun.

The scent of blood had gone tantalizingly distant so she'd stopped at a general store for supplies. The shopkeeper, a tiny, strong-jawed old woman named Gracie, took pity on the dark circles under Elena's eyes. She offered her a hot meal and a chance to take her anger out on some tin cans in her backyard.

Elena was a terrible shot. The bullet sailed through air, never coming close to hitting a can. She didn't like the way the barrel jerked back or the soul-shattering *bang*, and she wished she could feel empowered by those things. But Elena was not some vengeful thing hardened by death, suddenly capable of feats beyond her own physical abilities. Death did not improve her constitution or her aim.

Elena brought her free hand to her cheek, more surprised than irritated at the tear streaming down. Suddenly ashamed, she turned away from Gracie. "I don't know why I'm crying. Forgive me."

"You've got poison in you, dear."

Elena's head whipped toward Gracie. "What did you say?"

"I said you got poison in you." Gracie said calmly. Her gnarled old hands fiddled with her pistol. "Generations of poison from the looks of you, something real vicious too. Makes me wonder what a young thing like you did to get that kind of poison."

Elena knew exactly what. But her one rule on this journey was this: she would not tell anyone of Hal's death. If she didn't tell anyone, if the truth of what really happened to the love of her life just stayed in that town, Elena could almost pretend he was still alive. She could drive her hearse back into town and there he would be coming out of the pharmacy, big stupid grin on his face at the site of her driving such a ridiculous car. But if she told anyone? If she dared speak the words, "Hal died," the hole in Elena's chest would erupt into a chasm.

That could not happen. She had too much to do.

So she didn't tell Gracie. But part of her suspected that Gracie was the kind of woman who didn't need Elena to tell her to know what tragedy had befallen her. But Elena asked, "How do I get rid of it?"

Gracie looked at her with such pity. Elena didn't want her pity; she wanted *answers*. "Getting rid of something that old ain't easy, child. The way these things go, poison like that eventually consumes you or..."

"Or what?" Gracie was silent. "*Answer me.*"

Dark clouds had gathered over Gracie's backyard. The air buzzed in anticipation of the coming thunderstorm. Gracie gazed out into the distance, her thoughts someplace far that Elena was not allowed to venture to. "You drain it out. And lose yourself in the process."

Elena exhaled slowly. Driving alone gave her lots of time to think, and she thought most about if this slapdash plan of hers was really going to work. Or was she just chasing a ghost, too stupid to accept her lot in life like Mama did? But then she thought of Hal bleeding out in her arms. What justice was there in Elena blindly accepting the misery wrapped around her shoulders? She'd drain this poison out. And if she lost herself along the way?

Well, she'd take Hal's murderer down with her.

On the count of, "Nine," just when Elena's finger puts the slightest bit of pressure on the trigger, just when the idea of shooting herself starts to sound real nice…

The scent of blood floods the church.

Footsteps creak down the aisle. Elena lowers the gun. Heart pounding, she stands to meet him. Just because she's about to kill him doesn't mean she can't show a little common courtesy. Her breath shudders seeing his decayed form once again, but she holds her ground.

"Why?" she says.

Why her? Why her mama? Why her entire bloodline? Elena's voice is soft, too soft to sound menacing. The stranger in red doesn't react to such meekness. He… doesn't react at all. He merely stands, waiting.

Why is his jacket wet?

Slowly, with trembling fingers, Elena peels back the jacket. Where his heart should be is a—"Oh."

A bullet hole.

Oh. Elena draws back, because the monster who shot her fiancé isn't supposed to look like this. He isn't supposed to be hurt. And he must hurt tremendously. Even now, a steady stream of blood trickles out of the open wound. How long has he wandered the earth like this, forever bleeding out?

"You've got poison in you too," Elena murmurs. The stranger in red bows his head, the slightest bit of sympathy too much for his rotted soul. What does she do with a creature with poison in him? The answer is simple.

You drain it out.

Elena grabs him by the lapels of his jacket and kisses him.

She tastes the poison of a man who once loved a woman very much. A man who wasn't from the right family, who didn't have a dollar to his name, who had no business marrying a woman like her. And when he put his faith in his love for her and tried to elope, the man's love was no match for the bullet the woman's family put through his heart. And while he rotted in the dirt, the woman he loved married someone else. So that man took his pulverized heart and returned a revenant. A revenant existing only to wrench away the happiness of every descendant of the woman he lost.

The poison of heartbreak tastes coppery and bitter.

Elena drains every ounce of poison out of the stranger in red and in turn, it rushes past her bloodstream, past her bones, to the very core of her soul. The coldness seeps into Elena's body. The blood on Elena's wedding dress blossoms outward until her entire dress is crimson. The skin around her ring finger pales for the wedding band that will never grace it. Her body starts to shake, desperate to spread the hurt she's carrying, to hurt *him*—

No.

He's spent enough time hurting.

With one final inhale, Elena releases him. She pulls away, and the only thing left of the stranger in red is a pile of dust at her feet. When she puts a hand to her chest, she feels no heartbeat. But she feels the poison coursing through her veins, a poison that she can use to make sure no one ever suffers the way Hal suffered. And she'll do it.

For Hal, she'll do it for eternity

Author Bios

- **Tiffany Morris** is a Mi'kmaw/settler writer of horror fiction and poetry from Kjipuktuk (Halifax), Nova Scotia. Her work has previously appeared in Uncanny, Vastarien, and Abyss & Apex. Find her online at tiffmorris.com or on twitter @tiffmorris. [Inspired by: "Hounds of Love"]

- **Die Booth** likes wild beaches and exploring dark places. When not writing, he DJs at Chester's best (and only) goth club. You can read his stories in places like LampLight Magazine, The Fiction Desk, Flame Tree Press and The Cheshire Prize for Literature anthologies. His books *My Glass is Runn*, *365 Lies* (profits go to the MNDA), *Spirit Houses* and *Making Friends (and other fictions)* are available online. He's currently working on a collection of spooky stories featuring transgender protagonists. You can find out more about his writing at diebooth.wordpress.com or say hi on Twitter @diebooth. [Inspired by: "Hounds of Love"]

- **Leo X. Robertson** is a Scottish process engineer, writer and filmmaker, currently living in Stavanger, Norway. His work has been published in *Year's Best Hardcore Horror, Best of British Science Fiction* and *Flame Tree Press' Urban Crime* anthology, among others. Twitter: @leoxwrite [Inspired by: "Hounds of Love"]

- **Katie Young** is a writer of dark fiction. Her work appears in various anthologies including collections by Nyx Publishing, Ghost Orchid Press, and Fox Spirit Books, and her story, Lavender Tea, was selected by Zoe Gilbert for inclusion in the Mechanic Institute Review's Summer Folk Festival 2019. She lives in West London with her partner, an angry cat, and too many books. You can find her on Twitter @pinkwood. [Inspired by: "Watching You Without Me"]

- **Adrienne Clark** is a writer and editor from Seattle. Her nonfiction work has been published around the web (*Nightmarish Conjurings, A Nightmare on Film Street, Wool*) and for institutions including the Museum of Pop Culture and the 5th Avenue Theater. Her short story "Make Friends" was published in the University of Washington's *Stratus: Journal of Arts and Writing*. Adrienne is a proud queer author working to place her unique lens on the horrors of the modern world, seen and unseen. Twitter: @Adrienne_Edits [Inspired by: "Cloudbusting"] o **Leee McHugh** is a writer, a witch, and a weirdo from Boston, Massachusetts. They enjoy cats, Kate Bush, and things that smell good. They are deeply inspired by the life and work of Jack Terricloth, who departed for the astral plane so recently, and far too soon. RIP Cloth. Leee can be found posting cat pics on Instagram @three_of_cups. [Inspired by: "Eat the Music"]

o **Remo Macartney** lives in Seattle, Washington with his girlfriend Brittan, their cat, and their dog. He loves collecting books and records. Some of their favorite writers include Amy Hempel, Donna Tartt, Chuck Palahniuk, Bret Easton Ellis, and Jenny Offill. [Inspired by: "A Sensual World"/"The Fog"]

o **Sarah Karasek** mostly exists in rural Pennsylvania, where she enjoys staring at the river and talking to stray cats. She's an assistant editor at *Space Squid* magazine and the author of *The Little Punk Princess: A Fairy Tale*. She can be found on Twitter @haunted4always when she's not exploring abandoned buildings. If you need someone to order a pizza for you, you've got the wrong person. [Inspired by: "Cloudbusting"]

o **Patrick Barb** is a freelance writer from the southern United States, currently living (and trying not to freeze to death) in Saint Paul, Minnesota. Previously, his short fiction has appeared in Boneyard Soup Magazine, Not One of Us, and Dose of Dread, among other publications. In addition, he is an Active member of the Horror Writers Association. For more of his work, visit patrickbarb.com. Twitter: @pbarb [Inspired by: "Running Up that Hill"/"This Woman's Work"]

o **Nikki R. Leigh** is a forever-90s-kid wallowing in all things horror. When not writing horror fiction and poetry, she can be found creating custom horror-inspired toys, making comics, and hunting vintage paperbacks. She reads her stories to her partner and her cat, one of which gets scared very easily. Instagram: @spinetinglers Twitter: @fivexxfive [Inspired by: "Sat in Your Lap"/ "Running Up that Hill"]

o **Joe Koch** writes literary horror and surrealist trash. A Shirley Jackson Award finalist and author of *The Wingspan of Severed Hands*, *The Couvade*, and *Convulsive*, their short fiction appears in *Year's Best Hardcore Horror*, *Not All Monsters*, and others. They co-edited the collection *Stories of the Eye*. Find Joe online at horrorsong.blog and on Twitter @horrorsong. [Inspired by: the music video for "Don't Give Up" featuring Kate Bush by Peter Gabriel]

○ **Paulette Pierce** is a queer Pittsburgh-based writer currently working on their first novel and trying to preserve their local film community in their off hours. Their work has appeared in *Anti-Heroin Chic* and *Gayly Dreadful*. | paulettepierce-writer.com | Twitter: @GrannyRocko [Inspired by: "Babooshka" and folk song "Sovay, the Female Highwayman"]

○ **Chris Hewitt** resides in the beautiful garden of England, Kent, UK, and in the odd moments that he isn't dog walking he pursues his passion for all things horror, fantasy, and science-fiction. | mused.blog | Twitter: @i_mused_blog [Inspired by: "Jig of Life"]

○ **Thomas Thorogood** lives and writes in Seattle, WA, and has short fiction published in *Robbed of Sleep, Vol. 4*, and *The Corner Club Press*. In 2014, he stayed up until 3am to get tickets for the *Before the Dawn* concert residency. It was one of the greatest performances he's seen live. Twitter: @tathorogood [Inspired by: "50 Words for Snow"/"Snowed in at Wheeler Street"/"Pull Out the Pin"]

○ **Susan Vita** is a writing tutor currently living in Nashville, Tennessee. A handful of her speculative and contemporary works have been published. | vitahighviewstories.com | [Inspired by: "Get Out of My House"]

○ **Madeleine Swann**'s recent collection, *The Sharp End of the Rainbow*, was published by Heads Dance Press. Her recent novella, *The Vine That Ate The Starlet*, was published by Filthy Loot. Her collection, *Fortune Box*, was nominated for a Wonderland Award and her stories have appeared on various podcasts and anthologies, including Splatterpunk nominated *The New Flesh: A Literary Tribute to David Cronenberg*. Twitter: @MadeleineSwann [Inspired by: "Babooshka"]

○ **Sam Richard** is the author of *Sabbath of the Fox-Devils* and the Wonderland Award-Winning collection, *To Wallow in Ash & Other Sorrows*. The owner of Weirdpunk Books, he has edited and co-edited several anthologies, including the Splatterpunk Award-Nominated *The New Flesh: A Literary Tribute to David Cronenberg*, *Beautiful/Grotesque*, *Cinema Viscera*, and *Stories of the Eye*. He slowly rots in Minneapolis. | WeirdpunkBooks.com | Twitter: @SammyTotep [Inspired by: "Wow"] o **Maria Abrams** is a horror/suspense novelist living in Colorado. With a graduate degree in Psychology, she tries to incorporate psychological terror into many of her works. Her short stories have appeared in anthologies and magazines such as *Weird Horror*. Her novella, *She Who Rules the Dead*, was released in 2021 by Weirdpunk Books. Her novel, *The Doctor's Demons*, is out now from CLASH Books. Maria is the co-chair of the Horror Writer's Association Denver Chapter. | abramstheauthor.com | Twitter: @AbramsWriter [Inspired by: "Running Up that Hill"]

o **Max Turner** is a gay transgender man based in the United Kingdom. He is also a parent, nerd, intersectional feminist and coffee addict. Max writes speculative and science fiction, fantasy, furry fiction, horror and LGBTQ+ romance, and more often than not, combinations thereof.. He has been published in *Bodies Full of Burning: An Anthology of Menopause-Themed Horror* from Sliced Up Press, Carnation Book's *Imaginary Creatures, an anthology of Queer Paranormal Romance* and Cloaked Press's *Summer of Speculation: Catastrophe* anthology. Look for other works by Max being published in anthologies from Dead Fish Books, Bell Press, Cleis Press and Fanged Fiction. | maxturneruk.com | Twitter: @MaxTurnerWrites [Inspired by: "Wuthering Heights"/"Running Up that Hill"]

o **Kirby Kellogg** is a journalist, music critic, and horror writer from the great state of Maine. Her work's been published in *Belladonna Horror Magazine, Morbidly Beautiful, Black Rainbow vol. 1,* and her novella, *Trampled Crown,* came out through Unnerving Press in 2020. You can find her on Twitter @sugarbombstim. [Inspired by: "Mother Stands for Comfort"/"Breathing"]

o **Wendy Dalrymple** writes cute, low-heat romances and sometimes spooky stuff too. When she's not writing happily-ever-afters and tropical thrillers, you can find her camping with her family, painting (bad) wall art, and trying to grow as many pineapples as possible. | wendydalrymple.com | Twitter: @wendy_dalrymple [Inspired by: "Violin"]

o **David Busboom** was born and raised in and around Champaign County, Illinois. He works as a science editor and is the author of the novellas *Every Crawling, Putrid Thing* (JournalStone, 2022) and *Nightbird* (Unnerving, 2018), as well as more than a dozen short stories appearing in such venues as the *Saturday Evening Post, MYTHIC,* and *Planet Scumm.* | davidbusboom.com | Twitter: @DavidBusboom [Inspired by: "Hammer Horror"] o **TR Hitchman** has been writing for 20 years. Her influences stem from a childhood love of ghost stories, vampires, and the dark side of life. She has been inspired by classic gothic novels such as *Dracula, Frankenstein*, the work of Edgar Allan Poe and the twisted tales of Roald Dhal. She had a collection, *A Child of Winter* published by Corona Books UK, and had stories published in the first and second volumes of *Corona Book of Horror Stories*. Most recently, she's had a novella, a ghost story entitled *Little Bird*, published by Demain Publishing. Twitter: @TRHitchman [Inspired by: "Wuthering Heights"]

o **Zac Hawkins** is a photographer, critic, poet, and writer of the weird and the horrific. Based in Manchester, NW England. He has a story featured in *Fingers: A Bizarro Fiction Anthology*, and two collections: *Rebirth and Other Aberrations* and *The Ash and Bone Sanctuary*. Twitter: @ZC_HAWK [Inspired by: "Babooshka"]

o **Jameson Grey** is originally from England but now lives with his family in western Canada. His work has been published in *Dark Dispatch, The Birdseed* and in anthologies from Ghost Orchid Press, Black Hare Press and Black Ink Fiction. He can be found at jameson-grey.com and occasionally on Twitter @thejamesongrey. [Inspired by: "Leave It Open"]

o **Wesleigh Neville** doesn't believe in ghosts despite being absolutely enamored with ghost stories. A self-taught writer, she grew up in a small town in southern America and spent her free time wandering through graveyards and making up stories about road ghosts when driving down the backroads late at night. Along with narrative fiction, Wesleigh enjoys writing scripts, and her most recent show, "Troop 1627" was featured as the winning script in the production *Resilience: Three Plays About Women*. She currently resides in Los Angeles where she can be usually be found at the library or The Mystic Museum. | wesleighneville.com | Instagram: @wesleighdownahill [Inspired by: "The Wedding List"]

o **Evan St. Jones** is the editor and owner of Heads Dance Press. They're from Louisiana; they work at a nonprofit agency providing services to folks living with HIV/AIDS by day, and they read and write and edit book stuff by night. Evan co-founded QUEERPORT (LGBTQ+ arts and resource organization) in their hometown of Shreveport. | evanstjones.com | headsdance.press | queerport.org | Twitter & Instagram: @evanstjones

www.ingramcontent.com/pod-product-compliance
Lightning Source LLC
Chambersburg PA
CBHW031149160726
47991CB00004B/1597